Presner the Remarkable

Don Eron

Contingency Street Press

Library of Congress Control Number: 2023913100

ISBN: 978-958015-04-9 (pb)

ISBN: 978-958015-05-6 (eb)

Logo art: Janet Glovinsky

Cover Designer: Suzanne Hudson

Cover Image: *Dempsey and Firpo* by George Bellows, 1924. Whitney Museum, New York, New York.

For E.J. Meade and Bridget Klauber (1957-2014)

Part One

It wasn't that Presner spent so many years living in the past, so much as that the past made more sense than the present, mattered more in the ways that *mattered*, and thus was more pleasant to contemplate. Under the *circumstances*, few blamed him for not jutting out his jaw and daring the winds to whoosh another blow. After all, life was a Chekhovian comedy. Some admired him for his standards, but *deep down*, where you know things, Presner knew.

Even before the circumstances, he wasn't one to hop a float and settle in for the parade. "You're a contemplative man," a girl he knew in college told him. "You think about things. I like that." At the time Presner didn't know what kind of man he was, or if indeed at twenty he was a man at all, and he didn't think he thought about things any more than anybody else; nor was he certain what she meant by "contemplative," other than that he hadn't yet tried to kiss her. They were sitting on the floor outside his dorm room after a loud party down the hall where Presner had drunk too much. Even in his pleasant, inebriated state, he didn't think the girl was beautiful, yet her green eyes sparkled and her long brown hair bounced suggestively when he'd seen her walking on the campus green. He didn't think she was taunting him. He'd nodded and smiled in contemplation of her observation, then closed his eyes and fell asleep, the back of his head leaning tentatively against the wall. When he awakened—it couldn't have been more than a few seconds later—she wasn't there. Yet she'd liked it that he was contemplative, if indeed he was contemplative, and he'd often think since that if she hadn't said she'd liked it, or had observed instead that he was a different kind of man, a quick study, perhaps, or a loner, and said she'd liked *that*, or even if he hadn't fallen asleep just then but had kissed her and she'd kissed him back and they'd made love in the hallway, as Rob Kedzer had been seen doing the week before with Marjorie Kemp, or if she'd said that he was a take-charge guy, a doer, a comer, a plucky ne'er-say-die presence (the kind of guy, in fact, that a girl with sparkling green eyes and bouncing brown hair would naturally want to make love to in a dorm hallway), that he might have thought of himself differently. *And if he had?*

Who can answer these things? The only thing more pointless than contemplating such questions is not contemplating them, if you're Presner. If you're somebody else it's your call, but you may be surprised where it takes you. If the Honorable Roxanne Trusk Cramer hadn't barged through the doors of Tyson's 24-Hour News and Smoke, where he'd worked the counter for thirteen years, usually graveyard, shouting "Counselor!" Presner shouting back, "Your Honor!" would *Tales of Presner the Remarkable* (the play wasn't *really* about Presner, but his late, disgraced pal, Fitz) stand today as the most rejected play in America? If his parents and sister had lived longer, would he have married sooner? ('Stuff they don't cover in law school,' he can hear Fitzhugh say.) If Roxie hadn't walked into Tyson's to tell him the news about Marx, would Presner be sitting at a huge oak desk in the bungalow on Cherokee—in fact, once *Fitz's* law office, his brother under the skin—staring at a pile of class action documents—impressive sounding, but really a piece of change Gary Marx sent his way to help him along—mostly wondering if he can steal an hour to work on his new play, *Murray the Remarkable*, which was about a guy like his dad, a lowly CPA by day but by night upholding the very foundations of the world with his cryptic wit and wisdom. More immediately, *if* he steals an hour can he cross town in time to hang posters and set up the chairs and scrub the toilets—ah, the privileges of owning a theater company—before dress rehearsal for *Three Sisters*? Opening tomorrow night at the Sara Burton Theater. No royalties due, Chekhov being public domain. A marriage of artistry and low overhead, that's the SBT. With volunteers always hard to come by, Presner was down for head usher. Ticket taker, too, which means looking everybody in the eye: "Please enjoy our show."

As for the *Murray*, so far there was a lot of Murray shrugging bemusedly, "Like father like son," but there was also sagacious dialectic:

"Son, the only questions worth asking never have answers."

"Pop, do we answer them anyway?"

"That depends on if you have a choice."

"How do you know when you don't?"

"At the breaking point, *bubbe*, you'll sing like a bird."

Back to the contemplative college kid. Sometimes he wasn't sure if his life was his own. If he were the central player, it was always in a game that he couldn't begin to fathom. For example, Presner went to the small school for two years before transferring to the State University, and once he'd left, he so quickly and thoroughly lost contact with everybody he'd known there that as soon as two years later it occurred to him that, were he to take a road trip back to the small college, nobody was likely to recall his name. 'I'm Presner,' he'd say if he stopped a familiar face walking across the green. 'Sure, Presner,' they'd say, shrugging, moving on their way to class. He already couldn't strike up a conversation at that school with somebody who looked vaguely familiar without somebody patronizing somebody. But that was two years later. Tack on another fifteen, and you'd have another Presner, who wouldn't give a thought to the notion that nobody back then was liable to remember him now—'So much the better,' Presner would be liable to think—but that at the time he didn't make more of an effort to get to know them could sometimes overwhelm him. Certainly—like almost everybody—he was shy. But he'd dismissed them pretty quickly. Possibly as early as his first evening on campus. A bunch of the floormates were gathered in Chuck Hill's room and somebody—Dink Mathers, in fact, who'd been assigned to share Presner's room (he couldn't quite think of Dink as a *roommate*)—suggested that it was high time to head into town and get drunk. That was it, it occurred to Presner now. He'd dismissed them, as of that moment, as thoroughly as you can dismiss a floor full of guys you eat with every day and share the communal bathroom with and speak civilly to and quite often exchange observations with about classes, and whose papers, for 80 cents a page, you'd type and improve. But he'd wanted to be an intellectual, a real student, a guy who learned, a serious scholar (but a doer, engaging the great issues of the nation), and fancied himself attracting girls who were passionate about guys who were intellectuals, real students, learners, doers, etc., and these guys on the floor were exclusively out to simulate happy-go-lucky fraternity life. That's what they wanted out of college life. "I'm out of place here," he'd written to his parents in his first letter home. "These guys are just *kids*." A quick study indeed, Presner thought, looking back at the kid he'd been in the early eighties.

In view of such disposition, it's not surprising that Presner chose to study the law. This was after he'd taken a double major in drama and sociology at the U, where he'd transferred after his two years at the small college. Writing papers on the nature of comedy in Chekhov—which occurred when the characters took themselves more tragically than their circumstances warranted—opened a window through which young Presner could view himself with a semblance of fresh air: Presner, Comedian.

These were the kind of eureka moments he was always reading about in novels. He understood sociology to be the confluence of circumstance and event, and in viewing the urban underclass, for example, studying populations whose circumstances were far more tragic than his own,

Presner sometimes wondered if the purpose of his interest might be so that he could feel better about himself. 'Presner, it could be worse. You weren't born a one-legged raccoon. Buck up.' But between these moments when his pulse quickened and he felt in the presence of a comprehensive understanding, as if by dint of sheer concentration inspired by readings on the alienation of the "outer directed" he might reel in the unified field theory of human longing, Presner drew blanks, fearing these probings offered not insight but self-portraiture. Too much Presner, too little air. Beyond that, he found the readings as pleasantly tedious as his professors found his term papers, and his friends—those few kindred spirits he didn't summarily dismiss as unserious—found him, and Presner found them. Very well, Presner decided. The stage it would be.

Talk about drawing blanks! 'Deja vu all over again,' Presner eventually shook his head in defeat. Or reality? They amounted to the same. As an actor he lacked both the presence and the skills of projection for a career on the stage. As testimony to his presence, few of the young women who majored in theater ventured a second look at Presner—or a first, from what he could tell—while most other guys in the program never went ten seconds without a beautiful coed theater major tethered to their arm. Even those theater guys who—predictably enough, Presner later heard—turned out to be gay, were lady killers at the U. "What's wrong with this picture?" Presner, the comedian, found himself saying aloud, before instructing friends to inscribe the remark on his tombstone.

As for becoming a director? "There are big picture guys and little picture guys," his friend Stephen Monday told Presner one day as they sat on the theater steps. This was shortly after Presner's proposal for directing *The Seagull* was turned down without comment by the department chair. To Presner, Stephen Monday was pleasantly tedious, in that way that having a sibling who was a rock star might become pleasantly tedious after the initial euphoria that you knew them when, and that there might be some small boon to be gained by association. Still, this was one of those perfect moments, when somebody so accurately sums you up that you have to pause a moment to wonder if your life is entirely your own, or if you were instead a standing cliché manufactured by the zeitgeist, accessible at a glance to anybody—any quick study—bothering to take a gander and perceive. All you can do at such a moment is to sit there on the steps and hope they reveal more, perhaps (though unlikely, one can nonetheless hope) a nuanced refinement cancelling out the initial judgment. It was like the moment years later when an acquaintance took Presner aside. "There are two kinds of men in the world," he said, jabbing a thick finger at Presner's chest. "Leg men and breast men." The acquaintance's observation revealed not so much about taste and attraction (Presner had long ago learned where women were concerned that it takes all kinds, even if some kinds were in far greater abundance than others) but that he had spent his entire adult life, if he gave it a thought, believing he was *both* a breast man and a leg man. But you can't *be* both, the finger jabbing his chest pounded home with such urgency Presner understood that his acquaintance wasn't talking about breasts or legs or women at all, but a darker truth that required utterance before receding beyond grasp into the realm of abstraction and—the fate of all abstraction—disappearing into thin air more quickly than it had emerged. 'You can't be both. You may want to be. You may want to hide behind your mother's skirt and suck her tit, too! You're one, you're the other, or you're nothing. *Bubkes*,' the acquaintance didn't add, but may as well have.

Stephen Monday was a big-picture man. Many years later, Presner read his life story in the Arts & Leisure section of the *New York Times*. Stephen was directing a version of *Richard II* at Casper's Point, a prominent venue in New York. In Stephen's interpretation, the characters dressed in business suits or other conservative, if contemporary, attire. The play was set mostly in an airport lounge. "Otherwise, it's a costume drama," Stephen Monday was quoted as saying, a line that Presner took to repeating to himself over the next several days as he walked to work or to the grocery store or—less often—to Lisa Caner's apartment, then back to his own apartment. "He's calling all of Shakespeare a *costume* drama," Lisa Caner said after Presner got around to showing her the story.

"That's not it," Presner said. His tone was regretful for reasons too complex to reel in. "That's not it," was more or less her response to everything Presner uttered during the two months they'd gone out the year before. It also assumed the worst about his now famous former friend; that time had turned Stephen Monday into an arrogant know-it-all, a solipsistic egotistic polymathic iconoclast—a smarty pants. "Lisa, he's not saying that Shakespeare had it all wrong—a transcriber of costume dramas, that's all—and Stephen Monday knows best; he's saying the play's so great you can do it in a business suit in an airport lounge. And if you can't, or if you raise a commotion and throw a big temper tantrum because he's being sacrilegious, then *you're* saying it's just a costume drama." Still, Presner considered the notion. Was there one essential thing in the midst of grandeur without which it wouldn't *be* grandeur but ordinary, make-believe pretending to be genuine, a costume drama?

"Interesting interpretation," Lisa Caner said.

"Stephen Monday's a big-picture guy," Presner explained.

Lisa looked at him oddly. She was a tall woman though compact, with long red hair—"strawberry blonde," she called it. Maybe Monday nailed it those years ago back at the U, Presner thought. Stephen Monday was big-picture. That's why they were reading about him in the *Times*. Presner was small-picture, went the corollary. Everything about him was small-picture. Was there one essential thing missing in him, with which he'd be big-picture? Instead there were blanks. This was nothing he'd be regretful about. He wouldn't take his predicament more tragically than warranted. Lisa Caner was small-picture, too, by definition, because she was having coffee with Presner in her kitchen, and because—more definitively—she had gone out with him briefly the year before. The only thing big-picture about Lisa Caner, as far as Presner could see, was that she'd dumped him after two months. That she still saw Presner occasionally—even if on a strict friendship basis—for a movie and quick cup of coffee afterward in her kitchen suggested that the big-picture gesture of unceremoniously letting him go was an isolated incident, a singular act of inspiration in the midst of her own pleasant tedium. The *Times* article, after cataloguing Stephen Monday's numerous directorial triumphs, mentioned he was married to the actress Jane Beverly. Presner never heard of Jane Beverly, but you could bet she was big-picture.

"You're probably right about what he meant. I'm wrong," Lisa said to Presner. "You should have been a lawyer."

Ah, lawyer: Lisa Caner's favorite sobriquet for Presner. Her familiar trope. Her way of saying, 'Don't that beat all,' or, 'I'll be a monkey's uncle'—this Presner appreciated—but he wondered now if he hadn't ladened the trope with significance it didn't contain; for all her You-should-have-been-a-lawyer rejoinders, putdowns, comebacks, was it possible—it hit him now—that Lisa Caner was unaware that Presner *is* a lawyer?

If you major in sociology and drama, absorbing enough to understand that if there were two careers you're spectacularly unsuited for, they were sociology and drama, you go to law school. As far as Presner knew, the command was delivered at Mt. Sinai. It seemed to Presner that everybody he knew in law school had majored in sosh and drama at their respective U's, where they'd learned, if nothing else, precisely what Presner learned: Law school is the accommodation for those children of abundance who can't find anything else more accommodating. It's the little picture that remains after the big picture recedes. It's also what his parents would have wanted, or so he assumed. He'd wanted to do something *productive* with the money they'd left him. When he wasn't walking around dazed, it was the best time of Presner's life. Later, he wondered if he might have taken it more seriously if someone else had been paying his tuition. But it was his to blow.

That there were other kinds of law students, those with a real fever for discerning the criteria applicable when one constitutional right conflicts with another constitutional right, or possessed a legitimate fascination with hearsay exceptions, students who tossed and turned in bed with visions of clerking with the circuit court or a white-shoe law firm, devoting their careers to the intellectual contortions necessary to help rich guys sustain their wealth, or even quixotic students dreaming of springing the wrongly accused or otherwise doing their bit in the big-picture dance to provide a fair shake for those disadvantaged, Presner had no doubt. Perhaps they had their own friends. Like seeks like, kindred spirits coalesce. Sometimes Presner would watch them in class, eagerly expostulating the contradictions in tort law or the tensions between federal and state jurisdiction, forging common ground between disparate opinions, citing disparate precedents, and wonder to himself, 'These people *like* this stuff. Gee,' sometimes with a kind of impersonal envy, other times with that sense of superiority peculiar to law students—though not unlike what he felt in the dorm room back when the rest of the floor fled to get drunk their first night at college—that Presner still sometimes felt even as he fought it in himself: He had seen the big picture recede, mournfully accepted who he was, while these believers were still preening in their costume dramas, their big-picture pretensions. 'Gee.' Now, of course, fifteen years later, he understood the sense of superiority masked his own fear and disappointment and grief, but, at the time, being 1) little-picture, and 2), knowing it, evoked its own irresistible, tarnished romance.

All his friends in law school were similar children of abundance, going nowhere at approximately Presner's own negligible pace. Still, when you graduate last in your class at law school, what do they call you (assuming you pass the bar, too, even if barely)? *Counselor!* There was Pepe, who had spiked black hair, wore a dark green leather jacket embroidered with tiny chains, and had an unexplained but profoundly articulate scar lining the crease of his forehead: Pepe scoffed at the cornballs with a pious indignation not even Presner could summon. He was from inner-city Detroit—Pepe *was* inner-city Detroit with all the gritty toughness and surly knowledge and incipient anger at everything *not* inner-city Detroit. Presner never doubted Pepe had seen things, even after he'd admitted one night, after a two-week Detroit-size drunk before finals, that while he was inner-city Detroit, don't think for a second otherwise, there was also influencing his personality the circumstance that his dad owned a series of supermarkets and thus a good portion of inner-city Detroit.

There was also Roxie, a stocky, tough-talking Texas gal—Roxie referred to herself as a broad—a Raymond Chandler addict who once confessed to Presner that she thought of herself as a "Philip Marlowe with boobs and hips." Roxie was a tough broad those days. Fifteen years later, she was a county judge in Denver, but back in law school, Presner remembered her as far more vocal about the penis sizes of every guy she had a nodding acquaintance with. "Guys didn't have acquaintances with Roxie," he told Lisa Caner one night, over coffee. "They had jaw-dropping acquaintances." To Presner's knowledge only the guys in their group—her true intimates—were spared Roxie's scrutiny.

Gary Marx was in the group. Looking back, Gary Marx was the only one of them—Presner included—who didn't come across as a walking petition for psycho-pharmaceuticals, but Presner never trusted him. If you looked deeply enough into Gary Marx you could see his devious core. "But you could say that about anyone. You could say that about me," Lisa Caner protested, the same night he first reminisced about Marx in Lisa's kitchen. To this observation Presner smiled. Lisa got it. A year before, Presner told her he was falling in love; the next day Lisa called and said they were "going too fast," that she "needed time," that this wasn't a "good idea."

"I'll bet you're getting back with your old boyfriend, too," Presner had said glumly.

That Lisa laughed then was why he'd been inclined to fall in love with her, and why being with her now on a strict friendship basis amused Presner the Comedian far more than tormented him, but deep in her core she was devious, too.

Speaking of girlfriends, Gary Marx stole one from Presner in law school. Henrietta was a short, thin, well-dressed girl with curly black hair Presner found spectacular, and hazel eyes so searing with intelligence they emitted vapor trails; in her gaze you felt capable of manufacturing brilliance, if necessary. She couldn't talk to Presner without leaning her elbows and knees into Presner's. They'd met during Orientation, then sat beside each other in torts, with the seating arrangement continuing after class when they'd meet with others for a drink. You couldn't call her his girlfriend, Presner admitted. More of a Presner-*style* girlfriend. If you took away the elbows leaning into elbows and knees into knees, all they had was the seating arrangement. He called her up a few times under various pretenses, once leaving a message with her roommate, inviting Henrietta to a barbecue (she never got back to him), and told a few others of his infatuation. "You'd make a cute couple," Roxie offered, and while Presner shrugged, he agreed, too. He also told Gary Marx about her. Marx didn't say anything that Presner could recall later, talking about it with Lisa Caner, but a few nights afterward, Presner walked by Marx's house and saw Henrietta in earnest discussion on the porch, her knees and elbows leaning into Marx's as they swayed on the porch swing, Presner waving diffidently as he walked by. An hour later—then the next morning—Presner walked by as well. Her car, a burgundy MG, remained parked in front of Marx's rented bungalow. It had been the longest night of Presner's law school life, to be matched by the next night and several thereafter. 'How much can I take? How much can a heart bear?' he'd ask himself repeatedly, as if through sheer repetition an answer might emerge.

He didn't end up ambushing Marx and pounding his head repeatedly into the curb until it crushed like a cantaloupe. After all, he'd called Henrietta several times, lingeringly gazed into her eyes over beer after torts, understood his own brilliance in her gaze; it wasn't as if she was unaware of Presner's infatuation; she *preferred* Gary Marx, a bitter pill, but Marx was by acclamation the best looking guy in the law school, thick black hair and a chiseled face that had found its way into *Esquire* during an earlier, brief incarnation as a male model prior to taking up the law. Presner's demise took place in the first year of law school. Marx was still going out with Henrietta at graduation two years later, her burgundy MG still parked most nights in front of the same rented bungalow, but by then Presner didn't care. He had figured out Marx was devious. Once he said those words to himself, aloud, it was as if a lid had lifted. He was out of his league and into another, a Machiavellian league where people were unkind, cutthroat, vicious. ("You were expecting the School of Ed? It's *law* school, for crying out loud," Presner could still hear his erstwhile friend Fitz pontificate.)

He'd remained friends with Gary Marx after that, part of the same group, as was Henrietta. No words were exchanged between them, no accusations fired or explanations extended. Marx remained friendly to Presner, and Presner, after a brief interlude, to Marx. It was all very civilized, Presner thought later, and he liked the fact that he didn't do anything, really, didn't hurl accusations in defense of his pride or crush Marx's skull against the curb like a cantaloupe, or, even more piteously, petition Henrietta with the transcription of his longing, as Marx himself had done earlier in wooing her, thereby—Presner had no illusions here—defining him for all time as the epitome of little-picture. He *admired* that about himself. Presner wasn't without pride at his restraint, at being civilized, not taking the wild swing, not a cross word uttered. Also, he reminded himself, he'd been through worse, and often felt he'd betray his parents' memory by getting so upset about losing a girl who'd never been his. Afterward, being friends with Marx was like being friends with a child: you knew what you were dealing with. You expected less, even found yourself surprised, charmed by the occasional gestures of consideration. When word got back to Presner during the last year at law school—through Pepe—that Marx regretted the erosion of their friendship, regretted that they no longer huddled together to discuss, through the prism of tarnished romance, the turning world, to mock their professors and the cornballs discussing con law with such straightforward earnestness, Presner felt obscurely triumphant. Well, you couldn't blame him for salvaging what he could. Marx was a scuzzbucket. And when, a year after graduation, Henrietta abandoned Marx for an assistant United States Attorney—"It was in the works," Marx told Presner. "One day she wants time to herself, the next she's already moved in with Shrady"—Presner being Presner regretted Henrietta and Marx's demise.

Pepe. Roxie. Presner. Marx. Henrietta. Norman Fitzhugh was the heart of the group, the center, the wheel, the *sine qua non*, as Fitzhugh himself might have said. You can only excoriate the pampered suburban kids for so long, scrutinize so many dick sizes, contemplate passively through the sheen of tarnished romance, or—as with the lovers Marx and Henrietta—stare burning into each other's eyes in a snug booth as the others share the adjacent table—before it's the one time too many. Familiarity breeds contempt, jokes turn stale. There are 1,000 variations on the theme but not 1,001. Even Presner, who balanced out the group by spending time with his sister and her theater crowd in Denver, wearied of the smarter-than-anyone cynic routine. Without Fitzhugh there wouldn't have been a group by third year, that's what Presner thought. Fitzhugh was adventure. You didn't necessarily share in the adventures, but you heard about them and swapped the anecdotes with the others and offered your psychological analyses and huddled together when Fitzhugh broke down, then the day would come very soon when Fitz—only sometimes did they call him Norm—rose Phoenix-like from the ashes of humiliation and you had another adventure to discuss. Well, you wanted to be more like Fitzhugh yourself; Presner knew that even then. He was a big, red-faced guy, 6-2, husky, prone not to over-statement—that was Presner, pressing the issue under stress, trying to make a point—but *oversentiment*. An excitable guy but not angry, at least not like Pepe. Fitz wouldn't court women so much as overwhelm them, living and breathing their virtue—and everything about them was virtue—until one month down the line, two months, they'd break down and accept that they were the most beautiful, brilliant, tantalizing spirits in human history. It would work, too—some of the prettiest girls in law school slept with Fitzhugh and planned their joint futures, briefly—because he wasn't selling but proclaiming. He would tell these beautiful women what they always secretly suspected about themselves, or never dared to. Another month down the line they'd begin to think all they had with Fitzhugh was oversentiment. No substance, just praise. When the song gets old, your vanity hardens, Presner supposed. You didn't hear the words. You look across the pillow and see not a seer but a fool. Then it was down in the dumps for Norm, a spectacular fall. He suffered like nobody else Presner knew. He'd drink a lot and sit across your table drenched with sweat as if physiologically draining the woman from reference. You'd reason with him that he was missing too much class, that there would be other women, and Fitz would look at you, his eyes expanding on his thick, sweaty, red face, as if you were talking him into a pyramid scheme. "Presner, I just want to talk about her," he told Presner a dozen times, about half a dozen women.

At one end-of-semester party, Fitzhugh puked in the dean's bathtub, then wiped himself with the dean's monographed silk towels. But he didn't have to be drunk to cause a spectacle. He was beaten up, at least twice that Presner knew about, for expressing his oversentiment in the wrong place one time too often around guys who didn't want to hear. Fitzhugh wasn't a fighter; he was a proclaimer. You wanted to drive to his house in the middle of the night and knock on his door to check if he was still alive, which Presner did one night after a despondent phone call and found Pepe pacing back and forth on Fitzhugh's porch. Nobody answered the locked door after repeated shouts and louder knocks. Presner and Pepe were taking off their shoes to knock out a window when Norm Fitzhugh came to the door wiping his eyes, surprised to find them there. "What are you guys doing here at 2am?"

Presner looked at Pepe. What could you say? We're here to keep you from slicing your wrists? Neither said anything until Pepe said, "We're here to keep you from slicing your wrists, Fitz."

"Come on in," Fitz smiled, then made the two of them the greatest hamburgers and eggs in history. His house was a wreck, coffee tables overturned, laundry on the upholstery, books and law journals toppled everywhere, pages of the journals torn and scattered as if Norm found solace in the esoteric posturing, and dust upon dust so you were afraid to touch anything. But he could clean his house. And a month later he was sleeping with the most beautiful law student you'd ever seen. It was stories like this that kept the group together, gave them something to talk about and laugh over after they'd already talked and laughed. Fitzhugh was famous for his exploits, his mood swings, too, and he was theirs. "We fed off the guy," Presner told Lisa Caner.

"Do you think he knew that?"

Presner considered. "He knew it and liked it."

Later, after law school and the bar, when the group saw each other at functions or parties or after locking their cars, walking to the theater—Presner the only one not a practicing lawyer of some kind—it was Fitzhugh they talked about immediately. "What's with Fitz now?"

You always knew you could count on a story. When he looked at Roxie or Pepe or Marx or Henrietta reminiscing, though often it would be a year now between chance encounters, at such moments, Presner was looking at a friend.

———◇———

Presner graduated law school 119th in a class of 147.

"Ain't the top three quarters. That's what I was shooting for," he told everybody. "What do they call you when you graduate last in your class at med school? Doctor!"

"Room to spare," Roxie said of his ranking. She'd finished 32nd in the class.

"They call you shmuck," Pepe said.

Pepe ranked 109th. Since after each semester Pepe was listed behind Presner, and Presner turned on the lights to "full brightness" the last semester, lighting his way into the law career, he found the final list curious. "I'm going to request an investigation," he told Roxie.

"That's hard to reconcile with your not caring one bit."

"A scam's a scam," Presner said. "It's the principle."

"You know Pepe," Roxie said. Presner nodded, though he wondered what she meant. That Pepe had in his possession intimate glossies detailing Professor St. Clair's and Professor Judith Temple's sleeping arrangements—whereas the next professor who recognized Presner without the assistance of the seating chart would be the first? And if Presner ever landed on Mars, that would be as likely.

"The GPAs are bunched together. Everybody does about the same. So if you do a little better you shoot up, a little worse you fall back," Roxie elaborated. Roxie didn't say that Pepe, still slave to his inner-city pretensions after three years of law school, was sharper, the smarter cookie of the two.

They were sitting up front in the open air at a coffeehouse along the mall, watching the people walk by. It was a windy day, late spring; Roxie wore a long red scarf that waved chaotically when the wind shifted. Presner was reminded of the legendary dancer Isadora Duncan, whose long scarf caught behind a tire and broke her neck as she sat in the passenger seat of a convertible. Though Roxie wasn't in a convertible, Presner felt like grabbing her scarf and holding it so it wouldn't blow in the wind. You could have told Presner that after graduation he'd never see Roxie again, or you could have told him that he'd marry her, and each would seem as likely, but at the moment, he wanted all of them to be safe. Sentimental? By then his parents had been killed—going on four years ago—in a plane crash that may as well have finished off Presner, though the insurance bankrolled him through law school and a few excursions. Within another year his sister would die, cancer, and you couldn't have told him that. Or that he wouldn't be equal to it, and for a dozen years afterward would attend each day as if it were his own beheading. Then after another sleepless night he'd walk outside and see that Chekhov really was right: In the general run, one fate relentlessly mirrors another as characters play out their psychodramas made clownish by the intensities of subjective longing. What would he ever be but another character in the play? What were circumstances but *tsuris* you read into them? What were mountains but molehills misperceived? What were love and ambition but illusion cut out of the same mirror?

If it's *reasons* you want, Presner had plenty.

Roxie, Pepe, Fitzhugh. Even Marx, even Henrietta. 32nd, 109th, 54th, 62nd, 86th in the class. If it were possible to feel sentimental for a moment, not only in retrospect but as the moment occurs, Presner did.

Fitz, Roxie, Marx, and Henrietta landed good jobs before the bar exam. Presner found work, too; a clerk at Tyson's 24-Hour News and Smoke. The night shift, though he was flexible. He still had plenty of money of his own but needed to stay occupied. When he wasn't selling

magazines or cigarettes or shooting the breeze with Pepe, who didn't
work at all—"That's what happens when your dad owns Detroit," Roxie
reflected, looking Presner over skeptically—Presner memorized statutes
and exceptions and subclauses for the bar exam.

"At least in law school reasoning was required. Logic, resolution, the
whole deal," Presner told Lisa Caner, when Presner told her the full
story. "Plenty of memorization, too, of course. But the bar? Strictly
rote."

The bar exam was a matter of turning yourself into a computer for
six months, storing endless information into the computer drive, then
hoping like hell that when you press the button the information spews
out. Because everybody's schedules were different now that work entered
the equation, everybody attended different bar prep classes and study
groups, except Pepe, who tagged along with Presner three afternoons a
week. "Pepe wasn't much help. I helped *him*."

Lisa nodded skeptically.

"I also collected for UNICEF when I was a kid," he added.

The night before the bar they all called each other up—Fitzhugh's
idea—to wish themselves luck. Presner was moved. "We're going to kick
ass!" he proclaimed (they all agreed), but he showed up at the exam with
a headache. Presner broke into the first and last cold sweat of his life.
His teeth chattered to his vibrating torso. He couldn't concentrate as
he pushed the computer button—nothing. He pushed it again. *Bubkes*.
Were there anything in it for him but a broken toe, Presner would
have *kicked* the computer. He steeled himself to concentrate—"Your
future's at stake, that's all. Tough it out. Why? *Because character matters*"– then looked around him throughout the massive lecture hall at
the U, a couple of hundred law school graduates of various ages from
every law school within a hundred-mile radius, burrowing into their ex-
ams, pressing the buttons, information spewing out, or frantically—like
Presner—re-pressing the buttons, and stifled the impulse to laugh.

Afterward, convinced he'd failed spectacularly, Presner didn't hit the employment trail—realistically, what was the point? His law resumé, not promising to begin with, sprouted in his desk drawer. By the time the results arrived two months later—Presner kept the official registered envelope on his kitchen table for a week before opening it—he passed—he'd decided he wasn't cut out for the law, when he confronted the matter honestly, through the prism of his abilities and interests rather than through his emotional desires.

"That's what you've been doing?" Lisa asked.

A week later all of them—Pepe, Roxie, Fitz, Marx, Henrietta, Presner—drove down to the state Capitol in Fitzhugh's station wagon. On a freezing day in early December 1987, Presner stood on the Capitol steps, raised his right hand, and—in his first act as an attorney-at-law—took the oath of admission to the state bar.

He'd stayed on at Tyson's during the two months before the registered envelope lay for its week upon his kitchen table, and it was still there thirteen years later. Presner discovered that when you don't spend every spare second every day, plus huge chunks of every evening, memorizing statutes, exceptions, subclauses, until you're correcting your mistakes in your dreams (that's *if* you can sleep), your desperate mind on desperate autopilot, processing the data, racing long after you've urged the monster to quit, that huge vistas of time open up. How could he not have known? You haven't scratched the surface of the day. If you're not hooked into television, if you can turn off the contemplation and not interpret your circumstance too tragically, if you've a job with regulated shifts that require nothing more than the capacity to withstand pleasant tedium, there's time for everything you could possibly want, provided you don't want too much.

He read. He took long walks around town, day and night, often with a cigar from the company stock teetering half-smoked from his lips. People had a way of not bothering Presner as he walked through crowds with his dangling smoke. In the midst of congestion, pathways magically cleared. This especially after he started lifting weights. Presner bulked up. "A bruiser," Fitzhugh called him. "Just the sort of thing you do when there's time in the day and you're a single guy," Presner shrugged modestly, but he liked the sobriquet. How could he resist? *Bruiser*. Nobody else had ever called him anything but shmuck. He began running—a byzantine route of five miles through jogging paths and sidewalks and alleys ending in a bonus lap around Presner's apartment building. As for his reading, between manning the register, stocking the shelves, marking the inventory, and playing 'Make believe we're Bogart and Bacall' with the distributer's dispatcher, Mag, who took every syllable he said for a punch line, there wasn't as much time as you might imagine. Once he ventured to Mag over the telephone line, "I'll bet you have piles and piles of red hair." To which the dispatcher replied, "Don't be fresh," accompanied by a laugh reverberating from so deep in her imagination, touching a corresponding spot in Presner, typically deadpan, so that he laughed with corresponding convulsions—at what he hadn't a clue; that Mag had out-quipped the Comedian was his best estimate. Neither mentioned the laugh again; a moment so genuine can only diminish in the retelling, a tarnished relic of better times—Presner was barely willing to take it in at the time, so tenuous are such triumphs, so voracious the suckhole, so unforgiving the whirlpool of the human comedy—well, on the job Presner had time to half-read a dozen newspapers a day. He came to consider himself something of a half-expert on local issues in a dozen locales. "Maybe I wasn't getting rich practicing the law," Presner said to Lisa Caner, once he spilled the beans about the purported legal career. "But I know as much about Council Bluffs as anybody in Denver."

Still, your expertise in a dozen locales, that you're now a bruiser, a runner, a reader (though Presner admitted the high falutin' stuff he'd begun had given way to less high falutin' detective novels), that you're capable of such authentic moments on the phone with Mag that they serve as anchors in your memory, that you're the best inventory-marker, shelf-stacker, register-manner Tyson's 24-Hour News and Smoke ever saw? *Bubkes*. 'I left you money for *this*?' he'd imagine his dad, who had liked to imitate the inflections of corny Jewish comedians, wailing dramatically.

'I'm a failure,' Presner explains in his imagination.

'A failure?'

'A failure and a shmuck,' Presner clarifies.

'But *why*?'

Presner wondered if that's why he was still an attorney, in good standing with the state bar. Never earned a cent, never filed a paper or bought stationary, few of the people he knew since knew—Presner not hiding anything, it just wasn't something anybody was liable to bring up—half the time that it might be worth bringing up, Presner didn't think of it—Lisa Caner a case in point; go out with her two months, get dumped, then a year later fill her in on the rough outline over the kitchen table—but every year he snuck into colloquiums or seminars on the latest in contract law or sexual abuse investigation, looking around from the back row for somebody he knew—not Roxie or Marx, but recognized from across the counter at Tyson's—thinking that everybody in attendance knew he was something of an imposter—*something*?—wondering if he'd blow their disapproving minds by raising a hand and blurting, 'What about *Siegal v. the State of New Hampshire*?' Often—with these seminars and colloquiums taking place in the off hours, the lawyers attired casually—Presner, the bruiser, in his Yom Kippur suit, was the best dressed guy there. Afterward he'd walk up to the table smiling, unabashed—you didn't work night shifts at Tyson's if you couldn't talk

to people—and signed his name to the roster on the table. He was no
less a lawyer than any of them, officially speaking, he told himself, his
dander up over imagined frowns. Thus, Presner earned the required
convocation points to maintain standing with the state bar, along with
the yearly dues he paid.

Roxie was the only one of the old crowd he saw with any frequency
these days, outside Fitz, who was usually out of the country. Every few
weeks the Honorable Roxanne Trusk Cramer made a point of stopping
by the shop; they were practically neighbors, the courthouse several
blocks west.

Now Roxie burst through the double doors, shouting, "Counselor!"
Presner shouted back, "Your Honor!"

In law school Roxie, according to self-description, was "built like
a brick shithouse." These years later she'd expanded into a municipal
building. A courthouse, Presner considered, not unkindly. The Cramer
she'd married and divorced was also a judge, in the State District Court.
His miserable dick was the only one Roxie was excoriating these days.
Being a judge was a mixed blessing man-wise, Roxie said. Everybody no-
tices you when you walk into a room, but they cower. Not that Presner
supposed she stopped over because she was lonely.

Roxie kept him abreast of the latest. "Have you talked to Marx lately?"
"Do I look like I've been in an accident?" Presner said.
"Very funny."
"You work in a courthouse. I work in a smoke shop. To me it *is* funny,"
Presner said. Marx was a personal injury lawyer. A couple of years ago
he'd run those ads where downtrodden if innocent-looking accident
victims beamed into the camera, "Gary got me $20,000." Then Marx
himself was facing the camera, looking more like Gary Cooper on his

best day on the range than an ambulance chaser. "I'm Gary Marx. Call if I can help. No promises. Just results."

One thing Presner adored about Roxie: her pretensions that they were still a group. That Marx was liable to call up Presner to say hello. That Presner took the time to email Pepe (at the Family Law Offices of Peter Murray, out in Aurora) with his current ruminations, and that Pepe—Peter—bothered to read the email between depositions. That he'd occasionally meet Henrietta after work—Presner's the smoke shop, Henrietta's the Public Defender's Office—for collegial cocktails before Henrietta drove home to her duplex in Boulder and Presner walked back to his weights and detective novels. Maybe Roxie really believed this? That if she thought it so it was so, or as so as any other reality. In fairness, it was clear from Roxie's monthly bulletins that the others stayed in touch, more or less knew what was what about each other, weren't averse to making a phone call for additional perspective, continued to be moved by currents of warmth and affection. Presner, out of the loop, felt the currents of affection, but it was a sentimental deal. For old time's sake. These guys, except for Roxie and Fitzhugh, tuned him out a long time ago.

For a couple of years after the bar, they'd all stop by Tyson's, even Henrietta, as if nothing had changed: Peers-in-arms. Then less often, then never. This was even before his sister became sick. Presner admitted the estrangement wasn't all their doing. He became a handful. "These guys bring out the chip on my shoulder," he told Lisa Caner. They'd all get together at parties at Roxie's over Christmas, Presner included, ostentatious greetings, perfunctory hugs, but the conversations still-born—how often can you repeat yourself?—mundane stuff, too, that you didn't want to hear in the first place. Presner couldn't help feeling they felt sorry for him, and he felt sorry for them if that's what they felt.

"You're not a mean-spirited person," Roxie reflected. "It's about time you got over it. Why didn't you punch him in the nose fifteen years ago? You should have, instead of taking potshots at him for fifteen years. Don't think he doesn't know. It's embarrassing, really."

"That's because you cross Presner at your peril. He'll hunt you to the ends of the earth, day and night. You'll never rest."

"Well, he's learned his lesson."

It was nice of Roxie to say that. Presner would have leapt over the counter to kiss her if it wouldn't violate the social contract where she was the county judge with the heart of gold and Presner the incorrigible ne'er-do-well. Anyway, if he leapt over the counter to kiss her, Roxie was liable to catch him and throw him back. It would be embarrassing, really. Sometimes Presner wondered why he bothered with the social contract. Nothing against Voltaire; in general, it had its function; precluded anarchy, etc. It kept you from urinating in public or leaping over the railing at Coors Field during the 7th inning and running out to left field with your baseball glove to assume the position. Stuff Presner wouldn't do anyway. But with old friends? These weren't absolute formulations. That Roxie was the judge with the heart of gold and Presner the incorrigible may not take into consideration Roxie's view. Just last month, Fitzhugh confessed to Presner that he'd slept with Roxie periodically over the years. Presner was startled. At the time, he couldn't think of anything that would surprise him more. He knew they'd both slept with plenty of people—Roxie less so in recent years—but what of the implicit social contract between old friends, the assumptions that allowed you to be yourself without worrying that they were playing an angle, viewing you as potential roadkill? You could flirt your heart out with Roxie, you could be outrageous, because Roxie wouldn't call your bluff. Or you hers. You knew it was harmless, that she'd be there the next month flirting away, the old Roxie if fifteen years moreso. That was Presner's formulation. A definitive interpretation? Well, the bruiser mused to Lisa Caner. Evidently Fitz and Roxie perceived the social contract differently.

Fitzhugh also slept with Henrietta after law school, after she'd broken up with Marx once and for all and married Shrady. This went on for several months, though, as ever, Presner didn't find out until later. 'Not much social contract in evidence there either,' he guessed. Fitz was apologetic when he told all, as if he'd cut into line in front of Presner. Everyone but Presner knew it was a sore point with Presner. But Henrietta was different from Roxie. Presner understood, contract or not. With Henrietta, you couldn't help yourself. Ask Marx. Ask Fitz.

"Gary doesn't care if I take potshots at him. I haven't been on his radar for years."

"He may not care, but I do," Roxie said. "At first it was understandable. Now it's just annoying. And tiresome. Plus, don't sell yourself short. Gary doesn't find your disapproval pleasant. Anyway, he's getting married."

"How'd he convince Jill to sign the pre-nuptial?"

"Presner," Roxie frowned. A warning: One more crack and you're out with the bath water. Presner didn't enjoy being this way. He'd be surprised if anybody but Marx didn't consider him a good guy. 'Somewhat lacking in ambition,' but otherwise princely. The bruiser made a point of this: '*You need something done, ask Presner.*' And he didn't begrudge Marx, hadn't for years; they'd each endured their subsequent shipwrecks. But around Roxie—if Presner recognized this for the canard it was, he felt it nonetheless—the old feelings were summoned, subsequent shipwrecks be damned. She saw you a certain way, so you trotted out the old home movies, with the same old wounds, the same desires, the same tarnished romances. Well, he couldn't deny either that it meant a lot that Roxie still liked him.

"Mention Marx and I go berserk. It's involuntary."

"I'll take that under advisement," Roxie said.

"That's clever, Your Honor."

Roxie smiled. "If you can mind your manners you're invited. Gary wants you to come."

"I'll be on my best behavior," Presner promised. Another thing he adored about Roxie: She thought he would *appreciate* hearing about Marx's wedding first, before the invitations were mailed. Or afterward, too, which was just as likely. Marx was up to a lot of stuff he never heard about. But traditional milestones were observed. That was the old gang, strong as ever.

"Good, that's settled. Now, how's your play?" Roxie wanted to know.

Never let it be said you could pigeonhole Presner at a glance. Lawyer-in-good-standing, news dealer, bruiser. Playwright, too. This last development only over the last few years, but Presner understood it connected him to his youth, those days back at the U pouring over Chekhov, memorizing line inflections, envisioning the big picture, contemplating a life in the theater. Tying him to his dead sister, too.

A few years ago, he saw *Oleanna* at the Denver Center. The play was about an entanglement between a professor and a female student, in which they both misinterpret everything about each other. In the final image the professor raises a chair into the air as the student—now his accuser and blackmailer—cowers. "I only wish the Professor had crashed the chair down on her skull. That would be a more satisfying ending," Presner told his date as they walked out.

"You're crazy. He should be castrated," his date said.

"*You're* crazy."

Similar exchanges characterized the conversations of every couple walking out of the Edison Theater. That night you couldn't take a middle ground. You understood both views, but you had one or the other as you walked out of the theater, as if the drama itself reached out from the stage and clutched your viscera and squeezed until you screamed, for your own sake. For the sake of humanity, also. It reminded Presner how overwhelming the theater can be. It was a one-time shot, too. A week later he went again, with Roxie—she was still married to Cramer then, but the judge, for all his ubiquitous pretensions Roxie was pleased to catalogue, was no culture buff—and that time everything was different. The tension dissipated. Perhaps because their seats were different (more expensive, still the orchestra but further back), or because he didn't spend the night half-anxious with anticipation over putting the moves on Roxie, as he had with his date—a plan doomed by their cut-throat exchange leaving the Edison, needless to say—or the actors were human themselves and not programmed to hit every note the precise way, their intensity diminished the second night, the inflections flat; it wasn't the same. Roxie walked away wondering what all that commotion was about. Still, the theater's not about averages, Presner thought. It's not about the net sum. A night where you cry out for humanity isn't cancelled because next time out, you're not similarly moved and sense the fakery. The first night was still real. Presner thought, you don't forget times like that wherever you find them. If anything, the second night was encouraging, as if it weren't just about genius—beyond Presner's ken—but the stars in alignment, also. If for Mamet, why not for Presner?

There were other considerations. Presner admitted the urgings weren't exclusively high-tone, swayed-by-the-grandeur-of-the-human-comedy, gee-that-could-be-little-ol'-Presner-up-in-the-lights stuff. "You still have to consider there's plenty of time in the day, even after the work shift selling magazines and smokes, then running, then lifting weights, the detective novels, the long walks contemplating women and other relevant matters," he told Lisa Caner, over coffee in her kitchen. "You want to feel good about yourself, that you're a little more interesting than the ordinary run, that when they strip away the trappings and cut to the core, it turns out there's some Big Picture, after all."

Lisa smiled cryptically, not taken aback by the revelations but as if to say: 'Fancy that, Presner wants to be special.'

"It's something to do," he added. "You think I'm kidding myself? I know, it's been too many years. My joints ache shambling across the room. I'm winded. My mind blanks."

Lisa met Presner not as a news dealer or attorney, non-practicing, but as a playwright. He'd signed up for an acting class in the Continuing Ed division at the downtown campus. While Presner, the former theater major, had no pretensions of being an actor as well as an aspiring playwright, the additional insights he gleaned would hone his art. Lisa Caner was one of the actresses in the class, the third prettiest, by Presner's reckoning, but when they staged selected readings during class, he couldn't take his eyes off her, third prettiest or tenth or Queen of the May. Was it just Presner? He looked around the other desks. Nobody else was transfixed. Their teacher—an ancient director of the local stage who faintly resembled Omar Sharif and moved like Charlie Chaplin—appeared less inclined to interrupt than with the two prettier women reading for their scenes; Presner—a scammer at heart—knew from that. There was this disembodied quality to her voice which was riveting, as if each syllable was earned at hard cost. Breathy, earthy, tutored in the chain gang of experience. Every sentence she uttered intimated human knowledge Presner himself instinctively recognized but couldn't nail down. You recognized speech was shifty, true. There were symbols there you didn't notice when you read the stuff yourself, and extra dimensions evoked by those symbols. The two prettier ones weren't actresses but pretty young women who always thought—were always told, the playwright imagined—that they should give the acting scam a try. That their faltering attempts so mesmerized the teacher confirmed in Presner that he'd done well not to pursue the theater back when, been lucky not to toss his eggs into that basket, though he understood himself well enough to know most anything would have resulted in similar confirmation. At one point in the three-week Continuing Ed term, the ancient instructor made a list of everybody's phone numbers. "As actors we need to be in constant contact to foster our craft. Remember, the secret to art is not competition, but *community*," the old teacher said starkly. (Presner knew the kind of community he had in mind.) When the term ended, Presner looked up her name on the list and called Lisa Caner to tell her that of the several would-be's in that Continuing Ed class, she was the real actress.

"The real actor," Lisa Caner corrected.

He knew that. "Actor, I mean."

"If you can make it in Continuing Ed, you can make it anywhere," she reflected over the phone.

"But the secret's not competition," Presner said. "It's community."

Presner didn't expect to ask her out for dinner—his motives were pure, to tell her he'd been moved by her talent so that—What? Presner didn't know—if, perhaps, she wondered if she should continue, she should continue, she should really continue, Presner was prepared to say, and, "Talent like yours, Miss Caner, you don't find on the rack," he'd prepared to say—and did—but her sense of lightness about herself caught Presner off guard, and 'I'll look forward to reading your clippings' didn't seem quite adequate for closing the conversation. She took his testimonial for a valentine, assumed he was after a date, and, for the one and only time, Presner found himself meeting Lisa Caner's expectations.

Face-to-face, her voice was nothing like it was on stage. You could sense the actor's voice behind the one she used over dinner or when you walked her to the door, but only if you'd heard the voice before, and Presner couldn't be certain that wasn't just him revving up the extra-sensory equipment to clarify the discrepancy. "It was there, but you'd have to have dog ears to hear it," he told Fitzhugh. Later, when Lisa called Presner to tell him this little adventure of theirs "wasn't working out at all," during this moment of gravity and import he heard those inflections, though under the circumstance, Presner was too distracted to contemplate what the syllables evoked that the words themselves hadn't. Once he began dwelling on it, there were other considerations—such as exactly what she'd thought they'd been trying to work out in the first place—which took priority.

In a similarly curious development, over dinner on that first date, Presner noticed Lisa was vastly prettier than she'd been in class. It was as if Lisa Caner had made an important decision about herself—'I do character, not ingenue'—and showed up in acting class thus in costume to avoid confusion. Blanche Dubois, not Stella Kowalski. She was tall though compact, slim, mop-haired. "Ragdoll, with emphasis on the doll," he told Fitzhugh.

"What attracts you to the theater?" she said shortly after they were seated.

He was ready. Presner looked at his glass of merlot and squared his shoulders and held up his fist as if a radio mic, then cleared his voice. "At best it captures precisely the human comedy; the pity, the dignity, the quiet acts of grandeur so understated that only later upon reflection can we comprehend the immensity."

Lisa furrowed her strawberry blonde brow.

"I majored in theater at the U," he clarified.

The woman looked him over. Presner returned the compliment. Her mouth was a small scar, her eyes huge and round and slightly astonished. Presner sensed something studied in the intensity, an actor's pose refined over a series of classes. He was half tantalized and half self-conscious, as if he might have a huge wart on his nose.

"I wonder what you do for a living."

"It's not *theater*, needless to say. I work at Tyson's 24-Hour News and Smoke. Shift manager. Graveyard! The distinction—shift manager vs. regular clerk—is nominal, at least as reflected by my paycheck." Because he didn't want to leave it at that, he told her a story so she'd know he wasn't *about* the job, but enjoyed watching the customers. Usually, they'd ignore the bruiser when he watched; others got antsy and fled. The men who were immersed at the porno rack never noticed, of course. They were the ones he'd learned to keep half an eye out for. On the worst night he had on the job, a guy who had to be over seventy whipped it out, right at 2am with four other people in the shop. Presner couldn't believe what he was seeing. The guy was rubbing the picture then rubbing himself. "Hey!" Presner shouted when he realized he was seeing what he was seeing. "Hey!"

He walked around the corner hoping that the guy would disappear into thin air before he got there. But he was *immersed*. The guy's head was cocked, and he was rubbing, carried away a million miles beyond admonitions. "Hey look, you can't do this here. Zip up. Hey!" The four others in the shop hadn't caught on yet to what was happening and looked frightened as the bruiser bustled toward the old man as if he'd blown a wire of his own. Presner placed his hand roughly on the old pervert's shoulder, begging himself not to look at his rooster dick. That's one memory he didn't need plaguing him the rest of his life. The old man spasmed at Presner's touch, dropped the skin rag on the floor and ran out, knocking over a display stack of new paperbacks en route. Presner didn't chase him or yell at him to place the display rack back upright.

A semi-regular who'd caught on to the action walked over as the bruiser stood by the skin rack, collecting himself. "Was he really doing that? Takes all kinds."

Presner pointed at the semen-stained foldout opened on the floor. "Care for a complimentary copy?"

"It sounds interesting," Lisa Caner said.

With Presner and women, sometimes it was the timing. When they went out with him, they didn't want a guy like Presner. At any rate, there weren't many of them. Too often he talked over their heads; he'd smirk when they talked, as if ready to burst into semi-permanent catatonia. But he didn't mean anything like that, or like anything. All this was before Lisa Caner. When they *wanted* a non-practicing attorney who worked at Tyson's 24-Hour News and Smoke for years, a bruiser who wrote plays on the side, those times he was working on something else, or too much water had rushed under the bridge to stroke back upstream. The lost women sensed that Presner regretted this more than they. Or he was the perpetual runner-up, sometimes placing third. What they liked in Presner—or wanted more of—the other guy had in abundance. This was case-by-case. It never occurred to Presner to blame the gender. The women who liked him liked a lot of guys.

Since this was their first date, Lisa Caner thought to ask about his play. "Is it autobiographical?" she teased.

"Tales of Presner the Remarkable."

"Really, what's it about?"

He couldn't tell her it was about too much time in the day, or attracting women like her, or the way he'd felt when he walked out of *Oleanna*; about reconnecting with the younger Presner he'd been back at the U. before his parents and sister died, about big picture versus little picture and taking yourself more tragically than circumstances warrant. He couldn't tell her—though he suspected Lisa Caner would find this less evasive—that it was about the characters and the language and a commentary about dramatic structure and narrative and what happens when what you always thought was one thing becomes another thing entirely, the nexus of imagination, reality, perception, that ball of wax, Presner versus Presner, what he believed pitted against what he knew, or what he knew one day cancelled out the next, or two guys sitting in a bar glibly commenting on the passing parade, which was where the play was first set.

What's it about? What's a rose about, or the very air itself? "It's about Fitzhugh, this nutty guy I know."

"I saw *Marat/Sade*," Lisa said.

"Not that kind of nuts, though I've wondered sometimes," Presner allowed. "Well, Fitz is a guy with large appetites. Enthusiasm Incarnate. Nothing phony about him, though. He means it. Even when he's being phony, he means it. He puts himself out there—always—and trusts his wits to sustain him. Who can live like that? You know in football games when they toss a Hail Mary pass on the last play—that's his *modus operandi,* his game plan, if plan it is. More often than not, he topples over, humiliated—ashamed, too—but he meant well, his motives were pure, and that counts more to Fitz, I guess, once he's back on his feet. He gives us plenty to talk about with his misadventures, I'll say that. Even his rough patches are notable. Friends stay friends because there's always Fitzhugh to laugh about and commiserate over. Still, he's a sponge. You sort of want to be more like Fitz but not *be* Fitz, that would be too painful. But Fitz has more bounce than most. He always gets the girl. Fitz always loses the girl, too, and that's part of the play. Not that it's really about Fitz, exactly. It's about what he'd do."

"A hypothetical Fitzhugh?"

"His life's his life. *Modus operandi* aside, it's not a play."

Lisa Caner nodded. Her mop hair bounced. Presner noticed she'd stopped gazing into his eyes like he'd invented conversation. Of course, he knew you could only look into somebody's eyes for so long, with just so much intensity, as they gesticulate and bray about the nature of drama and otherwise sidestep the issue about their play, but Presner couldn't help thinking he'd said the precise opposite of what she longed to hear.

"Does Fitz know you're writing about what he'd do?"

"Fitzhugh thinks every play is about what he'd do," Presner said. "Novels. Movies, too. Soap operas are stolen from his diaries."

"He's so vain."

Who can explain why two people find something funny at a given instant? Presner? Lisa Caner? Perhaps it's an expression of the instant itself, that at another time you'd look across the table—if you're Presner—at the same person—if she's Lisa Caner—who'd say the same thing in the same way, and you'd understand that you shared a frame of reference with her and she'd been clever. Things you didn't find particularly funny, but you'd appreciate the college try, tickled by her *effort*, as if she were your niece or a student. But funny? You'd smile and snap the books shut. Enough's enough. But in the instant you do find it funny—this was the thing to Presner—it's not the crack itself but the circuitous route you've taken to find yourself across the table from this woman who's the product of her own circuitous route, against all odds the miraculous has occurred and you share a frame of reference, even if it's as negligible as an old song, and if that's not about the funniest thing you've ever heard it's only because in that moment—Presner again—you're more taken by the warmth, which has overcome you like a seizure. It doesn't mean you want to fall in love with her or resume the studied intimacy of staring into her huge round eyes or touch her rag doll mop, or that this instant means anything beyond a nice moment between two people, but Presner knew when he walked away from that table that he'd see her again. The circuitous route finds the two of you here, and though you may know better (after all, it's circuitous) you suddenly want to see where it leads.

Eventually they stopped laughing and looked at each other, now bashful. Presner said, "I know that a theater guy working at Tyson's makes me kind of a walking cliché. A lot of times when customers have questions about the merchandise—porno magazines or pipe racks—they shout out, "Hey Playwright!"

"I'd like to read this play," Lisa Caner said. They'd recovered now. She was wiping off her brow, touching her blushed cheek, running her hand through her strawberry blonde mop. Though Presner had no pretensions—a perennial runner-up, sometimes placing third—in that moment every woman in the restaurant envied Lisa Caner.

As for where this circuitous route led? "Fitz, when you call up a girl and ask her to dinner at a nice restaurant or a movie she wants to see or a party where the two of you will show up with a bottle of merlot and a plastic container of chocolate chip cookies"—Presner staples—"is there not the presumption that you're asking her on a *date*? Yes or no?" Presner frowned. He doubted that Fitz understood the question. When Fitzhugh asked a woman for the time, there was the presumption they were dating. Why he was asking Fitz, Presner didn't know, other than to communicate to his friend that he had had a few adventures of his own. Whereas Fitz was operatic, Presner's romantic misfortunes were muted, as were his triumphs. "Case in point: Lisa Caner," he told Fitz. Over two months he saw her fifteen or twenty times. "Good times, usually better than good. Good was the *worst* it got." He'd pick her up in his Taurus. They'd talk for fifteen or twenty minutes in the front seat, parked, engrossed in the latest, before Presner would think to turn the ignition and back out.

She always surprised him. For one thing, she hadn't formally studied acting in school—"Too theoretical"—but went from audition to audition, learning through trials-by-fire in community setups from Arvada to Aurora, character roles, not ingenue, taking the occasional class when she didn't have a part going. "To keep my hand in the cookie jar," Lisa told him. Also, they both had the same favorite Gordon Lightfoot song from the same obscure album neither had heard in years. "That's one example," Presner told Fitz. She was a waitress and temp secretary and teaching sub—this Presner expected, low pay but autonomy being the actor's Faustian deal—but also a trust funder who didn't need to work. *This*, Presner heard second-hand from a friend of Lisa's he ran into after they'd stopped seeing each other. How much? Presner, who'd once been rich himself, wondered but couldn't ask. Anyway, not even there was she what you'd expect. A trust funder, but she had to skimp. This Presner admired.

Lisa told him that he reminded her of a guy she'd been deliriously in love with, also a theater guy, also a playwright, Presner a low-rent version, cut-rate (this implied). About the only place she didn't surprise him was at her door afterward, when she'd box him out like a shaggy dog who had followed her home and cut inside her door before Presner could get any ideas.

Usually, as they drove to her place after a good time at the worst, usually better than that, she'd instruct Presner to let her out at the stop sign in front of her building. Presner, the gentleman, would insist on parking and walking her to the door. They'd debate briefly, Presner winning, a muted triumph as he'd walk her to the door where she'd deftly forestall any Presnerian ideas about her compact, mop-haired, prettier-than-anticipated actress's body, and box him out like a pisher.

Presner thought—if not on a minute-by-minute basis, then hourly—about asking her what was going on, but after the third or fourth time it was too late. Asking would only seal his fate by that point. "You *knew*, but you didn't want to know," he told Fitz, recounting his losses. When Presner, going nuts about the song and dance, resolved not to call her again, enough being enough, she was guaranteed to call Presner, as if on cue, to ask him out. Did she sense this was peculiar? Presner wondered. By then there was a discouragement about Presner, a muted, doomed perseverance. He lacked Fitzhugh's bounce. On the day Lisa called and told him, "This adventure isn't going anywhere," Presner, for once, wasn't the last to know.

"It wasn't going anywhere," Fitz pronounced absently when Presner called with the full report, to question whether there was some signal he'd missed. Two heads were better than one in scouring the ambiguity. Fitzhugh sounded disappointed as he voiced the postmortem, as if even at being a loser Presner was something of a loser. "What's your deal? Nothing ventured, nothing lost?"

A year later he ran into Lisa Caner in the Post Office. Her back was turned to him as she slipped the key into her box, and Presner—in a moment of weakness—thought of walking out without saying anything. He could leave easily; she'd never know unless she turned that same split second. What's more, Presner was late for his shift. (Not *technically* late; later than he liked to be, Presner preferring to *ease* into his rhythm, deliberately, browsing in the stalls customer-style. Even at the shop he had his way of doing things.) But, finally, he didn't sneak away. "I wanted to blow her mind."

"By saying hello?" Fitz asked, when Presner told him he was seeing Lisa Caner again—Presner without the romantic pretense now. To Fitz, as a method of mind-blowing this was decidedly low-key, like surreptitiously sipping from the same water glass; Presner figured Fitz'd probably enter her from behind as she bent over to look into her mailbox. Presner tapped her on the shoulder. She turned, startled, took Presner in for a moment before recognition registered. Ah, Presner. Not disappointment, though. Now that Presner thought of it, he'd never looked in Lisa Caner's eyes and seen disappointment. Her face was smudged below the huge round eyes, as if she'd been reading Chekhov and crying, as she carelessly inserted her envelopes into the appropriate slot, metered or stamped. Her loose work shirt and jeans, torn at the knee, were smeared with streaks of paint. "Have you switched to stage design, Ms. Caner?" Presner said, pointing at the paint smears. Lisa Caner laughed.

That's all it took. She drives you nuts for two months—you driving her nuts, for all you knew—though probably not, realistically—you don't see her for a year which may as well be ten, you run into her, make a mild quip, call her "Ms. Caner" aping an antiquated formality—Presner from the old school—and snap, you're back in her good graces as if nothing had happened. "I remember what I liked about you," Lisa said to Presner in front of the mail slots.

"I didn't think you liked anything about me," Presner said, which is as close as they got to discussing those curious two months last year.

They went to Vic's Coffee, quickly filled each other in on the latest—Presner still due at work, but this was worth breaking up the routine for once—anyway, it's not as if you had to psych yourself into a maniacal frenzy to sell magazines and file invoices and count inventory—then a movie two days later without the pretense, discussion after the movie in her kitchen. (*Inside* her apartment. A first in his Lisa Caner adventure.)

"You know what it was?" Presner told Fitzhugh over the phone, his low voice catching, as if the bizarre word came to him, but an hour after he'd recycled Tuesday's paper with the crossword puzzle. "Fitz, she was looking for a friend."

"Jesus, screw her," Fitzhugh said.

"How's your play?" Roxie wondered now, after telling him the news about Marx's wedding. She looked concerned, like an aunt who wanted to be encouraging but nonetheless couldn't help finding the enterprise both pitiable and transparent, as if in middle age Presner had announced he was a communist, or a grass roots candidate for mayor.

Presner shrugged.

"Well, keep at it," Roxie said encouragingly.

"When it plays on Broadway you can star."

Roxie smiled distractedly. "I'll settle for tickets opening night."

Though the odds against Roxie getting house tickets opening night at a Broadway play that Presner wrote—calculated as zero in 2,000,000—weren't much better then the odds against Roxie starring on Broadway in the play—zero in 5,000,000—the possibility struck the bruiser as more realistic.

A line was forming behind Roxie. A well-dressed man two customers back frowned impatiently, then looked away when Presner petulantly frowned back. Presner glowered an extra second, then looked at Roxie and shrugged. Roxie didn't notice the drama. This happened sometimes at the shop. It wouldn't astonish Presner if the guy initiated a short conversation when he reached the counter—"Broncos sure looked good yesterday, wouldn't you say?"—out of embarrassment over the sheer pettiness of his impatience with Presner (a working stiff, doing his best to make ends meet), and if Presner himself, ringing up the purchase, encouraged the talk—"But does Griese have the arm strength? Those receivers get strung out over the middle"—it was because he was similarly abashed at the bruising frown he'd shot back at the well-dressed guy, suddenly not wanting to ruin the guy's day because the guy stepped in for a paper and smoke (better bring your sabre along if you talk to Presner), or ruin his own good opinion of himself—sky high when he talked to Roxie, despite the dips and swerves and hoops she pushed him through—as well as because it was an *honest* question. *Does* Griese have the arm strength? "I should go," Roxie said.

"Congratulate Marx for me."

"He really wants you there. He told me that. 'Wouldn't it be great if we were all together again? Those were the days.' Fitzhugh's coming back from his travels, too. Pepe's driving up from Aurora with his wife. Your lass Henrietta will be there. As will you, Counselor, or I'll hold you in contempt."

"I get it," Presner said.

"Think about it over at the Pleasure Palace."

His place.

"Presner's Pleasure Palace," Fitz called it. His joke with Roxie. At least Fitz had been there. Roxie never had. Caner, once.

The Palace was a second-floor apartment at the end of the hallway in a brick building, with amenities including a bedroom, a living room, a kitchen and a bathroom. The kitchen was large enough—*palatial* enough—for a card table in the corner, where the bruiser sometimes sat and wrote. He had a huge copper pot that he got at a garage sale that he used to cook everything in until he discovered the microwave and the George Foreman grill. He still kept a pot on the stove, the way he still kept his Cubs cap on the dresser. The bathroom had a shower stall, and a fluorescent light above the sink and mirror. He loved the bedroom because it wasn't the living room, and Presner loved the living room because it wasn't the bedroom. Sometimes on summer nights, he'd turn out the bedroom lights, open the window, and, kneeling on his bed, lean his forearms to the window well and stare out over downtown Denver as if something interesting was imminent, a meteor shower or somebody screaming for help. The living room was also large, with a desk, a couch, a wood coffee table, and a TV set with excellent sound but no picture to speak of. Most of the time, when he wasn't at the desk, he was lying on the couch reading, or lying on the floor with the back of his head cushioned by a pillow against the couch leg, reading or staring at the ceiling or the picture-less TV or listening to the boom box purring softly from the corner; sometimes he performed all four activities simultaneously. He had an overstuffed chair across the living room that he seldom used. He had a portable phone and a computer and piles of books and magazines. He had dozens of pictures of his parents and sister that he kept in a box on the shelf in the living room closet. He'd discovered that when he lay on the couch talking on the phone, he was far less intelligible than when he sat up, but generally sank into the cushions and kicked up his legs anyway. Six years ago, the place was a steal at $390 per month, and was still a steal at $620. If they raised the rent again, next year the Palace would be a steal for somebody else.

Presner had three posters on the wall that he'd also gotten at garage sales. Two of them—Hopper's *Nighthawks* and Rodin's *The Thinker*—he loved but never noticed any more than he'd notice the background music in a movie. The third poster, Bellows's *Dempsey and Firpo*, though, could stir him, and sometimes the bruiser would find himself staring at the images as if discerning the pentimento underneath them. Perhaps the difference was in that, even to Presner's untutored eye, the thinker was pondering profound considerations; similarly, in the Hopper it was evident that the lonelies in the diner were attending to their loneliness—"Each to their own shipwreck," as Ortega y Gassett said—but in the Bellows there was no evident emotional statement at first blush, just a journalistic depiction of an actual event at Madison Square Garden when Luis Firpo, the Wild Bull of the Pampas, knocked Jack Dempsey clear out of the ring. The painting itself, unlike the Hopper or the Rodin, wasn't generally considered to be great art—a mostly failed experiment in dynamic symmetry, which was Bellows's contribution to twentieth-century American painting, according to what he'd read in an art magazine at Tyson's. Also it was *sports*, portraying gravitas the guys who made the decisions didn't understand or considered to be kid's stuff—*this* is profoundly moving; *that's* immature; etc. Presner wondered if what shook him wasn't directly in the painting itself, but in his knowledge that the fighter catapulting through the ropes toward press row wasn't Firpo, the clownish pretender who'd been known mostly for his fanciful nickname (most viewers assumed it was Firpo, thereby further dismissing the artistry) but was instead the great Dempsey. This was a fight for the heavyweight championship, a designation that during the Depression ranked in prestige somewhere between the King of England and the President of the United States. Even Jewish kids would tell their moms—"I'll be heavyweight champ someday"—and their moms would *kvell*. What Presner *knew* is the historical record: Within seconds Dempsey, here apparently senseless, life endangered in a helpless fall, would rise and climb back through the ropes and onward in his ascension into popular legend and myth, knocking Firpo out cold and back to poverty and the Argentine pampas where eventually the Wild Bull would find work as a sideshow with a traveling circus—a fate not anticipated by the depicted moment itself, when Firpo could be excused for believing that he was on the verge of transcendent triumph. Yet it was all *there*.

Did you have to know all of this ahead of time to understand that the painting was a portrait of Luis Firpo's imagination? It was as if in this depiction of Luis Firpo's temperament that he'd walk by several times daily, pacing through the Palace, and occasionally stop to contemplate, that Presner glimpsed what he glimpsed, and what he glimpsed was the raw intersection of character and fate. "See?" he said to Lisa Caner, the one time she came over. Caner stared at the poster respectfully as the bruiser pontificated. "Here Firpo *knows*. He'll permit himself no illusions!" Thus he wondered—here's what shook him—if Bellows's Firpo wasn't a greater character than any in Chekhov's plays, where illusions were the guiding force?

Caner glanced at him like the sirens went off, smiled quickly, then turned back to Firpo.

But Presner saw it in Firpo's *frown* as the great Dempsey flies through the ropes—not the exhilaration you'd expect, but a slightly pained expression one might wear while watching a child misbehave. Or a momentary confusion as if the 2:47 bus pulled in when the 2:35 was scheduled. And then he'd notice again the fat smear of Firpo's pupils, his cauliflower right ear, the rasped, chipped bridge of his nose, all communicating that he knows what's in the cards and what isn't: After all, he's only Firpo, not a legend but a colorful footnote. Dempsey was immortal. At second blush, the poster says to Presner, Firpo's the prisoner of his interior life where boundaries are drawn with barbed wire.

But did you have to know Firpo's fate to be so moved? To be able to *predict* from the look on somebody's face? To the playwright, art came alive the second time through, when you already knew what had happened and now viewed what occurs in the shadow of that knowledge, as in *Three Sisters* all the longing for Moscow is made more poignant by the knowledge that it's futile.

Gary Marx's wedding would be in June, two months away. Once Presner received the formal invitation three weeks after Roxie stopped in at Tyson's, he anticipated the wedding with an eagerness and resolve previously reserved for the next Scott Turow novel.

"It's not your high school reunion," Lisa Caner said when Presner showed up in her kitchen limping from a strained groin, the fruit of doubling his mileage. "You don't have to knock yourself out. Nobody cares."

"*I* care," Presner said.

Lisa nodded. When Presner said he cared, either Presner cared, or else nobody in history cared less than Presner about the reunion of his old group—that's what the "*I* care" communicated—but he'd knock himself out anyway.

But it really was like a high school reunion; his response not only startled Presner but swung into high relief much he'd assumed he'd moved beyond. For a few days he was disappointed in himself. It brought back too much for the bruiser. You didn't find Fitzhugh taking time out during his travels to lift weights like a maniac. You didn't find Henrietta, who like Roxie had put on weight since those days, paring down to her old size four so she could show old Presner—old Marx and old Fitz too—that she was still the stuff to melt young men's hearts. You didn't find Pepe breakdancing before the mirrors at the Family Law Offices of Peter Murray in Aurora. You didn't find Marx stabbing Presner in the back, same old Marx, or Marx auditioning for anchorman at Channel 7, his true destiny. Or Roxie, who fixed many a memorable dinner for the guys back when, declaring she'd cater the wedding by herself out of her kitchen at the Belvidere.

"I can't put my finger on why," he told Lisa Caner. Still, he took a stab. He wanted, for once, Fitzhugh to tell stories about *him*. ("But chronicles of triumph, not humiliation.") He wanted the Honorable Judge Roxie to be slightly less patronizing in her affections, and Peter Murray out at the Family Law Offices in Aurora to not just vaguely recall that they knew each other in those days—by itself a distasteful notion, Presner'd bet—but that they'd been *outsiders* together, pals in grievance and mayhem. He wanted Henrietta to look in the mirror and pause languorously, suddenly knowing she'd missed her ship back in those days, that she'd bet on the wrong horse, that she'd do well even now to call around to inquire if Presner's seeing anybody. He wanted Gary Marx to size him up and think, 'Gee, I underestimated Presner. Always have. I'd do well to watch my back. Luckily Pres didn't tear me limb from limb.' "I guess I want all of them—except Fitz—Fitz doesn't do this—to stop viewing me as the shadow *nightmare* they would have become were it not for their gumption, resolve, and all-around great character. A tragic figure, Presner; that's what they think," he explained to Lisa Caner.

"Are you sure you really want to see these people?" Lisa Caner asked.

"I exaggerate," Presner admitted. He reminded her he was a comedian, Chekhov-style.

Lisa asked him if he wanted another cup of coffee. Presner nodded and watched her walk to the stove. She often wore long dresses when she went out with Presner, stuff she picked up at garage sales or second-hand shops. For all her slenderness, her compact round rump swayed as she walked to the stove, more the stage walk of a woman trying to communicate sexiness—a '50s blonde bombshell version of sexiness—than the natural walk of a lusty woman. This was a two-way street. He sometimes found himself flexing his bruisers—his biceps—for nothing more and nothing less than Lisa Caner's admiration. If to his knowledge she didn't notice, to her knowledge Presner never noticed her rump-featured choreography in the tight dresses. But just because they were sworn friends—nothing more—who wanted more?—didn't mean Presner's mind wouldn't wander. At the stove, Lisa Caner turned toward him. "I understand," she said. "You're disappointed in yourself."

"I'm not disappointed in myself," Presner clarified. "I may have once been but I worked through that." After all, isn't that what big picture/little picture was about? To look at yourself and see little picture toe to crown, no regrets. Anyway, who cares? "Now I get the wedding invitation and I want to go on Oprah for a makeover, which disappoints me in myself, yes, but I'm not disappointed in myself, typically. Only in the invitation-to-the-reunion sense of the term."

Lisa Caner yawned as she returned to the table. "At the supermarket this afternoon the cashier gave me back an extra ten-dollar bill. Usually, I return the bill when that happens. Today I didn't bother. I'm not disappointed in myself," she told Presner, "except in the short-changed-the-cashier sense of the term."

"But you're still a good person."

"Yes."

"I believe we've discovered the essence of purposeful self-esteem," Presner said. "The Presner Method."

Lisa said, "Otherwise known as denial."

Presner nodded. "The secret to my success."

As glib as they were being, who's not disappointed in themselves? If not over the long haul, then occasionally over the short run? Presner wondered, taking inventory. And if you can't pretend it's not *you*—without breaking into gales of Chekhovian laughter—you're also not the one thing but several. You couldn't pigeonhole Presner. Sure he's a loser, but he's also an attorney (if non-practicing), a playwright

(non-produced), a weightlifter and runner (non-Olympian), a reader
of detective novels (not literature), the manager of a solvent business
(newsstand, sometimes afternoon shift, sometimes graveyard), the com-
panion of a beautiful actress (friendship only). Not big picture, maybe,
but an album of little pictures, murkily developed.

Naturally, Presner put himself on a program. Increased his roadwork,
letting up so the quads wouldn't snap, pushing the pace when the groin
mended. Upped the poundage on the weights. 'I'm not a bruiser. The
Incredible Hulk's a bruiser,' Presner told himself with grim determination, adding an extra plate to the barbell. He had two months to work
with. *Time enough to make the world ten times over*. That's if you're God.
If you're Presner it's a start. Enough to make a difference? He thought
of putting out a shingle in front of the shop: 'Tyson's 24-Hour News
and Smoke. Plus *Presner,* Attorney-at-Law!' Not that he'd know where
to begin, but he could read a few books, purchase the software to guide
him step-by-step. Fitz would answer questions if he had questions. "But
the software's probably so good I won't have questions," he told Lisa
Caner. He'd start with small stuff, filing quit claims and writing ominous
letters on impressive stationary to discourage bullies, but soon—given
the seedy clientele walking through the double doors at Tyson's—he'd
graduate to spectacular murder trials, all from his office in the humidor.
That's where the rumination stalled.

He thought—Lisa Caner's influence—of starting a new play. It would
be hard-hitting and relentless, but spiritual and tempered with mercy, a
Chekhovian comedy—such was Presner's nature—but funny, not just
conceptually but with laugh lines. "Neal Simon meets Eugene O'Neill"
he told Lisa Caner, discussing the possibility. And if the new play came
back in the mails—"Hard to do all this in the next two months," Presner
conceded, "but it's a start"—he'd rent a hall, audition the actors—a part
for Lisa Caner; the play itself a showcase for Lisa, so everyone can feel the
immensity he'd felt the first time he'd seen her project her interior long-

ings, back in Continuing Ed—direct the thing himself, set up the chairs and register, and the tables in the lobby tottering with wine, cheese, crackers, cookies—chocolate chip, oatmeal raisin—the works—this was doable—because if they didn't need Presner, he didn't need them—their loss—he'd find backers, too (possibly Fitz, or the Tyson of Tyson's, who tolerated Presner paternally), or set up a non-profit to get the ball rolling. The Presner Players, he'd call them. It's not like he couldn't find a *lawyer* to do the paperwork cheap.

———

Sometimes on his walks Presner veered toward the Platte and stood contemplating the water.

They were stars, the lot of them. Maybe not with their names in lights, their faces on billboards—though Presner had seen Marx's visage on a bus stop bench—"No promises. Just results"—Presner seems to recall a pointing finger now, Marx posing like Uncle Sam—but big shots, lower case. When they spoke, people knew. Even Henrietta. Maybe not—in Henrietta's case—garage mechanics. Presner figured garage mechanics would take a whiff of her perfume and roll their eyes when she spoke. 'There's a sound in the thingamajig.' 'Yes, lady. Can you leave it?' Garage mechanics were more inclined to listen to Presner, the bruiser, until he opened his mouth—'Fellas, there's a sound in the thingamajig'—revealing himself even there, Presner the shlub, a fuckup; but when you knew who she was, you noticed Henrietta. She was in the news occasionally, earnestly photographed by the side of a despicable-looking defendant. Presner had this way of spilling his coffee on the picture, as if it were that or stick it on the refrigerator with a magnet. Several times her clients—technically clients of the state—walked on murder charges. "*Walked*? Does that mean they're out on the streets, running free?" Presner, concerned for community safety, asked Fitzhugh, who kept him abreast of the gang's developments when Roxie didn't.

"No. 'Walked' means they were acquitted of murder, first degree. They may have been convicted of second degree, or even manslaughter."

Presner wanted to get it straight. "So she didn't win, she *lost*?"

"When you save a guy's life it feels like a win. I'll tell you one thing," Fitz told him, "the prosecutors weren't celebrating."

If the garage mechanics knew that there were guys behind bars who'd be dead if it weren't for Henrietta, they'd get right on top of her noise in the thingamajig, Presner bet. No 'Lady this, Lady that,' guffawing behind their grease-smeared hands. She was still a pretty woman, too, not a looker who turned heads at twenty-five, but one you'd appreciate later, with more to her than met the eye.

To Presner, all of them were in that category, huge successes who looked it. Marx looked like a movie star. "I'll bet when he walks down 16th Street people think he's a movie star they can't quite place. A personage, definitely. Is it Harrison Ford? Is it the governor?" Presner informed Lisa Caner, his pitch rising. Well, Marx could still get him worked up. The guy face-to-face wasn't so bad, the last few times Presner had seen him. But the *idea* of Marx was grating. "Then they remember. Ah yes, the TV commercials! The bus benches! They'd farted on that handsome face!" Pepe, too—Peter Murray—had millions several times over, Presner'd been told. "There's big money in divorce and probate. Plus Pepe—Peter—knows people who know, apparently. Not insider stuff, but he invests wisely," Presner told Lisa. "More, when his folks retired, they cashed in half of Detroit. That didn't hurt. Money makes money."

Lisa frowned, "But are any of these people happy?"

"As any adult," Presner said, stiffly. He could criticize the old gang. Fitzhugh could. Roxie could. With anybody else, even Lisa, he got defensive.

"Pepe looks like a TV preacher these days. When he does your will, you think God's on your side."

Roxie was the least successful looking, though that wasn't an issue, Presner imagined, when people genuflected—"Your honor, your honor! Good to see you, your honor!"—wherever you went. She had to be disciplined to keep her head on straight. Roxie looked formidable, a tank—though a sexy tank—in her long shapeless dresses (he'd never seen her in her robes), though the formidability might be more the effect of the genuflection than her appearance. "Fitz tells me that sometimes she wears the robes in court, sometimes she doesn't. She's a new-style judge, doesn't go for the pomp and circumstance. Roxie figures they don't respect her for the robes, but the office. They know if they look at her sideways, she'll rule against them in two seconds flat. Who needs the symbolism? When she wears the robes it's because she looks good in black."

Presner thought it wasn't so much that Roxie looked successful, as that you couldn't imagine her as anything other. You knew there was more to her than met the eye, and you applied that knowledge when you looked, so when you looked at Roxie a second time, your imagination magnified. A dozen times more successful on second glance.

Fitz was like that, too. Big and gregarious but rumpled, with a sincerity bordering on the sentimental, he always gave the impression of dressing down, so that when you met him—this Presner imagined, staring at the Platte River downtown—you took Fitz for a record-setting Lincoln-Mercury dealer on his day off, or the head football coach after six hours of dissecting film. There was no place for Presner on this all-star team, though he contemplated triumphs as he stared at the Platte. He felt like Pete Best, the fifth Beatle cut from the band shortly before they became Big Picture, but still friends. Who can begrudge his resentments? But those kinds of reveries suffused him: He'd show 'em. Maybe he couldn't turn the earth topsy-turvy in two months, but Marx's wedding could be a wakeup call, like an attack of angina. This, too, would be in the Chekhovian script.

It was inescapable that there was less to Presner than met the eye; in the event somebody found the shabby bruiser impressive on first glance, on additional scrutiny he may as well string a placard around his neck bearing his fate: newsstand clerk. Even Presner wondered how this had come about. At first, he'd just wanted to get by, to free his sights of the murkiness that everybody else groped through. He didn't intend to wear the placard. If it were Pepe—with his black leather jacket, his chains and perpetual scowl expressing inner-city contempt for everything not inner-city Detroit—Presner could see Pepe acting out his rebellion for a decade or two, working the newsstand gig, doing the class system analysis to death, living every inch the political statement about where he'd stand when the barricades were down. But Presner knew it was a pose *back then*. Half the reason he had mocked the cornballs who got fired up over con law is because he could picture Bogart mocking the cornballs, his amusement always more with himself contemplating Bogart than with the cornballs. Back then, while he was as disenchanted as the next guy and played the disenchanted law student like he was a paid consultant on the prototype, it wasn't like Presner was *really* disenchanted. Sure, his parents were dead, but you couldn't blame the world. Presner knew the difference. Sometimes, when Pepe went off on a diatribe, Presner would look at his angry friend and think, 'Gee, this guy really believes this stuff. Time to back off.' Presner, you can bet, played it for laughs.

He'd thought—mistakenly—that he'd flunked the bar, but that (even if so) just backed him up a few steps that nobody else would notice. Plenty of guys *really* flunked the bar and spit and scowled and stared down the fates then dared the fates to hit 'em again, pulling themselves up by the bootstraps—Presner pulling himself down—before signing up for another go. Then Sara's death threw him for an endless loop, but he was hardly the only one. It hurt to think he was little picture, Presner admitted that now—"Perhaps I resented those who hadn't figured that out about themselves," he posited to Lisa—but the realization was a small hurt, not fundamental. He wondered now. 'I didn't double major in drama and sosh without realizing everybody hurts just as much, or worse,' Presner thought. 'But they didn't wear the placard. I did. What happened?' and wanted to weep on the grassy banks of the Platte in his blue jeans and green t-shirt with his shabby bruiser biceps amidst the cyclists and joggers on the bike path and the rush of traffic on Speer Boulevard, ashamed not that he was a newsstand clerk, but that he'd let it happen to himself, as if a bystander, stunned and unable—unwilling? Presner knew—to lift a finger, even, to the rushes of fate.

Part Two

Well, Fitzy was the reason he couldn't let the old gang go. He was prepared to tell Lisa Caner as much when he walked back to his apartment from the Platte. He knew sometimes even she looked at him and thought, 'Poor guy. Parents dead. Sister dead. A tragic figure.' Everybody who knew did. You couldn't escape it. She didn't necessarily get the comedy. He'd call her for a movie and afterward they'd convene in her kitchen. "Our session," Lisa liked to call it. The actress was unusually interested in everything Presner told her, and Presner thought she was the best listener he'd ever known. He tried not to abuse the privilege by calling her day and night with his 'Lisa-drop-everything-I had-another-thought's, but in the months since he'd seen her at the Post Office, he'd found himself automatically turning loquacious around Lisa, as if she were a forum he'd paid for, or a studio audience. The playwright—he felt like a playwright around her—didn't fear this signaled a deep loneliness so much as that when you lived in the Land of Plenty you found yourself taking plenty. It was circumstantial. If his friend were a great horseback rider or obsessive cherry picker but run-of-the-mill listener, they'd ride horses or grow cherries and talk less.

Ordinarily, *outside* the job, where casual conversation about sports and politics and weather forecasts was coin of the realm—Presner sometimes viewing himself as a target, sometimes a shrink—these sessions as important to the job as running the register—he was typically reticent. Close-lipped. He didn't like boors dampening his solitude with their ubiquitous views and was no more inclined to dampen theirs. But Lisa made you larger than life—Fitz-like—with her attentions. It was easy to feel important and interesting when she watched you across the table and lifted her coffee as if in affirmation. She didn't tell you much about herself, turning every query—a Presnerian trick—into additional questioning—"But what I don't understand is where you get the idea?"—until right before the very instant that Presner might remonstrate himself—'Gee, I should lay off. This is too much Presner for her'—he'd recall that she was a dedicated actress—character roles, dependent upon profound understandings. Presner was himself a depository of quivering protoplasm, grist for her art; her friend, certainly, but also her research project. Whether this was a good deal or a bad deal or who got the best of it, Caner with the front row seat at the Chekhovian comedy, Presner with the rapt audience, depended upon his mood.

That explained Caner.

But the *group*, who collectively could send you weeping on the banks of the Platte? The All-Stars, Presner liked to call them, out of tribute to their current status. It was Fitz. It was Roxie, too, and the boyhood fantasies of evening the score, making 'em notice, guys you got me figured wrong. Big Picture. But mostly it was Fitz. Not just that Fitz called him monthly from his travels and delivered bulletins, though how Fitz knew the latest from across continents while Presner knew bubkes from up close was never made clear. He had his ways. Possibly he still had something going with Roxie? Sometimes Presner wondered, sometimes he suspected. Even with Henrietta, who was divorced now as well. Henrietta seemed unlikely only in that Fitz was so apologetic the first time around—there remained the impression that Fitz thought Presner was still waiting in line for Henrietta and wouldn't break his pal's heart with a second crack. Fitz could be an exciting guy on the phone and Presner could imagine Roxie and Henrietta both getting caught up in the commotion. He'd call hourly with amplifications, modifications, refinements, praise; Fitz always made you feel like you were in the mix. It would be easy not to notice—if you were Henrietta, Presner imagined—that he had Roxie balanced on the other hand, and if you were Roxie not to care that Henrietta was getting the mirror version of the same amplifications and refinements. Roxie *expected* as much, whereas Henrietta had this air of not knowing what was going on. "She wouldn't know even if you told her," Presner explained to Lisa Caner. "She gets that way from being a criminal lawyer, I guess. Those guys don't want to know too much."

"Have you done that?" Lisa wondered.

"Balanced two women? Or talked to defendants?" Presner—womanizer, non-practicing; attorney, non-practicing—asked, unsure of the thread.

"The women."

"Well, you know me. I'd discombobulate." Lisa laughed at the image: The bruiser discombobulating. "Plus, they can tell by looking at me. They don't even need to look at me. I'm not Fitz. I'm meat and potatoes. So's Fitz, really. He wouldn't be lying to them. I mean when he tells Roxie and Henrietta—*if* he's balancing the two—Jeez, Lisa, I don't even know if he's seeing either. I've no grounds for suspicion. No standing, either. Just wondering—when he tells them that they're the center, well, they're the center, but of separate universes."

The one time Presner went out with two women at the same time—"Not two on the vine, playing the field, one against the other," he told Caner, but encouraging first dates—both had sensed Presner's divided loyalties and lost interest. "It's easier when you're rich and out of town a lot."

Was Fitzhugh rich? This Presner wondered about, though the curiosity made him feel shabby. Fitz had helped him with his sister when she'd taken ill about a year after they'd passed the bar, and after that Fitzhugh could do no wrong with Presner. Before then Fitz was one of the gang, the glue, but not much more to Presner; an adventure, a colorful guy closer to the others. It was Pepe he related to, Henrietta he dreamed about, Roxie who kept him laughing. He could *ask* Fitzhugh if he was rich, Presner knew. Fitzhugh was liable to answer candidly, but Presner suspected the answer would be different if he asked him a second time, different yet a third. What's more, Fitz was so forthcoming it was only a matter of time before he furnished the information himself to fill out a story. He told you things in that manner, so that later you'd shake your head and say, '*Wait*. Did Fitz say he had eight million?'

Still, inferences could be drawn. The legal trade of Norman Fitzhugh was an odd potpourri. "A little of this, a little of that," Fitz called it. A little? The scope of a dynamic firm, the attentions of a solo practitioner, was Presner's reading. Fitz used to have three or four associates—he'd stop over at the office in a refurbished bungalow on Cherokee and they'd be bustling about importantly—but now flew solo. Not a generalist, Presner surmised. A polyspecialist. Fitz knew whom to call and they'd accept his calls. (Presner assumed this, too, about the rest of the Stars.) Was he rich, not by Presner's standards but by those of the Stars?

Presner, who'd once been rich himself, was ashamed of the consideration but curious. Possibly Fitz may not have had any more but spent it on travels rather than equity and salting away. Presner knew Fitz did a lot of contracts, not only business acquisitions and agreements, but flashier stuff: concert promotion, negotiating stadium leases for sports teams. He'd done athlete's contracts, too, a couple of guys on the Broncos, not big stars but even the minimum was substantial, and Presner doubted Fitz did it for the experience. He had a hand in intellectual property, Presner heard from Roxie. Fitz did some defense work, too, personal injury. He made angry phone calls on a guy's behalf. "Whatever comes through the door that's not a dog," Fitz told him once. If so, sometimes what came through the door was lucky. A few years ago, he represented a woman—the friend of a gal he met in a bar, Fitz (ever the networker) told Presner—on a sexual harassment charge against a prominent public relations firm. The trial was covered on the nightly news, Fitz soberly providing earnest spin straight into Presner's living room. Before final arguments a substantial settlement was reached, the news announced, with Fitz and the coiffured plaintiff smiling deliriously at Presner in his living room, courtesy of 9 News at 10. Presner waved at his friend. Details were confidential, both as to the nature of what must have been a monumental smoking gun—a smoking *cannon*—and the dollar amount, rumored to be more than twice the plaintiff's original request. Fitz wouldn't tell Presner; usually for Fitz confidential meant 'Be careful who you tell after I tell you.' (The irony was as substantial as the settlement, Presner thought. The kind of full-court press, 'You're the center of my dreams—prettiest woman since Helen of Troy—brighter than the sun' treatment Fitz specialized in, pulling out the works, wasn't always welcome at first. These women had their lives. Sometimes their love interests. But with Fitz they caved in, eventually overwhelmed. With another guy, another setting, you had a lawsuit and the dismal aftermath. Presner figured that was half the reason Fitz smiled so deliriously at the camera.)

For a while after that, Fitz was on the news every time Presner turned on his set, providing expert commentary on matters from high-court decisions on school vouchers to high-profile jury trials, local and national. "It's a media circus," Presner recalled Fitz once disdainfully exclaiming into his living room with no apparent irony in the assessment.

In person, if it was a circus Fitz knew who the clown was. "I can't sell a newspaper without there being enclosed the legal observations of Norman Fitzhugh," he complained to Fitz once.

Fitz puffed out his big cheeks in self-mockery. He agreed. "It's a disgrace." Fitz face-to-face or over the phone was always a lot more fun than the guy on TV. "*You* try reducing Supreme Court decisions—split votes at that—to sound bites." Fitz spread his arms bemusedly when Presner raised the issue.

"Can't see any reason to, or I would!" Presner joshed.

"Fitz in person's expansive intimacy," he told Lisa Caner. "That's what Fitz is about. Hear him talking for ten minutes and you want to hear an hour. Hear him with the twelve-second stint on the TV news and you want to hear less. Five seconds would do, if not fewer." Unless he's your friend. "He's been on less often lately, considering his travels. He's more a senior consultant now, when he's in town. There's another guy they call first."

With his international business contacts Fitz was a liaison now, Presner guessed, a middle guy, greasing the works for import/export. Multinational acquisitions, media deals, the imagination ran rampant. He didn't really know. Fitz liked smoking Parodis in Palermo, gazing from the docks to the water; that's what he talked about. Riding motorcycles down the Amalfi coast, meeting glitzy women with readymade plans to fly to Corfu; he'd tell you about that, not the deals. He was an international type these days but lonely for Denver, Presner guessed, since when Fitz called he seemed to know more about what was going on locally—with the old crowd—than Presner. There were calls on Presner's machine when he came back from his shift, as if the one thing Fitz didn't know was Presner's shift hours: "You're probably not answering. You're busy working on your play," Fitz liked to tease to the machine. Since news of Marx's engagement there'd been three messages a week. More than that to Roxie and Henrietta, he'd bet. "Or doing your pushups. You'll be the strongest guy at the wedding, mark my words."

But when he'd helped Presner with his sister, Fitz was none of that. Certainly he had plans, and Presner back then had no trouble envisioning Fitzhugh cutting a romantic career swath. Everything that happened—the media commentary, the international contracts—Presner might have foreseen, if he'd thought about it, and you could bet Fitz foresaw as well, but at the time, fresh from passing the bar, he was doing piecework with two or three general practitioners; stuff they'd farm out to Fitz then cut him half. He'd hire out for investigations at an hourly rate. Fitz had hopes one of the practitioners would take him under his wing, but it was sink or swim. As for the quality and efficiency of his legal work, "I'm pathetic, I'm a piece of crap," Fitz told Presner often.

He hung out a lot at Tyson's those days when he wasn't doing piece-work or investigation—almost always, in other words—especially after Presner's sister took ill, Fitz not saying too much—unusual for Fitz—but standing around, it seemed, in case Presner wanted to unburden. Some-times he even took a shift behind the counter, Fitz a quick study, when Presner went to the hospital on short notice to see Sara. Sometimes Fitz went along with him. Presner got used to him, the way the President gets used to the Secret Service. "I suck," Fitz would say about his legal efficiency. For every eight hours he worked back then, scrambling a thou-sand directions as he researched, feeling his way by trial and error, he'd bill two.

"Even I have a conscience," Fitz told Presner, who didn't doubt it. "In law school they don't teach you how to be a lawyer, they teach you how to think like one. The being comes later."

"So that's what I was doing in law school," Presner whistled.

"Well, you knew better. You knew what being a lawyer would be like. It's not fit for man nor beast." As Fitz explained, "Here's what it's about. You take something which doesn't seem to fit the criteria at all and swear to the heavens that it does perfectly, and then take something—the other guy's motion—that fits the criteria perfectly, and swear to the heavens—to the judge—that it's apples and oranges."

Presner waved his arms, Fitz-style, indicating the rows of magazines and newspapers and the humidor in the far corner. "Luckily I have this to fall back on."

Fitzhugh laughed. Since Presner's sister took ill, Fitzhugh had this way of not only crediting him with higher motives, as if the personal circumstance generated purity of soul, but of finding Presner more amusing. He wasn't being patronizing—though Presner wasn't as sensitive to patronizing as he would be in later years when Roxie and the others pretended to take him seriously. It was as if through Sara's illness it dawned on Fitz that Presner was a person worth paying attention to. Fitz stood across the counter from Presner in his overalls—Oshkosh B'gosh, Presner remembered, for every time Fitz walked into the shop in those same overalls Presner would yell "Oshkosh B'gosh!" Fitz would laugh at that, too—the same pair every day, a practice Presner found more inspiring than reproachable. And not—to be diplomatic about it—flattering to a big man like Fitz. To Presner—the former theater major, the future playwright—it looked like Fitz was auditioning for a role in *The Grapes of Wrath* or *The Beverly Hillbillies*. More likely—given the bulbous fit of the overalls—auditioning for a role as a helpless guy auditioning for a role. He'd spread a magazine across the counter—*Popular Mechanics*, *Commentary*, *Modern Maturity*, all stuff he read with interest—and turn the pages in total absorption as Presner tended to customers.

He'd tell Presner about his latest misadventure in the legal trade. Less often than in law school he'd talk about women he was pursuing, or women he was resisting. This must have been—unknown to Presner until years later—around the time he was shtupping Henrietta, though Fitz never mentioned Henrietta. Then he'd ask, "How's Sara?"

Sara was cycling through good days and bad. Presner would tell Fitz which it was that day, Fitz nodding solemnly in either event. He'd ask if Presner wanted company going to the hospital. When Presner wasn't at the hospital but at Sara's—Presner all but moved in with her after the diagnosis—Fitz might come over with him after the shift and often as not order pizza or Chinese for everyone, including Sara's friends who were usually around. Sara's place became a clubhouse. The Cancer

Clubhouse, Presner joked to Fitz. When it was the three of them, Presner could still see Sara gamely working on a slice, with Presner and Fitz finishing the box and then the other box of the Deluxe Special, then later Fitz and Sara holding court or—more often—watching TV.

Sara, an actress, was a year older than Presner. For a time when he was a theater major, Presner enjoyed envisioning riding his glamorous sister's coattails into the big time. Though her talent and her imagination were Big Picture—this Presner would insist upon to his grave, if not long after—her ambitions were less urgent; Sara sought to develop her craft not in New York or Los Angeles but Denver. "New York or LA can wait," she'd say when anybody asked. Plus, there was her marriage—a brief imbroglio to her college sweetheart that more closely resembled an experiment in living together, a last stab—as Presner understood the relationship—at staying together after college. Rick's family had numerous interests in Denver that Rick was being groomed to oversee. That kept Sara local. Plus, there were her friends, fellow members of the theater community, a purposeful lot with ambitions for Denver as a Regional Theater Mecca that Sara bought into and encouraged. Plus, her brother was in Denver. But she was *good*—this wasn't just the brother in Presner talking, though as her brother he was proud of her once they became adults. During one four-year period, there was never a time when she went without a role, usually as the lead ingenue, though as Willy Loman's wife—at the Arvada Dinner Theater—she won the Best Actress designation from the alternative arts newspaper. "Not a Tony but still," Presner told everyone.

Sara shook her head when Presner went on like this. "Still not a Tony."

He was a walking scrapbook. When Sara played Lemon—a complex, demanding role—in *Aunt Dan and Lemon*, the *Denver Post* critic preferred Sara Burton's performance—Burton her married name—to the Lemon he'd seen at Steppenwolf in Chicago.

"When is a Lemon not a lemon?" Presner asked Fitz.

She had an Equity card, which Presner kept in his wallet after her death, along with Sara's picture—a glamour publicity shot—and another picture of the two of them standing in front of his apartment building shortly before Sara's diagnosis. This shot was taken by a stranger walking by. Though by then she'd been exhausted for two years, she smiles radiantly at her brother.

Though a year apart in age, they weren't close growing up. Sara lived the imperial presumptions of a girl—later a young woman—who knows she's more beautiful, more talented, probably smarter than almost anybody in any room she was liable to walk into. Adolescence being what it is, she wasn't universally worshipped. There were rumors that got back to young Presner that she was stuck-up, a snob, and Presner, adolescence being what it is, didn't find these rumors unwelcome. Even those reporting the rumors—Presner noticed—reported them with a kind of awe. She was a target for beauty pageant promoters and scouts for model agencies. In high school, there was talk around the dinner table of Sara's appearing in television commercials. If she ever did, Presner couldn't remember. Presner in contrast was an athlete earnest in all seasons; from Little League through high school there wasn't a sport he couldn't be second string in, unless he was third string. Sara took the advanced curriculum, Presner grappled with the regular. From what he could tell, she didn't actively despise him. They didn't have much in common. Presner liked to recall one time when they were in junior high and their parents were out for the evening. The two of them were sitting in the living room, ten feet apart, Sara curled up on the couch reading *Crime and Punishment*, Presner stretched on the ottoman reading *The All-American*, by John R. Tunis. For over an hour, not a word was exchanged. Later, when Sara walked out of the living room, she turned out the light.

When their parents were killed in an airplane crash shortly after Presner's graduation from the U, everything changed. In an instant the siblings were transformed from polar opposites to life supports. Presences rather than existential curiosities. Though their parents were lifetime Chicagoans, they buried them in Denver, where they could visit the graves, and though their reasoning was understandable the guilt they shared over that decision tied them together more.

They didn't know how to stage a funeral. While the mortuary handled most of the details, how would the *mortuary* know, for example, if their parents would want a rabbi for the service? "What do you think?" Sara asked.

Their dad stopped going to shul the same time Presner stopped—right after his bar mitzvah. Their mom was far more active in the League of Women Voters than Hadassah. "I don't know. We should probably err on the side of safety."

"They were Jews through and through," Sara recalled.

"Remember Murray the Remarkable?"

Sara shook her head. Over the years, he'd asked her the question, but Sara never remembered. It was the name their dad called himself in stories he'd tell Presner. Was it possible that Murray never told Sara those same stories? She often remembered their childhoods differently. Presner wondered. Maybe he'd thought little Presner needed the tales? Years later, when Presner would read up on Jewish folklore during slow times at Tyson's, or at the Pleasure Palace, kicking his legs up on the couch with a thick book, he'd think that Murray the Remarkable was a Jewish archetype, derivative of the Golem, the shapeless mass, the monster who'd protect persecuted Jews, or of the lamed vovs, the thirty-six hidden saints upon whose virtues the continued existence of the world depended—as long as there were thirty-six out there, the place was worth preserving.

That's how Presner felt when his dad told him the stories—that some-body was protecting him, and that there were guys out there pulling their weight—but as he'd reel in the stories he could see that the tales of Murray were remarkably pedestrian, recounting walks with his dad where Presner the tyke identified caterpillars and robin redbreasts, or the time that they rented a cabin in Wisconsin when Presner caught the biggest fish—Presner always the star in Murray's stories. "Tell me Murray Markable," he'd blubber, and his dad would put a finger to his mouth and whisper *shhhhh*, then softly tell him about the day Presner woke up the earliest of all four of them in the family, or of the time that Presner found Mom's slippers.

"Let's err on the side of safety," Sara suggested.

Sara called a director friend who was known to be active in the Jewish community. The director got them a rabbi.

In an instant it was as if Sara and Presner had never been anything but best friends. It was clear to both of them that their concerns for each other were genuine, yet nonetheless a way of placing the enormity of their parents' sudden deaths at one remove. You couldn't blame them for salvaging what they could. Years later, Presner would feel he still hadn't confronted the enormity, though sometimes he'd dream of them alive, often with Sara alive, too, the four of them around the breakfast table, and wake up enraptured with happiness, as if the dream were the reality and everything else the dream, then gaining his bearing—his bed, his apartment, he'd been dreaming—he'd feel again the overwhelming disappointment of waking to the everyday world.

Though his parents hadn't been wealthy, with the insurance their estate was surprisingly substantial. After taxes, Presner and Sara each in-herited over $300,000. The windfall—a mixed blessing in Presner's reck-oning—heightened the anesthetic. It seemed that in a calamitous instant he went from being an aimless twenty-two-year-old with neither equity nor particular prospects, a recent drama washout at the U, a guy who saw himself implicated by every sociological theory, working odd jobs when he worked, plotting future scenarios with more resignation than vigor, with two doting parents who still provided a monthly allowance along with the infrequent bailout as circumstances warranted—"What about law school?" his dad suggested in every conversation. "What *about* law school?" Presner carped back—and with an idealized glamorous sister to whom he was (at best) distant, to being a twenty-two-year-old with enough money to stake him to anything he desired should he desire anything, but no parents and a devoted sister who called him five times a day to catch up on his least musings.

Sara used her bequeathal to flee her mismarriage with Rick and commit herself with more determination and passion to the Denver theater. She soon began her fabulous four-year run. She rented an elaborate, elegant penthouse where she hosted fundraisers. He'd stop by to visit and walk in on a fundraiser for one or another theater cause, or for an unfortunate, impoverished, invariably uninsured actor. But there were plenty of other parties not strictly for the revenue. More than once Presner saw Sara Burton referred to on the society pages of the *Post* or *News* as the "Queen of Denver Theater." Her friends doted on Presner as if he were an adorable novelty item, Sara Burton's little brother. He was happy to sleep with a couple of the actresses, though he didn't imagine it was the same as sleeping with Hollywood actresses. They were both sturdy, attractive, older than Presner by several years, possessing remarkably precise enunciation. The sex was more cheerful than erotic, which was fine with Presner. He never mentioned either of these affairs to Sara, though in her last days he thought of asking his sister if she'd put them up to it. He was suddenly curious. Moments of lucidity in this final stage were infrequent, and Presner never got to ask. By then there was nothing of consequence unsaid between them, but there are always a thousand curiosities that remain.

As for *his* $300,000, Presner discovered how really difficult it was to make a dent in $300,000 if you don't spend it on anything. There were plenty of small-ticket items—a better television, a lot of eating out, a suede jacket—for a year he saw every movie or play featured within the city limits; he also flew over with Sara to London for a week of West End plays; extravagances Presner wouldn't have considered before the plane crash, but which together added up to relatively little in the $300,000 scheme of things. He indulged future scenarios with considerably more interest than previously—he'd begin his own theater group, the Presner International Players, or his own film production company (Presner, Boy Producer) but mostly what Presner liked about the $300,000 was the security of having it, of knowing he could take his time before deciding what to do next and know that whatever it was, there was a reasonable chance he could afford to do it without sacrificing too much more. He liked knowing that he had enough money that someday the right girl would marry him. This stuff was worth any number of extravagant purchases and adventures.

"I admire the way you live your life," Sara told him during this time, noting his austerity, that when they went to an opening night reception, he was liable to be both the most modestly dressed and the richest twenty-two-year-old in attendance. Years later, when he'd think of Sara telling him this, he'd feel immense, if temporary and rueful, pleasure.

Eventually he used a portion of his inheritance to purchase a good LSAT prep course, then Presner sent himself through law school, where he met a number of similar kids who were biding their time with seemingly more money than they knew what to do with, and a number of other kids much better dressed than Presner who sacrificed and scraped by for the opportunity to squeeze every ounce of knowledge from the law school sponge. He took plenty of time-outs to visit his sister and watch her act. He clowned around a lot with Pepe and Roxie and got the serious crush on Henrietta, was betrayed by Marx, and marveled with all of them in amused and envious attention at Fitzhugh's exploits.

Sara's four-year run was curtailed by exhaustion. The source of the exhaustion wasn't mystifying—the run of even a single play, given the endless efforts of preparation, memorization and descending—or ascending—into character, to say nothing of the nonstop adrenaline and surging stresses of putting the thing together—at numerous points every production appears doomed to disgrace and humiliation—then performing in front of paying audiences with the results published in ostentatiously discerning, sometimes mocking reviews (given the itinerant status of most theater companies and the superiority of most critics), can be draining and depleting. That's one play. To perform in a dozen consecutive seasons, in addition to hosting fundraisers and acting as the unofficial goodwill ambassador and self-described crisis advisor on 24-hour call to the local theater community—a phalanx of needy, temperamental types, Presner observed—in addition to conducting a personal life, a bit mysterious to Presner, where she fended off advances and sifted through men with such frequency that, despite several daily phone calls and weekly visits, Presner couldn't stay abreast—didn't want to stay abreast, Sara accused him once when Presner would confuse Darren with Nicholas or Kip—well, Sara was the one who inherited their parents' stamina, that was clear. Looking back, when he wasn't training for sports, it was always an effort to walk across the room. Sara became the Iron Lady their mother was, took real pride in assuming the mantle, Presner knew, a tangible legacy, but he knew she also loved what she was doing enough to do it all full throttle.

Years later he'd think of that when he'd think of her. He wasn't above idealizing Sara anymore in death than he was in life, but the fact was before him: twelve plays in a row. If there weren't a lot of people who would appreciate something like that, *he* would, just as he'd appreciate the kind of oracular conversations they'd have that he'd never have with anybody else. "Character matters," Sara told him once as a point of information.

"I don't doubt it."

"When I say that to myself, I gain energy. I'm not pretending I have any character to speak of, but it works. You should try it."

A noble sentiment, but wherever Presner went, he was still Presner; such tricks didn't summon dormant resources.

Probably her thermostat was set higher than Presner's. But her weariness became obvious. "Everybody burns out if they don't watch it," he told Sara when she first mentioned the exhaustion. He'd noticed it for a few months before she'd said anything. She'd looked tired always. She'd liked to walk up the steps with Presner—who never saw an elevator he wouldn't pass up—to her tenth-floor penthouse for the exercise, but now couldn't and took the elevator. Other small things you don't take in at the time. Spent more days resting—when she wasn't charging in a thousand directions—before driving to rehearsals. Strongly considered—the subject of many phone calls—not taking the Linda Loman role at the Arvada Dinner Theater, but it was *dinner* theater, a different audience than the small, cutting-edge crowds who usually saw her work. *Professional* theater, she'd explain, as if to convince herself; a chance to use her Equity card rather than a cut of what if anything was left after expenses. "Anyway, this will be my last role," she informed Presner. Sara meant for the time being. She'd take off a season or two to regenerate then come back gangbusters. Anyway, it wasn't just a health issue. Her *art* needed it. She feared she was growing slack, getting by on momentum, adding, "Nobody cares about my streak but you."

Presner was pleased she took the Linda Loman role. If she was exhausted, you couldn't tell. Linda Loman was herself exhausted from the sheer daily grind of maintaining the fragile egos of a deflated, defeated husband and two bums-in-the-making, year in and year out, with nobody else to keep the ship afloat, and always with a house that could pass for a showroom. The grandeur of theater is that it's always a one-time shot, but the half-dozen times he saw the play—watching from the wings once, the back row another time—she nailed it. Every couple of weeks he'd drive with her into Arvada in his Dart, in no capacity other than chauffeur, and end up working the ticket line or hustling around in the kitchen or shoving furniture around backstage under the supervision of the stage manager and director, a burly ex-public relations hack who repeatedly joked that Presner was around enough he could play an understudy. Although Presner *was* helping out, doing the favor good naturedly, voicing the occasional student-in-the-making legal opinion when applicable, he wasn't certain the needling was good-natured.

"Sign me up," he'd say, or "No, just happy to lend a hand backstage. It's interesting back here."

When he'd drive Sara back to her penthouse apartment—this was after she'd clear more dishes, then chat with the cashier after slumping in front of the backstage mirrors removing her makeup with the assistance of the Director ("You need a ventilator," Biff told her every night, curiously unconcerned), then helping out some more where needed—she'd be out cold before they left the parking lot. When they pulled in front of her place Sara would catch her breath for a few minutes before Presner walked her inside. For this performance, Sara Burton won the Best Actress designation from the weekly arts newspaper, the only award she'd ever win, but Presner would picture her standing around after her performances and talking, digging in her heels, being gracious while barely able to stand upright, soon to collapse backstage but for now playing the Iron Lady until the last Dinner Theater patron left, and think, 'Best performance? They don't know the *half* of it.' After the Arvada run there was a little item in the *Post* theater column commemorating her streak. "Now Ms. Burton is taking a hiatus," the columnist wrote affectionately.

"Now Ms. Burton is taking a hiatus," Sara would say after that, before hanging up the phone or when he'd leave her place after visiting.

During this time, it became apparent that her condition wasn't merely the natural effect of overwork. For the next year, until she was diagnosed, when the exhaustion was such that Sara couldn't leave the penthouse apartment except for movies or infrequent lunches with friends—staying away from plays for reasons Presner could only surmise—Presner chauffeured her to see numerous doctors. Some had no explanation for her condition, some had too many. Pretty much they'd look at Sara and her somber brother in their offices and shrug. The tests were inconclusive, repeatedly ruling out cancer but little else. 'Welcome to the litany of nickel and dime diagnoses,' Presner would think whenever Sara was given a new one. 'Welcome to the bullshit.'

But it wasn't *all* bullshit. He wasn't skeptical of doctors any more than he was skeptical of human beings. You walked into their offices because something was wrong with you and you waited to hear what, which was perfectly natural, and being human beings themselves, motivated by generosity and ego, the doctors wanted to tell you. They took the tests and took some more and interpreted the results and scratched their heads. While some did make their pronouncements with the air of absolute certainty, most admitted they were guesses. Each time Sara left their offices—with Presner along as the extra set of ears—relieved to finally know what she was facing. At various times she was pronounced anemic or hypoglycemic; she was diagnosed with Chronic Fatigue Syndrome (this Presner found plausible, though a physician Roxie was dating told her it was a "fad" diagnosis, useful when they couldn't pinpoint and didn't want to accuse the poor patient of malingering), endless colds, bronchial infections, pneumonia, walking pneumonia, double-pneumonia. "If you had a third lung you'd have triple pneumonia," Presner suggested when they drove back from yet another round of tests, interpretations, tentative speculations.

The pneumonia was real, but not really the problem. By then they both knew it. "Shut up," Sara said. "I don't need your wiseass humor now."

"Sorry," Presner said. "I know how frustrating this must be for you."

"You *know*?" Sara snapped.

"I have no way of knowing," Presner corrected. There were times, given her frustration, when you had to phrase things just so.

She'd say things to Presner she wouldn't say to anybody else upon pain of death. Sara sighed. It wasn't just her health, her energy, but that the various medications for the various diagnoses were bloating. Her face and body were puffy and sore all the time. While she'd always looked younger than Presner, now she looked years older. You wouldn't call her beautiful anymore—wouldn't suspect she was ever beautiful—unless you knew her. She wouldn't be the burning bundle of enthusiasm every second. In those moments she'd snap at you if you looked at her sideways, and though he couldn't avert his gaze, Presner tried not to snap back.

"Whatever it is I need to know," Sara said.

He was twenty-seven years old, Sara was twenty-eight; they were both adults by standard measures, but still two pishers playing grownup, improvising the dreadful script. Both wished that Mom was driving her back and forth to the hospitals for the tests, that Dad was in the back seat or reading the newspaper in the waiting room, along for the ride and emotional support, that Presner was wherever aimless Presner would be; they'd call him later with the results and urge him to call his sister. Eventually Sara would talk about this, at first that she wished Mom and Dad were there to hold her hand and take care of her and assure her everything was all right, then later—well after the diagnosis, when she was dying—that she was only happy Mom and Dad *weren't* there. Presner knew what she meant. At least they were spared this. But now

Sara said, "I have to remember that it could be worse. I need you to remind me of that."

"It could be worse."

That night she called up Presner. "*Now* I could use some of your wiseass humor."

"Shut up. I don't need your laughs now."

"I know how exhausting it must be for you," Sara said melodramatically.

"You *know*?"

"I don't know," Sara said quickly. "I have no way of knowing."

"Was I that bad?" Presner asked.

"Thank you for putting up with me."

During one bout with double pneumonia, Sara was hospitalized for several days. The antibiotics, as ever, were slow to take hold. One doctor decided (another judgment call) that her lungs weren't efficiently draining mucus and thought to try a procedure called a lung fusion where he'd irritate the lung lining. In response to the irritation—as Presner understood it—part of the lung would fuse together to mend the lining. If the concept—anticipating the behavior of the lung lining—was wistful, it was no more so than using leeches to prevent blood clots. You didn't ask too many questions if it worked. While the procedure was fairly routine, a general anesthetic was required, which also worried Presner. During the pre-op protocols, when Presner was stuck in traffic en route to the hospital, angry with himself that he didn't think to leave half an hour earlier, suddenly afraid that he wouldn't get a word in with Sara before the operation—the general anesthetic could be a crapshoot, Presner had read horror stories—he was suddenly convinced she wouldn't survive this thing—*knowing* you were paranoid didn't reduce your paranoia, Presner thought, pounding on the steering wheel, pounding the horn—still, when your parents are killed in a plane crash it's not paranoia anymore, but realistic assessment—Presner opening his window to scream, lest anybody doubted him—now that Presner started, other cars were honking for a mile of standstill down I-25, as if heralding calamity—with Presner thus occupied, the physician's assistant who prepped her for the procedure observed that Sara's spleen felt swollen. The PA had nothing to compare the swelling to, so she called in the surgeon, who agreed, who called in the specialist for further consultation, who wheeled Sara out of pre-op and down to Radiology for an emergency CT-scan. "Usually, you have to schedule weeks in advance. Lucky me," Sara told Presner later.

"Didn't they ever feel your spleen before?"

"It wasn't *swollen* before."

He was present for the diagnosis three days later, sitting beside Sara in the office of Dr. Peabody Claridge, "the most prominent oncologist in the region," according to the specialist, an oncologist himself, who'd referred them. Though Claridge was a short, stocky, blush-faced man who sputtered to the point that Presner felt like helping him out with leading questions to signal memory—'What kind of cells are they, sir? Benign? Malignant?'—he nonetheless had a sense of swagger about him, an authority that Presner found mystifying—even Sara would speak reverentially of Dr. Claridge—beyond that he ceremoniously removed his smock when they entered his office, nodded not perfunctorily but with genteel pleasure at meeting them, and once he stopped sputtering, unleashed gulfs of language as natural and fanciful and windy as ocean storms.

Sara's sense of humor accelerated far past Presner's. "You know the one where the physician's assistant scrubs up for the pre-op? 'How's your spleen?' she asks the patient. 'Compared to what?'" Corny stuff, impertinent. Cracks even Presner would suppress found expression from Sara's lips. Stuff he couldn't think up to say. Now it seemed to Presner that Sara shot straight past Kubler-Ross's five stages of grief—fear, denial, bargaining, anger, acceptance—to a sixth stage, not mentioned in the books friends impressed upon her: situation comedy. If the situation was always the same, variations were many. This was after Claridge's verdict—the eminent oncologist sat behind his modest desk with mounds of papers and two large computers, as if posing for a portrait or catching his breath. Mostly Claridge answered questions about treatments and "progress" of the disease and what they could expect—everything but an outright prognosis. "It's a chronic disease," Claridge said at one point, coughing. "Something you'll have to live with, like diabetes." Already the cancer, an adenocarcinoma, had metastasized through the glands from an unknown point of origin to her liver and spleen and the cells surrounding her lungs. As they left the great man's office, Sara turned to Presner. "Fuck 'em if they can't take a joke," she said, then burst into tears on his shoulder. "It's a chronic disease," she whispered, "like gout."

Presner grunted.

While she was frequently too exhausted to move and during the last month of her life could barely talk, between the time of the dozen diagnoses and the end, Sara was seldom down that Presner saw. She had good friends she may have confided in about her fears more than in her brother, though it was but a chronic disease, "like irritable bowel syndrome." After the diagnosis, Presner virtually moved into Sara's, the easier to drive her around from the hospital for her chemo treatments to the doctors to the store or just for rides—at first—out of town, once to Aspen, though after a while she was too sick to spend so much time in the car. At her place there was a steady traffic of theater friends, Presner opening the door and leading them to Sara holding court in the living room, then he'd duck out for the guestroom where he'd set up headquarters amidst the piles of laundry. An hour later he'd duck back in. They'd get the idea and say goodbye to Sara until tomorrow.

Sometimes, when he'd duck back in, he'd find that Fitzhugh had come over to pay homage and entertain the troops.

She had plenty of other friends who didn't come over, of course, who avoided Sara as if she were the messenger of their doom, or a monster they'd long thought they'd buried again rearing her ugly head. Presner, long on memory, kept a list in his head that twelve years after her death he could still recite.

It was one of her best friends, Audrey, a vaguely pretty hawk-faced woman who was a CPA and kept the books for several local acting troupes, who took Presner aside. "She's mostly worried about you."

Presner nodded.

"You don't have to worry about me," Presner told Sara after everybody left. They were watching TV in the living room; he knew that soon she'd fall asleep and he'd fold her in his arms and carry her to her room and put Sara under the blankets—although this was summer she was always freezing, an effect of the chemo, as was the constant sensation of insects crawling over her, intense soreness in every orifice (Presner always listened calmly, not wanting to hear), and heavy sleep from which she'd awaken trembling with exhaustion—"Mom and Dad said they'd buy me a Model T," she said once upon waking, and Sara seemed to believe it; Presner lacked the heart to locate reality, which she'd discover soon enough, once the murk cleared—after which she was on her own, though she had a bell for when Presner was out of the room. At the ring, Presner would hustle.

"I mean it. You don't have to worry about me. I'll be fine."

She looked at Presner like it was the most preposterous thing she'd heard since the day as a kid that he announced he'd play pro football when he grew up. Sara reached over and melodramatically placed her hand atop his and stage whispered, "And I'll be fine, too."

Presner couldn't dispute that she may have really meant it. He hoped so, and usually managed to believe it himself.

Perhaps she'd raced through her Kubler-Ross stages during the two years of exhaustion, the endless litany of misdiagnoses, and now that she finally knew for good placed the anxiety behind her, like the catharsis after making a serious decision, freed now to disregard the bullshit. Kubler-Ross was referring to the average case, anyway, not necessarily accounting for an actress accustomed to summoning the depths of her imagination to become somebody else, somebody who'd be fine.

Presner may have thought so, too, if it weren't that later that day—Diagnosis Day, he'd think of it—as Sara was dressing before getting discharged, Claridge tracked him down in the waiting room and tapped him on the shoulder, startling him from the brief moment of repose. Presner followed Peabody Claridge down the corridor and into the stately office and sat again across the modest desk with the mounds of papers and the two computers and took the deep breath yet again.

The look on Claridge's face said enough. "I'm sorry, but I lied earlier. I've never done that before in this situation. Your sister was—is—so lovely and so upbeat and so confident she'll lick this invidious thing, I couldn't bear to tell her. I couldn't see what good it would do. But it's not my decision. What do I really know? Her adenocarcinoma's not chronic. I suggest that you get a second opinion—I'd recommend MD Anderson in Houston or Sloan-Kettering in New York, and I'll be happy to grease the works if that's what you wish—but there's no doubt."

"I'm not following," Presner managed.

"It's not a disease she can live with, like diabetes. I'm very sorry to tell you."

For days afterward Presner wept hourly; brief wrenching spasms that were so cleansing he could last out another hour without weeping again. "That's only when I'm by myself," he assured Fitzhugh, who looked leerily at Presner as if beholding a hand grenade. Now Presner nodded, thanking Claridge for telling him the truth this time. "Is there a prognosis?"

Claridge blinked and grimaced. "That's always the question I dread. I understand why it's asked, and I understand that I have to answer, but I'm not God. Okay. Typically, with adenocarcinomas of unknown origin with considerable metastasis at diagnosis, like this son-of-a-bitch, we're looking at three to six months at the most."

Presner nodded.

Claridge reached into his desk and pulled out what turned out to be a business card, which he handed to Presner across the desk. "As if he were a magazine supplier strolling into Tyson's," Presner told Fitz. He expected Claridge to insist that he call any time he had a question—'Any problems, you call me, and we'll take care of it'—but Claridge just held the card above his desk. Presner took it and turned the card in his hand.

"Do I tell her? What do you advise?"

"She's your family. It's your call."

A moment later Claridge excused himself and reached for the telephone. The confessional was over.

For days the question obsessed Presner. Fitz called in hourly as a sounding board. It was stuff he could have talked over with himself, walking the streets, weighing the pros and cons, but with Fitz on the other end of the line, he stayed focused. "It's Sara's life. She has a right to know. Even if Sara doesn't want to know—I mean, who would want to know, Fitz?—even if it hurts her. Finally, it's a question of dignity, Fitz. It's not *fair* to her that I have the knowledge and she doesn't." 'And not fair to me, either,' Presner didn't bother to add. He'd pause. Finally, Fitzhugh would say on the other end, "I understand."

"On the other hand, she's buoyant, thinking it's chronic. She's up-beat, a joke a minute. Peabody Claridge said she was so beautiful and optimistic that he couldn't bear to inform her. They say attitude's important. It's not just me, Fitz. You should read this stuff I'm reading, the kind of difference that a fighting, buoyant spirit can make. Why let her become defeatist, under the circumstances? This cancer's unusual for somebody like Sara—she's atypical. Claridge didn't want to say because *nobody knows*. Usually it's men fifty to eighty, heavy smokers. She's twenty-eight. The standard measures don't apply. You see?"

"I say we should sue the bastard," Fitzhugh said. "Fucking Claridge should lose his license. It's 1988, for crying out loud. I can't believe the paternalistic asshole thinks he can get away with that kind of shit."

"He's doing his best," Presner said.

Within a week, Presner had gleaned thousands of pages of popular literature on cancer. "My sweet amateur oncologist," Sara called him. She left it up to Presner to do the reading and recommend exercises, such as visualization, Sara trice daily envisioning little Pac-Men attacking the cancer, Presner envisioning torpedoes cutting through the blue Pacific to explode a battleship of cancer cells, then whatever he happened to think next. Fitz also came in handy here. As soon as Presner finished a useful book he'd hand it to Fitzhugh, who'd read it for additional perspective—or mostly out of interest, from what Presner could tell—and they'd talk it over. Sometimes, when they'd do the visualization sessions, Fitz would sit beside them on the huge couch closing his eyes, obliterating cancer cells in his imagination. "All I see are Pac-Man ghosts," Sara said.

Beside her on the couch Fitzhugh said, "I see sitting ducks in my mind's eye, the three of us blasting the suckers. Bam. Poof. Pop."

Presner wished it so. "Gee, the shmucks don't have a chance."

Presner never told her that she was dying. After a while the ethical character of the question diminished, obsessing Presner less as they acquired their convalescent routine. Every two weeks, he'd drive her to the University Hospital where she'd take three regimens of chemo—Cisplatin, Adriamyacin, FU-5—through the IV. Two hours later he'd drive her home. She'd throw up for three days, tolerate the soreness after that, then two weeks later they'd do it again. Sometimes he'd still look at her, the knowledge he carried immense, but he'd made his decision, *de facto* as it was, and he'd carry the weight. A dozen years later, he'd occasionally feel ashamed that he didn't tell her.

Sara and Audrey, who often stayed with Sara when Presner was at work, went shopping for a wig one afternoon—"Plan B," Sara named the long brown wig, which Presner for years afterward would periodically encounter when rummaging through his closet—but Sara never lost her hair from the treatments. "The first concept behind chemotherapy," Presner explained to Fitz from his reading, "is to blast the cells on the first go with as much treatment as you can tolerate without it killing you—that first shot's the real opportunity, for like any living organism, malignant cells adapt and won't be sitting ducks the second time through. The process is repeated on the second go and the third go, with diminishing returns, though—hopefully—there's less work to do by then." That was Presner's understanding.

Fitz, from his own scanning of passages, concurred.

But in Sara's case after the first two "goes" it was clear that the regimen wasn't working. The best opportunity had never been a real opportunity. These cells were resistant. So one day—Presner there, pacing the hallway—a nurse showed up at the penthouse and inserted a catheter in Sara's chest. The chemo would work non-stop. "Twenty-four hours a day of pumping's now the hope. Never providing the cells with respite or a second's breath," Presner explained to Fitz.

By then, it turned out, Sara had long known the prognosis, and not just by inference. Audrey's brother, whose roommate was an oncological resident, mentioned the diagnosis. It so happened the roommate had recently read an article about adenocarcinomas of unknown origin with significant metastasis at diagnosis, which he tracked down. The medical journal found its way to Audrey, who showed Sara in all innocence. Two weeks later, Sara mentioned it to Presner; she thought her brother should know. "That means it's not chronic, like a sore back," Sara said. "Do you think we should tell Dr. Claridge?" Suddenly her face rattled with anger. She bit her upper lip then opened her mouth in tiny gulps.

Presner admitted he already knew the prognosis and told her what Claridge said. "But that's for fifty- to eighty-year-old men. You're atypical, so it doesn't apply."

Sara trembled a second longer—he thought, at his betrayal—but then smiled and patted Presner's hand. "Claridge really thought I was pretty and charming?"

"That's a direct quote."

"Of course, we've established that he lies."

Later that night she told Presner that her biggest regret was that she wouldn't have children. "The chemo ruins the ovaries."

"Probably not every time. And if so, you could adopt."

Sara nodded. "Baby brother, I could die. You know that, don't you?"

Still, they'd thought the regimen was working. Signs were positive. Sara had more energy than usual, her stomach slightly distended but she'd put on weight, and for a few days managed to look like her old self. One day she posed melodramatically in her living room mirror and smiled approvingly. "Why, it's Sara Burton."

They went to the University Hospital for a routine discussion of the third round when Dr. Wescott—the original specialist, to whom Sara was handed back after the Claridge consultation—announced that the results came back and didn't look good. Sara didn't have tumors but malignant lacerations that seared her lungs and liver, Wescott said. "I don't know what to try next. The cells aren't spreading, from what we can tell, but not going away either, from which we can infer that the cells are successfully resistant." Wescott furrowed his brow.

"I want an operation," Sara said.

Wescott was confused. He glanced at Presner then back to Sara and seemed to smile.

"I want an operation," Sara repeated evenly.

"There's no surgical alternative," Wescott said.

Sara grunted. The blood seemed to suddenly drain from her face—that's what broke Presner's heart—and for a moment she looked abandoned. "Oh."

"There's no primary tumor," Wescott said, in the apologetic tone he adopted when he wasn't sounding like he was reading Sara her Miranda warnings. Presner wasn't complaining; under such conditions what can you say? Wescott wasn't a grief counselor but an oncologist; one human being talking to another, but as a human being who'd best channel his energies to save other human beings because there's no magic bullet, no Plan B, no trump card, no chemo potion or surgical alternative he could give like a magical bowl of chicken soup to the other human being sitting across the desk—and *conversation's draining*, Presner understood. "We could remove your spleen but your spleen's not a significant factor under the circumstances. If we cleaned up your liver and lungs they'd only invade again." Wescott shrugged: Parts is parts. What can you do?

That's the moment Presner *knew*. That's the moment he knew Sara knew.

Sara nodded imperceptibly.

Three days later the nurse arrived with the catheter.

Audrey and Tara helped to carry her despair. Rick—Sara's former husband and college love—whom she hadn't seen since the divorce four years before, started coming by several times a week once he found out—Audrey called him with the news—and they'd spend hours talking affectionately, as if still a young couple but with a million years of brutal, tenderizing knowledge between them. She'd also talk to Fitz, whom she'd met only once or twice before her illness, about her fears. Sometimes Fitzhugh would tell Presner what she said, roughly, and Fitz would report back to Sara what Presner said, roughly.

"We should put Fitz on retainer," Presner told Sara. "Though as attorney or therapist, who can say?"

"Or friend," Sara said. "He told me the other day that you two were brothers under the skin. He'll look after you when I'm gone."

Presner pictured Fitzhugh in his Oshkosh b'Goshes. The guy who'd look after him. "Sub-epidermal twins, that's us."

Sara's project became keeping her brother amused. Distracted, if amusement was unrealistic. Sometimes, when she looked particularly ghastly, she'd stare into Presner's eyes and say solemnly, "Ms. Burton will now take a hiatus," then burst out laughing. It was hard to stay morbid. He knew they were both acting—worrying about Presner was Sara's own nervous distraction—but nonetheless their despair often played out in glee-like imitation, so authentic-seeming Presner thought you'd need to be either of them to know it wasn't. "Will you cry for me when I'm gone?" Sara asked, glee infusing her stare.

"Are you going somewhere?" Presner asked.

Not that she was never somber, but that was for lying in bed, Presner guessed, or talking to Audrey or Tara, Fitzhugh or Rick. He knew she told Fitz that hours would go by without giving cancer a thought, and then she'd remember—a thousand things around the apartment itself would bring her back—and she'd feel again the infinite deflation. Between moods she'd tell Presner, "Don't sell my dresses to your pretty gals."

"And your wig?"

"That's for you," Sara suggested.

Once, a couple of months after her diagnosis, Presner beheld her with mock credulity. They were camped out on the living room couch, as they always were by then when they weren't driving to the hospital. She was huddled in a flannel nightgown, a wool shirt Presner gave her, three blankets, wool socks. It was the middle of summer; Presner wore his shorts and muscle shirt. "Now that you're dying," Presner said importantly, as if he were Bill Moyers or Charlie Rose peering across the table at an important personage, "what's the key?"

"The key to happiness and the good life," Sara said with equal sincerity, then coughed, "can be acquired with the following steps. First, a curious nature expressed through many interests, providing you with numerous small satisfactions. Second, a vital emotional engagement with some person or thing, perhaps a cause or passion, preferably larger than yourself. Third, a good imagination."

"And fourth?" Presner chided, wondering if this were from an inspirational monologue she'd memorized for an audition, or a page from Dale Carnegie.

"Fourth, the right parents. Other questions, Mr. Moyers?"

Presner went back to rubbing Sara's feet. "I've got #4 covered. As long as you don't expect me to cover the others, I'm set."

Sara stopped smiling and opened her eyes and looked at Presner. "Please," she mouthed.

Then Presner said the most difficult sentence he'd ever say. "Remember the time we tried to figure out if we needed a rabbi for Mom and Dad? For the service?"

Sara nodded. "We erred on the side of safety."

"Hypothetically, do you want a rabbi?"

"I want whatever you want, baby brother."

"What do you want?"

"It's for you."

"Nobody wants to live more than me," she'd tell Presner, though as point of information or in prelude to something else she wouldn't mention, the brother was never certain.

Later, Presner would think of her final months as an ongoing party, punctuated by fits of dastardly coughing. "My cancer cough," Sara called it. Because she conducted her final months not as a dirge but a salon with her ever-present coterie, afterward Presner usually thought of his sister happily. After she died, he thought of her every minute, though over the next decade the frequency diminished until the time came when he'd stand behind the counter at Tyson's, as a bruiser contemplating the reunion at Marx's wedding, and try to calculate how often he thought of her these days. He didn't know. She was never *far* from his thoughts, he'd envision her several times a day, but actually *thinking* about her? Once, twice a day, he imagined, sometimes less. Still, Presner would always consider her last months one of the best times of his life. He met the challenge and was there—probably beyond what Sara herself expected of him—and did his best by Sara. Perhaps those four months she survived after diagnosis he'd had that "vital emotional engagement" his sister meant.

The Vigil Committee, as Sara called them, went their separate ways. Audrey got married not long afterward and now lived in Northglenn, still a part-time accountant. When Presner ran into her at a Sound-Track two years earlier—Presner shopping for headphones, Audrey a large-screen TV—they embraced and spoke warmly and caught up briefly. Neither mentioned Sara. Rick he read about occasionally in the Metro section of the *Post*—usually in tiffs with suburban zoning commissions—an even more prosperous developer, Presner gathered; Rick's inherited interests had expanded into an empire. Tara and Greta he never saw again or heard about after the funeral. He asked Audrey about them when he ran into her, but they'd long ago lost contact. Fitz was Fitz, of course. Presner was happy he could report on Fitz's success; Audrey knew, recognizing Fitz from his expert commentary on the TV news reports.

Twelve years after Sara died, Presner went with Lisa Caner to see a community theater production of *Wit*, the Pulitzer winning drama from a few years back. To Presner, the production was a phony piece of anti-intellectual buffoonery that everybody else—including Lisa—misunderstood as a profound, life-affirming statement and went crazy over. Death rips away everybody's pretensions, the play got that right, but the main character—an English professor who took a severe stance toward education as she built her life around the inspiration and consolation of words—was made to repudiate everything she ever believed in; an attack on ideas that Presner found as transparent as he found implausible. "They take the English professor, the intellectual, and make her a coward in the face of death. Gee, I wonder why everybody goes nuts," Presner told Caner. "Why stop there? Why not humiliate her more?" Still, he couldn't help reaching a counterpoint. Sara, similarly childless but not alone (Presner and the Committee saw to that)—though he'd never thought of his sister as *childless*, and before her illness it never occurred to Presner that Sara wouldn't marry again—didn't pretend to be anything but a good actress, a protective sister, an Iron Lady for acting and theatrical causes. No intellectual. A mass of potential who'd become a smart, pretty young woman interested in roles and her friends, not ideas. But she knew what she believed, which didn't wither when it was no longer convenient. When Greta broke down and sprinkled her dying Jewish friend, the *shayna*, with holy water, when Rick brought over a long-playing record that his mother (Sara's former mother-in-law) thought would help, a New Age production which anticipated in soothing tones an afterlife of fulfillment and simple pleasure, she appreciated their concern; the gestures were thoughtful, not coercive. (Presner found them coercive, but if they worked?) "There are no atheists in the foxhole," goes the homily, but that formulation didn't take into consideration Sara Burton.

"I wish I could believe that stuff if it would make everyone feel better. Do you want me to pretend I do?" he remembered his sister saying to Rick and Greta, Fitz and Audrey and Tara, *smiling* at Presner, as Presner told Lisa Caner a dozen years later.

Presner would think of that moment as much as he thought of her roles on stage.

The four months that Sara Burton survived after diagnosis wasn't all salon and mock discussions between bouts of exhaustion and deep "cancer coughing," and pointed, clever remarks and advice that Presner liked to recall, and confiding her fears to her friends while keeping her brother amused and distracted, and staying vigilant in the foxhole. The last weeks she couldn't talk or eat. Presner drove her one last time from the penthouse to the hospital, where she lay silently, except for the coughing, wasting away, her organs finally so lacerated they couldn't function, connected to an IV, during infrequent moments of lucidity trying to talk hoarsely to Presner or the others as the Vigil Committee gathered by her bed in room 23B of the ward, along with some nurses who were often there and had become friends long after Dr. Wescott wrote off Sara as a lost cause, the nurses sometimes gathering around with the Vigil Committee or making a point of stopping in to keep her company when their rounds were light. One of them, a towering brunette with a beehive, who'd been an actress in college, recognized Sara Burton—the name, anyway, for his sister now looked older than Mrs. Loman. This nurse especially went out of her way to visit Sara when nobody else was around. Sara acted flattered, but Presner knew the nurse would have done it for anybody. Years later, Presner still remembered her name: Leah Federman.

Presner took over now, giving them all moments of privacy, later (when it was time) clearing the room so each could have their final words with Sara. They'd walk out and tearfully nod, or embrace one another then gather back in the room until Sara awoke again. After the others had had their chance, Presner took his own, nothing profound by now—saying how sorry he was, thanking Sara for being his sister, saying how much he wished it were he instead—"No!" he imagined Sara scolding with her eyes—saying a thousand other things he'd never tell anybody; stuff just between them that would always stay that way.

Even in her last days, as she wasted away in the cancer ward, decomposing before Presner's eyes, there were moments of hope. On her last night, she sat up and looked Greta in the eyes and asked how she was. Presner was out in the hall discussing alternative treatments with the tall brunette with the beehive who'd recognized Sara. "She won't survive the flight to Bermuda," Leah Federman cautioned Presner, who showed her the brochure he'd ordered last week. "I'm sorry." Her eyes welled as she stared at the desperate brother. "These crackpots just exploit people's desperation," Fitz chimed in. "You never know," Presner said, handing the offshore brochure to Fitz. "Look at what it says." "If you want to go, I'll go with you," Fitz promised. "We'll camp out on the beaches." Presner nodded. Fitz read his friend's desperation. "It's worth trying." "Nothing to lose," Presner said.

By the time they returned to 23B Sara was out again. Until the final days, there remained tests to be run, procedures to be tried; by now the decisions were up to Presner. "*Only the gold standard*," Presner insisted to Wescott, when he could track him down. "*Only the best*." When the best didn't work, Presner ordered everything else, at last over Wescott's objections.

"There's always hope, but realistically nothing's going to work." Wescott sighed—Presner understood he had this conversation weekly, in infinite variations—then patted Presner on the shoulder and wearily looked him over. "Perhaps it's time to let her go. We have a quite excellent hospice at the University. You might want to talk to them. I'll get you the number. Call my office."

He had the rest of his life to let her go. "Sure."

The hospital didn't pay for these procedures and tests and the care in the ward. Sara's insurance coverage (purchased with the insouciance of a robust woman in her twenties) and bequeathal had long run out.

The final accounting—including a catered memorial service that Presner staged at Legion Hall (Fitz attending to the small details, bargaining down the prices, lining up a rabbi), attended by two hundred, and the funeral and plot beside their parents at Memorial Gardens—that the bruiser still visited weekly, dutiful son and brother, sometimes unloading, unleashing endless monologues, wailing his heart out on two feet or all fours—came to over $200,000.

Presner needed to borrow $100 from Fitz to purchase a floral arrangement and delivery to Leah Federman and the other nurses on the ward in appreciation of their interest and care.

Part Three

Presner considered attending Marx's wedding by himself—the better to carry off Henrietta?—but decided to ask Lisa Caner. Lately she'd taken him places—recently to a family reunion, where a cousin asked Presner when they were getting married; Presner shrugged conspiratorially, "Whenever she wants."

If going with Lisa wasn't the same as going with a *real* date, Presner had attended so many events by himself, unable to scrounge up a woman willing to pull on a nice dress and accompany him to the reception or the dinner and venture gracious small talk, or willing to weather speculation that she was spoken for by Presner, that he often didn't consider corralling a plus-one. Now that he had a presentable woman willing to appear on his arm, it seemed "inefficient" to waste the opportunity.

"I like efficiency," Lisa Caner said, looking up from across the table.

"That's why I'm asking. You make a terrific appearance. I'd like them to guess, mouths agape, then keep guessing until the cows go home, 'Is she or isn't she?'"

"It will obsess your friends throughout their honeymoon." Lisa smiled.

"Having nothing better to do to occupy themselves, right?"

"Midlife crises are boring."

"I don't rate a midlife crisis," Presner admitted. "Why start considering my choices now? Also, I like being older. But Fitzhugh, there's a guy who rails against the wind and the wind cowers. *He'd* rate a crisis. *There's* a play. I'll bet he shows up at the wedding with three nineteen-year-olds on his arm. That's if he doesn't bring Hankie and Roxie both. I mean the guy lives large. Take a look at Fitz and you'll wonder when the election is so you can vote for him. You'll volunteer to drive the elderly and the infirm to the precinct. Me? You'll figure I'm an election judge down at the elementary school. In fact, I'm loath to mention myself in the same breath."

Lisa laughed. Presner appreciated that. It was nice having somebody around who understood he was generating comedy. Possibly—in Lisa's view—*trying out material* for his play.

"You can certainly sound like a *nudnick*," Lisa said, "if that's what you're wondering."

Another thing about Caner: she used more Yiddish—probably knew more—than Presner. "Even the *goys* outquip me in my mother tongue," Presner muttered solemnly.

"Midlife crises are boring, Presner. Who wants to hear about another aging guy lamenting his youth, or who understands that he's going to die someday?"

"Or somebody's lousy childhood and the wounds she carries into womanhood," Presner smiled. Two could play this game.

"Or a guy looking at the world and blaming it for not being his imagination."

"That's the same aging guy, I take it."

Lisa Caner looked to the side of Presner, behind him to a poster on the wall of a play she'd been in before Presner knew her. You could make out Lisa in silhouette in the background behind the hero and the ingenue. Well, she was a character actress. If you practiced a scene with her on the page—this Presner recalled from the class at Metro—her "pale cerulean" eyes, a description furnished by Lisa herself when he'd asked her during the two months they'd dated—danced across your face like you were the Rosetta Stone made flesh. Otherwise, she always looked off to Presner's side when she talked to him, as if to catch his eye would only encourage him. Lisa continued, "Or an insecure girl chasing her illusions through love."

"Makes you proud to be human."

"But it still hurts, it's still real," Lisa said tragically. Presner noticed she stopped short of clutching her heart and spilling out of the chair.

"Well, you can't underestimate the loss-of-youth angle, the promise in the pretty young smile—I mean Fitz can't; he's the one they smile at—and me, Presner, the strongest guy at the wedding? *Bubkes*. And I'm sure it doesn't feel great to understand you're not going to live forever—I mean for Fitz to understand—*I* figured that out in grade school—I read somewhere where Saroyan says he figured that out at *three*, along with all the great philosophies of the world—all that's true—but what strikes you—me—you'll have to ask Fitz if it strikes him—is you can take back twenty years and it's like an hour ago. I mean, that's what hits you so hard. Your relationship with time changes. Quote unquote. I could blunder on another fifty years or I could keel over before I finish this sentence. Either way it's the snap of a finger." Presner wondered if that's what his play was about—not about a guy tackling midlife with Chekhovian melodrama, but a relationship with time.

Sometimes what bothered Presner the most about Sara's death—what hit the playwright the hardest now, anyway, beyond the usual heartaches extrapolated from the fact of it—is that if he lived to be a hundred—as he'd read in the *Post* last week was likely to become the trend among "boomers"—he'd survive her by over seventy years. Nobody who knew her would remember her or anything about her; even Audrey or Greta would draw blanks. He'd barely remember her as well, even though he'd desperately try. He'd already survived her by a dozen years; if anybody *now* ever thought about her or remembered her, they didn't fill Presner in, though Fitz still mentioned Sara sometimes. He used to imagine running into people who grew up with them, friends from back in high school in Illinois, for example—who hadn't heard the terrible news. He'd even worked up a few words he would say to them, but that had never happened, not yet, they were a long way from Illinois, and by now he'd forgotten the words he'd worked up. If he ran into them now, Presner, too, would be caught by surprise and didn't know what he'd end up saying. Probably if they didn't ask, he wouldn't mention it. "It would be a conversation stopper, I'll say that," he told Caner.

Second most—Presner counting—what bothered Presner is that when his sister died he saw an opportunity, and by now the window of opportunity had closed without Presner standing on his tiptoes and reaching up and grabbing and crawling through—for a chance to act like a fool or fail and not have to look over his shoulder at somebody he'd let down with his foolish actions, somebody who'd suffer his failures more intensely than Presner himself. "That's what family's for," he told Lisa Caner. "They back you up, they absorb. Where else do you get that?" Also, he'd pledged—had he mentioned this to Fitz?—that he'd make every minute meaningful. That in his sister's memory—parents' memory, too, though that loss had overwhelmed Presner differently, transformed him—overnight, it would seem—into a relatively wealthy young man introduced by his actress sister—suddenly his best friend—into theatrical circles, then a dazed (so it seemed now) law student who couldn't pause to look back, and briefly, a caretaker—everything he did would *count*: through his acts he'd build a monument to their memory. Everything he'd tackle he'd tackle double strength, as if his parents and sister were soldiers who died for his freedom and now it was up to Presner to live *free*. Well, who could live like that? Not even Presner with his speeded-up motivation ended up tackling everything double-strength. There were few moments in the day—when he wasn't running or working out—when Presner would venture with confidence that he was working at *single* strength. Sometimes still he'd remember about being all fired up. He'd take a walk, smoke a cigar, raise his fist skyward—he'd make 'em proud or die tryin'—but those windows closed fast, too. It wasn't stuff you could manufacture. You couldn't pretend the wounds were raw; they'd been scabbed over.

Third most, he had no idea. If somebody asked, he'd come up with something. The bruiser wondered now, looking at Lisa Caner, who was looking past Presner at the poster on her wall where she stood in silhouette. Nor was he being glib about himself; it was a question *Fitz* would ask, because he cared and also because—to Fitz—it would be objectively interesting to know what a guy who'd lost his parents and sister hated third most about it. Also, Presner could imagine Lisa Caner—not *this* Lisa Caner, but a future one who saw in Presner the romance she desired—asking him, and he could imagine telling her. Why stop there? Presner could imagine writing a play, *Ten Things I Hate Most About Sara's (And My Parents') Being Dead*, the drama a comedy because it's over for anybody at the snap of a finger, and thus the exercise in melodramatic self-indulgence, enumerating and amplifying the ten items, was, from a Chekhovian perspective, pretty funny.

"So I don't see the midlife stuff—the boomer bubbamagumba—if it's happening to Fitz," Presner said to Lisa, "as looking to regain long lost youth. Who'd want to do it again? You'd just get it doubly wrong. I see it more as looking for distraction, closing your eyes, looking away from the glare and the gloom. Who could blame Fitz for bringing the nineteen-year-olds, if this applies to Fitz?"

"Enough, Presner," Lisa Caner yawned. "I give in. I'll go to the wedding with you."

"If midlife crises are *boring*," Presner promised her, "I won't have one."

Now that he'd lined up his date for the wedding, Presner loaded, then reloaded. The miles, the weights, extra blocks walking. Line up Presner shirtless with a bunch of professional athletes, he wouldn't be the first you'd pick as the imposter. Not only would they wonder what Lisa Caner—should he introduce her as the Helen Hayes of LoDo?—saw in a small fry like Presner, they'd take in the new Presner himself and pause. 'There's more humanity—more vigor, too—in the two of them than in the rest of us combined,' Roxie would announce. 'More glamour and romance.' 'Certainly we pale in comparison,' Marx, the groom, would concede gloomily. The bride too would take in that Presner had the build of a twenty-year-old and lament, 'Why Marx? Why not Presner?' That very question would haunt Henrietta. Long term, short term, Presner didn't care. Fitz himself would marvel at the theatrical couple seated at the round table, larger than life. Later, Presner would offer a toast to the celebrants. 'Steadfast, trustworthy, those qualities *define* Gary Marx.' Ostentatiously, he'd turn to reveal crossed fingers.

Also, it would be nice to see these guys again after so long; not just, for example, to see if he could make Pepe squawk, but to sound him out about the mucky-muck law offices of Peter Murray and the phony suburban setup. Maybe the guy didn't change? Maybe this was a better deal for Pepe? That kind of stuff he could find out about everybody. Henrietta, too. Not only how things were going down at the Public Defenders, though he'd find that interesting, objectively—still, he'd gotten a good idea from Roxie—but what she thought about being a mother and middle-aged woman, not the Henrietta she used to be, the head turner, and more, if Henrietta felt she'd made the right choices—'Were they only the right ones at the time?' he'd ask—or, had she decided, Presner style, to bury her head in the sand until the choices made themselves? These were things he'd never thought ten seconds about. The times he'd seen Henrietta since law school it was through the sheen of Marx stealing her away. Time to forgive her for that? To give up the notion that she'd been holding out for Presner but became distracted, unaware of Presner's interest? Presner wanted to laugh out loud. He wanted to stand on his balcony and beat his chest and let 'em wonder what was up. Well, Henrietta knew what Henrietta knew. When Marx sat beside her on his dilapidated porch swing and put his hand on her knee—perhaps Hankie slipping the hand—Presner wasn't an issue. Presner tried to remember the last time he'd looked into a woman's eyes and there were no issues, just the shrinking expanse of thin air between them, then flesh to flesh; then the timeless instant is over, issues emerge again, but everything has changed, the issues suddenly seen through the sheen of that timeless instant. If it isn't all spark and dazzle and tingly sensations but soon enough becomes taking your lumps in the harsher light of trying to get along with someone you don't particularly know once that instant passes, there are still things you knew in that instant that no one can take away.

To forgive Marx for not being Presner with the contemplative man's compunctions and peccadillos? To forgive Roxie for not imposing herself when his sister was sick? To forgive them each for not making it their life's work to read Presner's mind?

Because he wasn't just about the athletic build and Lisa Caner on his arm, Presner sent out his play. He was a playwright, after all; why hide his light under a bushel? If a tree falls in the forest? (The bruiser himself didn't know. "Depends on the circumstance," he guessed aloud.) What if—not as comparison but to emphasize the point—the guys who wrote the mishnah kept it to themselves? Presner felt his energy *surge* and thought of writing a play tackling the theme; about a guy, a rabbi, perhaps, considered a tragic figure by initiates, one of the deep thinkers about the oral law but who keeps it to himself, never writes the stuff down or mails it off by goat wagon to the Sanhedrin or wherever, it's a secret, but—here was the twist—imagines *everybody knows*: "That's Rabbi Shugglepuss, the mishnah guy. A genius." The delusion that others saw you as a thousand times greater than you were, but at the same time *would be* if only you wrote down the commentary and let the word out. Not precisely the bruiser's dilemma, but the point held. In that instant the technical questions that had always discouraged him, the bruiser shrugged off: Were the themes well defined, the characters rounded, the structure sufficient to absorb the obsessive ponderings of Chekhovian-style comedy (at which nobody had ever laughed—at the one-liners, maybe, but not at the situation, according to Lisa Caner) before the climax, the touching denouement? The audience moved to recognition and tears? Presner didn't know. "Search me. The only thing I'm sure of, there are a bunch of people talking," he told Lisa.

Since he'd met her, it was understood that she'd read his play when ready, when *abandoned*, to quote da Vinci (art's never finished, but abandoned); even during their yearlong hiatus he had Caner in mind for this capacity—but now that he was sending it out Presner found himself *demurring*. "I'm just submitting it, a trial run, something—frankly—to have on the record for the wedding reception. It won't be accepted by then, but I can *say* I have it in circulation. When Roxie or Fitz says, 'How's the play, Shakespeare?' I can say, 'Guess what. It's making the rounds, Roxie, Fitz. With promising developments, too.'"

Lisa shrugged: "Okay, it's your wedding reunion."

"When it's ready you're the one I want to see it first and foremost. The first looksee."

"Whatever you want, Presner."

Still, Caner quickly got into the spirit. "Is this the undiscovered Arthur Miller of LoDo?" she asked next time Presner called.

"Ah, go on" Presner replied. Still, if this was but something to mention at the wedding, the bruiser wouldn't run the other way if somebody—a regional theater in Albuquerque; the New Voices Festival in Poughkeepsie—took it on for production. Presner went to Kinkos and ordered a dozen copies, hand-feeding each into the self-serve. He got the addresses from a resource manual, compiled the kind of cover letter the books recommended—"It's about one man's relationship with time. A comedy, in the Chekhovian sense"—which he quickly crossed out, and instead vaguely alluded to theater "experiences" and requested that they consider the play for production. One day, then the next, Presner stood in line at the LoDo Post Office, bundled each time with half a dozen packages, willing the woman in line next to him to inquire about what he was mailing off— 'Just my child,' he'd say. 'Just my lovely juvenile delinquent'—to no avail. One went so far as to look up, but only when first in line.

"I don't *want* to show Lisa," Presner admitted to Fitz. The phone was ringing when he walked into the Pleasure Palace after mailing off his half-dozen copies to the half-dozen addresses from the resource manual. Fitz would spread the word that Presner was in the mix. Otherwise, he wouldn't mention it. Lately, since Roxie told him about the wedding, Fitz had called twice a week, Presner seldom in, leaving no return number on the answering machine.

Presner pictured Fitz driving the Amalfi coast in a Fiat, overcome by inspiration, not just from the vistas over the Mediterranean but his thoughts, dialing Presner long distance from every phone booth to rehearse his idea, 'before it disappears into thin air,' Fitz would say. Not that the impresario saw Presner as a lifeline. From what Roxie told him, Fitz dialed her five times for every call to Presner. Doubtless there were others playing Roxie for Fitz, playing Fitz's Presner, but they were temporary receptacles for his epiphanies and onrushing curiosities. To Fitz, the others were annuals. The gang—including Hankie and Marx but not likely Pepe, except in spirit—were perennials. "What are you doing?" Fitz asked, as if they talked hourly and he was Presner's amanuensis.

"Just mailed off my play," Presner admitted.

Fitz let out a ceremonious whistle. "Has your pal, the actress—what's her name? I can't remember—read it?" That Lisa didn't sleep with Presner was unforgivable—incomprehensible—to Fitz; he'd banish her name from consciousness if Presner himself wouldn't on behalf of his own dignity.

"I don't want to show Lisa."

That was enough explanation for Fitz. "Sure."

Presner wondered, though. If *Fitz* read the thing, turning the pages while smoking a Parodi in a park by a hilly garden above Dante's birthplace in Sienna, concentrating while the cheers from the *futbol* stadium below rise through the open air—"Sien, Sien, Sien!"—an actual description furnished by Fitz—Fitz could turn the last page, hold it gingerly in the air like a dirty sock. 'Gee, it's not like I'm a theater major, an aficionado. I wouldn't know *Streetcar* from a poke in the nose.' Even if Fitz *liked* it that's what he'd say, though encouragingly.

And Roxie? Though Roxie offered to read it every time she stepped into the shop shouting, "Counselor!" Roxie'd read a page or two, put it aside, not pick it up, not mention it. Presner, embarrassed, getting the message, wouldn't bring it up, fearing the worst, though he knew Roxie wasn't a reader these days with her busy schedule; she was a *peruser* at best. Roxie liked to show the genuine interest—"How's the play, Shakespeare?"—but her genuine interest wouldn't extend to reading the thing. She had enough worries meting out justice all day down at the County Courthouse to have to worry over tactfully dispensing suggestions to her sensitive pal, Presner. She was no theater major, either. But Roxie trusted her gut, knew what she liked and what she didn't, would—if pressed—reveal the distinction (Presner's play the evidence) as if passing sentence on a pervert. Giving it to Roxie for a candid assessment—'If you have the time. No rush.' 'I may not get around to it for a while'—would be like asking Presner his views on the latest tort legislation. Why not Fed-Ex the thing directly to the Bermuda Triangle?

"There aren't too many places to turn," he mentioned to Fitz.

"That's the artsy life for you," Fitz commiserated.

Still, he wondered about showing the thing to the guys down at Tyson's. Or to a few regulars he'd thought fondly of. There were customers he'd had hundreds of brief conversations with over the years and never once sighted outside the shop. A few *would* be interested, Presner imagined, some were good people, salt of the earth if more sophisticated. Still, it would be like Bruce Wayne revealing over the counter that he was Batman. "You don't work at a newsstand if you have a lot of pretensions," he told Lisa Caner once.

But he *was* Batman. Why begrudge himself the delusion? If it would throw off the equilibrium down at the shop, he needed the idea himself these days. You look Presner over behind the counter, shirtsleeves rolled up, or walking the streets, running his miles, you'd never suspect it. A bruiser, you'd think. A guy who reads detective novels, sure, righto. That's when you saw him walking, doing his roadwork. But the undiscovered Arthur Miller of LoDo? While Lisa was joking, it wouldn't be a joke if it weren't also real. Both knew (Presner anyway; and knew Lisa knew as well as she could know without, possibly, *knowing*). They wouldn't have had all these conversations, analyzed the movies and plays—Presner with a critical eye, bordering (in the telling if not the appreciation) on contempt at the *contempt* the inferior products, the shtuss, the tripe, the lowest common denominator conveyor-belt fantasies peddled as plausible realities, showed for *his* standards, his own worldview. He wouldn't have cursed these massive conspiracies to defile his intelligence—and Ms. Caner's as well—there wouldn't *be* those conversations, all these discussions of Chekhovian comedy and the arc of tragedy and the difference between drama and anti-intellectual buffoonery, to say nothing of the leery tolerance Lisa Caner showed, then finally the pleasure at Presner's assessment of her talents—"You're the best actress I've seen since my sister," he'd told her more than once, solemnly—and her own genius you'd never guess by spotting her in a diner or shopping at May D&F, slipping on a pair of shoes at Target, or even seated with other aspirants, Presner included, in the Continuing Ed acting class—if Presner wasn't a *ringer*, the genuine dimension, the hidden legend set to burst upon the scene suddenly—a little too good, perhaps, for the crass contemporary conventions. There was always that assumption, his masterpiece on his desk but for a little sharpening, Presner the perfectionist—'Anal about his art,' she'd think—if both didn't know his Batman outfit was in the other room.

'Jeez, we're better, the two of us.'

This Presner didn't realize until he made the copies down at Kinkos and considered an extra one for her, inscribed with affection, "For your warm interest." Why begrudge Caner her delusion? He wasn't eager to let her know it was just another costume, Presner another cornball making the rounds.

"Great that I finally got you on," Fitz said over the phone. "I always imagine you're too busy doing your jumping jacks to pick up the phone, even when it's your Uncle Norm."

"As a busy man, I've learned to prioritize."

"You should learn to multi-task," Fitz said. "For example, do your burpees while answering the phone."

"That's asking a lot."

"Speaking of prioritizing, it's time to move past the actress. It's been fun, right? Enough's enough. Listen to your Uncle Norm. Just because she wouldn't sleep with you doesn't mean you have to devote the remainder of your lonely days to getting her to sleep with you, just to prove the obscure point. I know you, Presner. Not that I don't admire your self-sufficiency, to a degree. Your tenaciousness, whatever. I've been thinking about this. The smoke shop's your monastery. The actress gal's your divine spirit who will reveal herself—so you persevere in the forlorn, euphoric hope—after years of absurd penance and devotion. I'm talking metaphorically, of course."

"Of course," Presner said.

"Move on. If you want to work the actress angle on the side in your spare time, that's one thing. But there are plenty of bigger fish in the sea."

"Thank you for the advice, Uncle Norm." Presner really was touched that Fitz had taken the time to consider his predicament, doubly that he'd done so in metaphoric terms. Not even Roxie tried to set him straight anymore. Roxie communicated things with her dismissive glances when she walked into the shop as if beholding a public defender in her courtroom, but Presner wasn't *that* sensitive to patronizing judgments. Though he was certain *this* argument was specious—women who would appreciate Chekhovian comedy weren't lining up to date middle-aged news clerks, for example—plus, there were no shortages of women he'd go out with—'Fitz, there are shortages of women I *wouldn't* go out with'—Presner, out of deference to the time Fitz took considering the notion, briefly wondered if there might be something to what his friend said.

"Well," Fitz said, "since you're playing the field, Lothario, who are you taking to the wedding?"

"Lisa Caner."

"I rest my case," Fitz said, without conviction.

Presner liked it that he didn't know where Fitz was calling from. In recent years, since Fitz took up with his international interests, even when his friend was in town, he liked imagining that Fitzhugh was calling from Paris, the Eiffel Tower in the backdrop, an attaché case chained to his wrist.

"You think I have a complex, Fitz?" he asked. During Fitz's experience as a defense lawyer, his friend was known to mock forensic psychologists. If he couldn't locate—or afford—an expert, Fitz himself implied the expert diagnosis.

Fitz laughed at the inside joke.

"Nothing that requires hospitalization, I hope," Presner added.

"I enjoy it that there's nothing so serious it doesn't warrant a joke at your own expense," Fitz said. "But you don't fool anyone. After law school, after Sara, I could see lying low, cooling your heels, plotting your next move, but when you're good and ready. What better place to rest from school and yourself than Tyson's? Ten bucks an hour, free smokes, free copies of *Boxing Illustrated*, pretty gals lined up across the counter to make change for and comment on their reading materials—"What's new in *Cosmo*?"—flirting with the gals from the Benny. Remember when I used to hang out down there? I found it restful. Small wonder you run and work out half the day. Otherwise, you'd be hypotensive."

If Fitzhugh wanted to psychoanalyze Presner from halfway across the world, it was the impresario's dime. "That's the setup. But don't forget my play."

Fitzhugh didn't say anything. Presner was glad he didn't let out a melodramatic whistle. "This is for your own good," Fitz continued. "What are buddies for if not to rake each other over the coals every five years? If you want to point out *my* character deficiencies, be my guest. I could use the input."

"Perhaps now you understand why I don't answer when you call," Presner said evenly.

"I deserve that. How's Roxie?"

"You may be right about Tyson's. Maybe the place served its purpose. It's not beneath my dignity but beneath my aspirations? There are days I think so. Sometimes I think people need me there to talk to while they buy their smokes, but they'd talk to the next guy, too. As for Lisa Caner, she's not a mythical quest—the potential symbolic conquest by which I can justify my meager existence—do I got this right, Fitz?"

"Sure," Fitzhugh said from across the ocean.

"It's nice having somebody to do things with who's a good listener and if she looks good on the arm why hold that against her? Fitz, that you find that circumstance incomprehensible is *your* character deficiency!"

"No doubt," Fitz said. "Touché."

"Since you asked."

"Don't get your back up."

"As for Roxie, you talk to her more than I do." Presner wished he could defend his character deficiencies without sounding defensive. He imagined he could if he had more practice at it, though it wasn't the sort of thing he wanted to be in the position of practicing too often. Still, he sometimes thought that when anybody looked at him sideways, his instinct wasn't to look sideways back, but to quake in his boots while looking sideways back.

"I guess that covers everything," Fitz said, hurt by Presner's outburst.

The phone rattled in Presner's hand with Fitz's sigh.

Two minutes later Fitzhugh called back. "You don't get any retirement there, any profit sharing, minimal health at best," he began as soon as Presner picked up the receiver. "Am I right? If Tyson sells the place or keels over or turns dyspeptic, you're out of luck and no fond farewells. All I'm suggesting is that you need to think about these things for your own good. For my good, too, since I'm the one who'll be putting you up when the bottom falls out. You'll be calling your Uncle Norm. And if I find out you called Caner first, or Roxie, I'll kill you."

"Thanks," Presner said, moved.

"It's just nice that you can close your eyes and dream your artist dreams all day and play hooey gooey with your actress dreaming her actress dreams. What's the state of the world economy beside an insight about *Oklahoma* or snide comments about who plays Miss Marmelstein down at the Dinner Theater? I envy that. I'm jealous, Presner. I mean it. *That's* where your play comes in. It was one thing when you were a ne'er-do-well. Presner finishes his play? What if it's successful? I can't stand it! So I attack!"

"You considered this in the two minutes between calls?"

"I didn't have anything else to do. Once the subject of my character deficiencies emerges, nothing else matters."

Presner wanted to tell him he didn't have too much to worry about. "You sound like you're torn between hoping that the play's no good and wanting to produce it."

"That's an idea," said Fitz. "And I'll write it down. But I have a few other projects at the moment. I've been involved with—you don't want to know—some oil futures. A little import/export, too. Just putting people together."

"That's what it's about," Presner said. Another inside joke Fitz got. Fitz told Presner once that whenever he was stuck for a response to a proposition—an impossible circumstance, in Presner's view—he'd retort, "That's what it's about," to which, as Presner understood it, nobody had ever done anything but nod approvingly. "People coming together."

"Some bank funds. A real estate mutual, too. Maybe Roxie told you. I want to give her a chance to make some real money so she won't be setting juvenile bail and levying traffic points when she's seventy. Hankie, too. She's a state employee, does well, excellent benefits, but she'll never have the summer villa outside *Firenze*, not at this rate. Hankie's great, but the wealthy guys who could rescue her are looking for Henrietta ten years ago, not the matronly lawyer lady with the troubled brow."

Until a few days ago Presner never really thought of Roxie or Henrietta as missing out on their dreams. They were *living* their dreams. They'd had almost everything they wanted, as far as Presner could see, and despite a few bumps in the road—who wasn't divorced these days, other than Presner himself, or overworked and too tired to take in the latest movies?—still pretty much had everything and—to Presner—weren't much burdened by what they lacked. But to Fitz they were desperate at missing the boat. It was odd hearing Fitz talk this way. Well, Fitz knew them better. They confided in Fitz. They revealed their anxieties and wishes to the guy, not just the desires they were supposed to have.

When Presner was *interested*, he came across like he was hustling, scamming their secrets, perhaps to put in a play. Fitz seemed really interested even when he was hustling them. But who knew? To hear Fitz talk about the two, you wouldn't guess that Fitz *adored* them both and they'd adored Fitz from the day they met him. Still, Presner reminded himself that these speculations were nothing beside the way they all liked to talk about Fitz, whose travails and triumphs kept them all amused and tethered as far back as law school.

"I never thought of Roxie and Hankie as missing the boat and being upset about it," Presner admitted. "Or even as wanting to catch the boat to begin with. Marx and Pepe, now, I know *those* guys are grabbers. Perhaps I lack your moral imagination."

"Well, don't probe too deeply," Fitz said.

"Other than Lisa Caner and poor financial planning," Presner said, "anything else wrong with me you want to get off your chest?"

"Now that you bring it up, you do have another problem. Roxie and Pepe aside, you usually read into things. You intellectualize. I've been thinking about this, too. To quote Sigmund Freud, 'Sometimes a cigar is just a cigar.' But you like to make things more interesting than they are."

"Well—"

"Don't deny it, Presner. Sometimes when you do that you can miss that they're already pretty interesting."

"I'll make a note of that. *Thanks* for the evaluation."

"I'm just talking, Shakespeare. Don't get your dander up. You're an artist type. You have to go deep. Leave the surface pleasures and the big cigars for materialists like *moi*. Anyway, I'll be back a couple of weeks before the wedding. We can catch up, knock back a few, chase some ladies."

"Sure."

"Tell Roxie and Hankie I called."

"Why don't you tell them yourself that you called?" Presner said, but Fitz had already hung up.

A minute later the phone rang again. "I know, I know, I know, I know I shouldn't say this!" Fitz roared into the answering machine, "But about your play, I know a guy . . ."

Sometimes after Fitz called, the bruiser had to call Caner to lick his wounds.

"Interesting that Fitz accuses *me* of reading too much into things. All the guy does is read too much into things. But do I say, 'Fitz, isn't the pot calling the kettle black here?' Do I say, 'Tell me what channel you're on, Dr. Impresario, and I'll watch?' No, I just get up my dander and fume!"

"Selfish people are always quick to call others selfish," Lisa said.

Presner got defensive about that, too.

"It's only what you're saying."

Presner nodded, defeated.

Half the time that's how it was when Fitzhugh called Presner from Europe to catch up. Fitz's good-natured soul got lost in the transcontinental wiring. That this was all said in mirth wasn't as clear as when his friend sat across the table—or the counter at Tyson's—face to face, sweeping Presner along. The script said one thing, the body language another. When Fitz said stuff across the table, no matter the content, you were pleased to be included. "Across the table, 'You should walk your filthy mutt more often' comes across as, 'With a little work Ruff could play *Rin Tin Tin*,'" Presner told Lisa. "So that doesn't come across on the international wire? The guy's not perfect."

It brightened Presner's spirit to consider.

At the *shop*, as Presner had taken to affectionately calling the place (though when he used the term, even other staffers sometimes did a double take. "You know, Tyson's? The smoke shop? *Here?*" he'd clarify) Presner liked best the graveyard shift. He enjoyed the casual if tentative camaraderie with some of the regulars. If most people didn't want to be up so late, sometimes those who were—who had something so good going—wanted to with such an offhand joy that it was impossible for Presner not to be happy standing in the refracted light of their sordid anticipation; suddenly buoyant despite the hour, he'd make change for their Lucky Strikes. At such times the dank air and smell of doughnuts from Duncan's across the lot would lend him a kind of contentedness, and he'd return to the book or the magazine he was reading behind the counter or the chaotic conversation he had going with a regular—to be resumed three nights from now—and be almost pleased to be permitted these small satisfactions, pleased that his life had landed him in this. If it was all small picture, it was still a picture worth shelling out your cash for and taking your seat and seeing. During the night shift—"counter-intuitively," as he told Lisa Caner, who spoiled him once by stopping in at midnight (she was returning home from a rehearsal)—nobody was *busy*. Nobody frowned and winced when they were stuck in line, which happened all the time during day shift. Not only were the regulars great, but the guys who had something going, and others who'd rushed out at 3 a.m. to pick, of all things, a literary magazine off the stands (they stocked everything), and the hookers who worked the Benjamin Hotel across the street ("The Benny," Fitz called it), who'd manage to call the bruiser *honey* five times as he'd count their change and their mascara ran.

They'd size him up. "A pack of Salems, honey. Why, you do look tired."

"That's because I'm up all night working here, and I'm up all day counting my money."

"You sound like my pimp, honey. Only the way he works my little ass, he got the money to count."

"I guess I can't fool anybody. Shazam."

"If I couldn't fool nobody, Jack, I'd be serving fries at the diner."

There were also guys who'd come in looking like they'd be pleased to stick a Luger in his belly—just in out of the cold, usually—and they, too, became part of the numbing routine, so easy in their chaotic conversations that the bruiser would often leave, shift over, amazed that he hadn't heard so much sheer bullshit since law school.

Still, despite the subtle pleasures and the fact that he'd long ago set the unofficial world record—over thirteen years at Tyson's and counting—there were plenty of times he'd considered other jobs, other careers, over the last couple of years. The bruiser wasn't *all* sentiment. Once, though, the idea would have been unbearable. "I was in a black hole for a long time," he admitted to Lisa Caner. "The shop was my crutch, something I could do well without thinking too much. What was I like? You don't want to know." Presner shook his head, as if clearing cobwebs. "Same as now, I guess. It was nothing I did, just a lot of stuff I thought of and didn't do."

Now there were entire weeks he'd be fired up with alternate lives, usually about becoming a private detective but sometimes about various brokerage courses—real estate, stocks, mortgages—he'd catch wind of. ("So, Fred, how'd you break into the business?" "I took a *course*," went numerous conversations he'd had with regulars.) But the week would pass, and it would occur to him that he could do most of this stuff on the *side*, like investigating murders as a freelance, until he set himself up. That would be the prudent way. Then it would occur to him that he *already* worked a job on the side, *playwright*, that kept his hands full.

Of all the trades he'd kicked around during the long shifts, he never considered personal trainer.

On the next Saturday morning the bruiser found himself jogging with Roxie—Roxie running with a scrupulous attention to form, Presner barely trotting—on the bike path along the Platte. He was torturing Roxie by encouraging conversation, but Roxie would talk even if she could barely breathe, so Presner occasionally interrupted her breathy monologue. "After another half mile we'll walk if you want. The object is to run as far as you can and still want to run tomorrow." Presner recalled this from an article he'd read several years ago.

"Excellent form," Presner added, honestly. Perhaps it was Roxie's scrupulous attention? The bruiser had been running for years and didn't know anything about form other than not to list sideways. *Roxie* looked like she knew what she was doing.

"Tomorrow?" Roxie cried.

"Or your next time on the schedule," Presner said softly. As Roxie's newly hired personal trainer it was important to be understanding of her aches and pains and encouraging of her desires, yet firm. If she'd wanted a drill sergeant, she would have hired a real personal trainer, possibly one of the sheriff's deputies from down at the courthouse.

In her loose orange sweats, the Honorable Roxanne looked like a talking, huffing, form-adhering, rolling pumpkin. "I'm not a personal trainer," Presner told her flatly a few days earlier when she'd walked into the shop yelling, "Counselor! Counselor!"

"I don't want a real personal trainer. I want you. We can spend more time together. It'll be fun," Roxie smiled impishly, inspiring in Presner the vague suspicion that he was on *Candid Camera*. "You work out anyway. I'll just tag along."

"I work out *alone*."

Roxie placed her palms together and bowed in homage, a gesture Presner assumed she learned from attorneys genuflecting before her on the bench. "I'm on a self-improvement plan like you."

"Enroll in evening classes and take tennis lessons."

"The wedding's inspired me. A real personal trainer would quit the second I yelled at him for telling me what to do." Roxie smiled, lasciviously now.

"Don't confuse me with your bailiffs," Presner said.

"As a friend you'll take the vitriol in the spirit intended."

"Nice to see I'm qualified."

"I knew you'd understand."

It would surprise those who saw him stalking along Speer, deep in thought, puffing a cigar, but the bruiser *enjoyed* doing favors. When younger—back in law school, for example—he'd always do the favors if asked, but with an air of grim apprehension. Now he had something of a reputation: *Need furniture moved, call Presner*. Nonetheless, people still felt compelled to talk him into it even after he'd agreed. "It won't take long," Roxie pleaded.

"Fine."

"Plus, there's lunch in it for you."

"Cinched." Even with strangers he'd feel a warm glow upon giving directions to lost motorists, the glow only diminishing upon realizing the directions he'd provided were wrong.

Presner figured Roxie had something else up her sleeve. It crossed Presner's mind—with Roxie across the counter smiling lasciviously, batting her eyes, insinuating her way into Presner's heart, then later as he shuffled beside her on the bike path—that Fitz could be right. Maybe Roxie thought she'd missed the boat; the guys she'd be interested in didn't typically chase—to paraphrase Fitzhugh—middle-aged, overweight, authoritarian tyrants, even if they were foulmouthed and candid in their sexual speculations. "Guys used to chase after her body. Now it's her robes," Fitz said to Presner. Did Roxie want to look her best for Fitz? Next Henrietta would call him for workout advice: Fitz was coming to town.

Presner imagined there were health considerations, too.

"Lunch defeats the purpose of the workout. It's a simple formula, Roxie. Expend more calories than you take in, and see to it that the ones you take in metabolize efficiently."

"Terrific. That's the kind of advice I need. See? Thanks."

"Speaking as a friend, I can't promise you progress before the wedding. Three weeks is barely a start."

"It's not the destination but the journey."

Presner told her he'd write that down.

If she wanted Presner she'd get *Presner*. He took the project seriously. He bought a manual on discount off the Tyson's rack, *Workouts for Busy Women*. He bought a notebook and charted workout plans, as well as alternative plans for alternative goals. Presner went all-purpose, not one-size-fits-all. If Roxie wanted to shed a few pounds and get in shape, you can bet Presner would train her. If she wanted to run triathlons, he'd be there, chugging beside her, notebook in hand.

It turned out that Roxie mostly wanted her personal trainer to jog with her a couple of times to build her confidence, then demonstrate the machines down at the gym, a one-time shot. "I don't have a goal," Roxie finally admitted. "Should I have thought of one before I talked to you?"

"Yes."

"*I* don't want people to *laugh* at me when I run, or think I don't know how to use the machines."

"I don't know how to use half the machines."

"But you look like you do," Roxie said. Presner, the bruiser, beamed.

With lunch being counterproductive, a violation of the formula, Roxie took the bruiser out to My Favorite Alaska for dinner. You couldn't skip dinner, according to the manuals.

When My Favorite Alaska opened on 12th and Cherokee, it was felt by many to be an example of concept taken to the extreme: not just Eskimo pies and glazed sandwiches known as igloos, and speared salmon, which as far as Presner could tell was canned salmon serrated by toothpicks, and polar margaritas, extra icy (on special Friday afternoons) and complimentary sorbet served in wooden canoe-shaped bowls, but on the walls were huge murals featuring Eskimo clans hiking through the snowy wilderness clutching primitive weapons, and polar bears scooping their claws into the icy sea. The igloo sandwiches, Arctic salads, moose steaks, and serrated salmon proved to be nobody's favorite. Within a few months the only concession to the concept was the air conditioning, pitched full-blast year-round.

Fortunately, this was late spring, and they'd landed a table outside. No immediate view other than the old downtown bowery and further away the skyscrapers downtown and the mountains beyond. And of course the women in halter tops and the women off work in summery dresses sipping their margaritas. Still, the concept was on Presner's mind. "I'll go to Fairbanks—no, Anchorage—no, Fairbanks—and open My Favorite Denver. Buffalo steaks. Complimentary mints. Shoot-out pies. Huge murals with mountain lions leaping suddenly upon their prey."

"And Rocky Mountain oysters," Roxanne suggested.

Rocky Mountain oysters were said to be the testicles of young bulls, a local delicacy Presner had never sampled. "I see your point. And you could fly up and be the hostess when things get hectic. Though a legal scion like you would be liable to throw off the motif beyond repair."

"A *fit* legal scion." The judge raised her glass of merlot. "To Presner the workout maven."

The bruiser proposed a toast. "You did well this morning. I was really impressed. Keep at it. Build on it."

She reached for a chip and brushed it lightly against the salsa. "Are these verboten?"

"Not tonight if you keep the light touch."

"Fitz tells me you're sending out your play. Congratulations." Roxie raised her glass.

"Fitz tells me he's going to produce my play. 'I know a guy.' Quote unquote."

"If somebody's going to make a killing out of it, Fitz wants to be the one."

"A killing? I'd be surprised if somebody could read it all the way through."

"Self-deprecation's not as attractive a quality in a gentleman as you may think," Roxie said, as if quoting precedent. "And you're a gentleman. You always have been, even when it didn't square with your attitude."

"My attitude?"

Roxie shrugged. "You know, everybody's always kidding themselves about everything, every house is made of sand, that sort of insufferable stuff you used to say all the time. I wonder why. Though it's easy enough to guess. Still, I'd see you down at your store and people really like you there. You'd be like you were in law school, always with a smile and a quip. But even then, you'd always be available to do people favors, like now."

"You're buying dinner," Presner reminded her.

Still, he *enjoyed* that Roxie was working him, though why he couldn't fathom. Probably to hear if Fitz had said anything. Even Roxie assumed that they knew each other inside out. Roxie may have been a county judge and local diva with an iron-fisted and intrepid reputation, but as she sat across the table from him, even as other diners were gazing at her—it was impossible to walk ten feet with Roxie without somebody stopping her to chat or lobby—Presner appreciated that the flattering characterizations were her *fallback* position. Who knew? The old friend dimension cut two ways. His radar was up. She wanted to know what Fitz thought and figured best pals talk this stuff over, even across oceans.

"By the way, Fitz was in his sentimental mode when I talked to him a few days ago."

"His sentimental mode?" Roxie took a sip of water now.

"He gave me advice on tailoring my personality for success and fulfillment, just as you are."

"Don't be touchy. And you bring it on yourself, Presner. You never seem to enjoy anything. I worry."

"It was interesting. Fitz was worried about you. Henrietta, too. He had concerns that you haven't salted away enough for a rainy day. That you're missing out on your dreams. I felt—feel—idiotic, to tell you the truth, because I haven't spent ten minutes considering your dreams. Sentimental *that* way."

"Shame on you for not considering my dreams."

"He wasn't just worried about my personality. 'Tyson's is a good gig for summer vacation but it's time to grow up. Also, stop chasing Lisa Caner. Get a real squeeze.' That kind of thing."

Roxie studied him. "It must be annoying." Roxie took another chip and again lightly brushed it in the salsa. Between the two chips she'd taken, Presner had finished the bowl and now motioned the waiter for another. "If you're not chasing her, you should. Is she seeing anybody else?"

"She doesn't tell me things like that."

"Sounds like my ex-husband."

"Tyson's would be a good summer gig for *Fitz*, that's what he means. If *he* were chasing Lisa and getting nowhere, *he'd* find somebody else. Fitzhugh lacks objectivity, Roxie."

"Unlike us," Roxie nodded, but he sensed she was suddenly wary. Often Presner felt as if he was maligning people behind their backs when he was merely *describing* things about them. He fought the impulse to add irrelevancies such as, 'Even though he's projecting from his own concerns, Fitz is a really great traveller!' to even the scales.

"I still feel like a *shmendrick* for not spending ten minutes considering your dreams. From now on that won't happen!"

"You had your own problems. Did Fitz mention Pepe and Gary?" Roxie wondered.

"No, but if necessary, he'd invoke those guys. He'd say he'd just been talking to Pepe, who was also concerned about my laggard personality development."

"He's helping them out with their futures." Roxanne automatically pushed her enchilada combination plate toward Presner, who was famous among the old crowd for his appetite. (Even Fitzhugh, who had fifty pounds on him, would defer. "If you could make a living out of your prodigious consumption, you'd be rich," Fitz said often. "If you can think of how let me know." "Sure, I'll be your agent.") Presner took a fraction, then a full half when Roxie insisted, and returned to his fajitas.

"Don't give Fitzhugh money," Roxie said.

"What does that mean?"

Roxie stared back at the bruiser—straight into his sucker lights, shining bright—then took another chip. "Here's why I wanted to talk to you."

What got to Presner now, other than that he'd been wrong about everything in his life—that Roxie appointed him her personal trainer in order to shape up for Fitzhugh, that Fitz was worried about the old gang for *their* sakes, covered merely the time Presner finished off the chips to the time the entrees were delivered—it occurred to Presner that there existed a one-to-one ratio between his assumptions and the certainty that his assumptions were puerile—from now on not even what was before him front and center would the bruiser vouch for—when he was only kidding himself, he was being as true as when he looked at things squarely, which, in the new formulation, only meant that he was kidding himself—if he cared at all for the truth, whether absolute, relative, or momentary and conditional, 'Your guess is as good as mine' is how he'd answer every query, from his name to his innermost thoughts—the speculations will stop here, Presner resolved; at this rate whether his parents ever loved him would be on the table, a question of perspective—what's more, perhaps Presner was a foundling his parents discovered in the bushes?—'Is the universe really the tip of some big guy's pinky?' 'Your guess is as good as mine,' Presner would say from now on, when asked—is that Roxie detailed her findings and pontificated as if she were ruling from the bench.

He'd seen the tendency before. Schoolteachers could turn pedantic at the snap of a finger; Lisa—his sister, too—could metamorphose into almost anything in a blink; and resolved not to hold it against Roxie. When stressed, Presner himself would resort to instinct and try to sell you a newspaper or a bag of Borkum Riff.

Her voice was oddly detached and icy, as if Fitz were a principal in case law—*Fitzhugh vs. Colorado*, a state of affairs Roxie didn't want to see—and not a guy she'd adored since law school. What was truth? The bruiser himself went from seeing Fitz as a guy who'd always had the drop on him, the burly big brother under the skin to Presner, the tag-along, worshipful runt, though they were the same age, his best friend, to 'Poor Fitz. The hapless guy veered off-course.' This transition took microseconds.

"Gary and Pepe gave him $50,000. Henrietta $25,000. I gave him $75,000."

"That's $200,000 all told."

"Thank you," Roxie said. As Roxie explained, the Fitzhugh Ltd. Fund—the Fitz Fund, they called it—was Fitz's opportunity to branch out.

"Branch out from criminal defense, class action suits, concert promotion, sports agenting, television and radio commentary, merger acquisitions? He felt pigeonholed?"

"Fitz was feeling confined. He didn't really explain," Roxie said. "Everyone else was getting rich, why not us? 'People have gone from owning just the shirts on their backs to retiring at fifty.' That was the theme. If you had a pot to piss in, he would have included you, too."

Presner shrugged and began to open his mouth.

"Don't look at me that way. You'd do well to keep your disdain to yourself," Roxie said.

He deserved the scolding, not because Roxie was right, but in that Presner had *thought* those same thoughts so often. But it was the metaphor that turned the soul inside out. Even before his circumstances. 'Everybody else is falling in love, why not me?' he'd brayed to the moon from his balcony. 'Everybody else's team wins the World Series, why not mine?' he'd agonized as a kid. If there were differences in degree there were differences in kind, but each was a brick in the wall. As if what gnawed at you wasn't that you weren't rich or in love, but that you were left out of the fun, the kid picked last or not at all. If, in reality, he had been picked for sports teams, these years later the *metaphor* held. But rich? Presner wondered, even as Roxie watched him from across the table, sipping her merlot, assessing how he was taking the bombshell. How did he take it? Presner found himself thinking of Philo of Alexandria, the first-century Jew who believed that every story in the Torah, all the five books of Moses, every law was best understood as allegory. How else to make sense? Thus, Philo tried to conflate the forebodings of spirit with the laws of reason. But what reason was there with money, what allegory? *Other* people fell apart, became distortions;

you could handle it—the permutations, the bruiser thought, were the stuff of Chekhov—because it wasn't *greed* but longing. "Who doesn't want to be rich *too*? It's like Gus, this cat that Sara used to have," the bruiser recalled. "He'd scratch at the door whenever the dog was outside. Gus didn't want to go outside. All he wanted was to be with Sonny."

"Which means?"

"I don't suppose Fitz had to twist your arm behind your back."

"You're comparing us to cats and dogs?"

"No."

"I remember when you were rich," Roxie said. "We all thought you'd be the one to get the haircut and join the corporation with the thousand perks and move into your cubicle on the 27th floor and spend your life helping other rich guys hold on to their money. Henrietta used to complain about that. She thought Gary was more down-to-earth. She could relate to his values better."

"I don't think I once mentioned the word 'corporation' in Henrietta's presence. Or anybody else's."

If, to Presner, Roxanne was fitting together the pieces of his life, to her it was a throwaway observation. The judge shrugged. "He didn't have to twist my arm. I was hoping to help Fitz out. I know he's an operator. If the returns were half of what he guaranteed I would have been happy enough. Does that make me selfish? Does that mean he didn't steal the money? He didn't swindle his best friends? He's teaching us all Zen lessons about being slaves to materialism? Gary was happy to help him out. Pepe too. It took a bunch of phone calls—they knew better—but once he'd hammered it home to them, they were happy. Henrietta wasn't so happy. Henrietta he *shtupped*."

"Is that supposed to be Yiddish?"

Roxie smiled faintly at the bruiser's petulance. "Atop losing her daughter's college fund, Henrietta has to face being humiliated and pathetic."

"I knew they'd been lovers. You sound like the guy spent all those years setting her up."

"It's how operators like Fitz work. He's always had it at the back of his mind that if it came down to it, he could use us. We're friends, but we're marks."

"No, I don't think so."

Roxie closed her eyes, clearing the deck to try again. Presner could be opaque, even when he tried. According to her, they'd signed promissory notes—at Fitz's insistence—"Who's doing whom the favor?"—to keep the funds untouched for two years, after which they could withdraw at double their outlay. "He sent out quarterly statements. Fitz worked at it. Everything looked good on paper. If we wanted, he'd detail lists of every transaction in the fund. He *encouraged* that. It looked like we could double after two years. Mostly industrial concerns. Some long/short. Some options."

Presner took another drink of water. "I know your feelings are shaken. Still, he's a *lawyer*. You're a lawyer. *Caveat emptor*? Deals go south, Rox. That makes him a loser, not a thief. Why not bet it all on the Cubs at 50-1? Fitz isn't Midas. Who wants to tell stories about Midas?"

"Well, I know you like the stories. You were so pleased when I was appointed to County Court so you could have the pleasure of believing I sold out and ridicule me accordingly. I know you." Roxanne took another sip of her merlot. "I'm not talking about stories."

He said softly, "You don't mean that."

The other outside tables were empty by now. The waiter was watching from the kitchen, though he didn't otherwise seem in any hurry for them to leave. The situation struck the bruiser as familiar. Several years ago, Lauren Goldman took him to Pasquale's, a chic Italian place off Wazee that at the time never had an empty table, as the necessary setting to tell him that she didn't want to see him anymore. Even at the time, as Presner realized that she was taking him to the busy Pasquale's as opposed to a quieter setting—to say nothing of her living room, where he'd been staying since two nights before—because she knew that he would never make a scene or ask too many explosive questions or fall to his knees and blubber like a lunatic or throw his calzone in her face with so many other diners around enjoying their evenings—he wondered what in her life, or what he ever said to her, made her think she had to take such precautions just to get him out of her hair. Still, as she was letting him have it, Presner knew that she was *right*, though what was as annoying as being dropped by Lauren—he'd liked those nights in her living room, liked in those days having the prospect of a woman to go to at all, though each time he'd appeared at her door Lauren ventured (*now* it seemed) a double take—"Which should have told me something," he'd admitted to Fitz—what disturbed him more than being dropped—who wouldn't drop the bruiser?—and that she must have been *terrified* of him to require the safety of Pasquale's to break the bad news—it was a debilitating statement, even as he saw her point of view—she made it clear they'd leave separately also, so there'd be nothing to remember for the road, no opportunity to voice the opposing view by touching her face or running his hand through her hair—still, it was *nice* of her, far better than not returning his calls until he got the idea—*worst* of all is that she was wrong: He wasn't going to throw a calzone in her face or turn the table over. She'd overrated Presner, ascribed to him passions he'd do well to possess.

In Pasquale's he'd been a gentleman. "I think there was more to you than I was willing to see," he told her honestly, though by that time Lauren may have left the table.

In My Favorite Alaska, where he sat now across from Roxanne, they were not only the only diners left but may as well broadcast their voices over the sidewalk and public airwaves. Still, Roxanne wasn't worried about the bruiser throwing a fit. He remembered that when he was a boy, he'd believed that when somebody trusted you, you could say anything and they'd listen and wipe up your words if they spilled over where they weren't intended. "I was happy for you when you got the appointment, Rox. I'm still happy for you." Still, she was right *conceptually*. There were enough other people he'd ridiculed, why should she think she was exempt?

Roxie shrugged. "What's so exciting about Fitz to you? Perhaps this only adds to the legend. At any rate, I imagine he meant to pay us back. Double, if possible. But that doesn't account for the Fitzhugh Ltd. Fund. He had an opportunity he needed $200,000 for. If it earned a million, he could double our investment—a little favor, something for his friends—and clear $600,000 for himself for his concern. I imagine he didn't want to swindle us like he was selling linoleum siding to little old ladies. What do you think it was? Gold? Ponies? Hog futures? Penis moldings? Stolen art? I'm a judge, I know the United States Attorney. Fitz used to be famous around here. Do you understand? I'm saying this out of loyalty to Fitz, so don't look at me that way."

"Don't go to the U.S. Attorney. Let me talk to him first."

"That'll work," Roxanne sighed.

"Please give me the chance, anyway."

Roxanne looked at him sourly, then sighed again. Presner figured she had her mind made up, or that this is what she had in mind all along, once more playing him like a good hand of Crazy Eights. "Tell him to get our money back—swindle some more old ladies if he must—by Marx's wedding or we're seeking an indictment. I hope he likes Monte Carlo, because if he wants to step on U.S. soil again, he'll pay us back or I'll put him in Leavenworth. Why not you? You've always worshipped Fitz, at least since law school. You've idealized the guy ever since. In fact, you like to keep all of us safely in the past. Fitz likes that. You should hear what he says, 'I can always count on the bruiser to wag my tail.' He wants to be your hero. He tries harder around you."

"Is that so bad?"

"Also, you can be persuasive."

"This has been going on for weeks. Why didn't you tell me before?"

"I can barely stand to tell you now."

"So why by the wedding?" Presner said. "How about by New Year's? By Purim?"

"Gary wants to go on a honeymoon," Roxie smiled. "Presner, I've always admired your ability to keep your sense of humor about you, through thick or thin. But then it's not your $50,000, is it? But then, you're spiritual these days, an artiste, a playwright, living for the mind and muscle, not material. It's not your kid's college fund. Excuse me, you don't have children, I forgot. Or your honeymoon fund. Excuse me, I forgot, you don't have honeymoons."

"So arrest me."

"You're incorrigible." Roxie shook her head sadly.

"It's my *attitude*."

When Roxie sipped her water, Presner was pleased she didn't throw it in his face.

For a few days after the bombshell, the bruiser placed the phone by the couch. Occasionally he'd stare at it, as if willing the instrument to ring.

When he went to his shift at Tyson's 24-Hour News and Smoke or for a run or idle walk or, once, to a movie with Lisa Caner and then later to Lisa Caner's kitchen for a cup of joe—all of which he attended reluctantly—he checked his message machine immediately upon returning to the Pleasure Palace. Seeing that Fitzhugh hadn't called and left a message, Presner sank to the couch, to his disappointment, in relief. He didn't want Fitz's call to come in when he wasn't there—who's to say when Fitz might call again?—he knew Fitz *would* call again, for the renegade wouldn't turn his back on his friends—though Presner understood every word in the sentence was open to interpretation and perspective—his own perspective steeped in nostalgia—it was Fitz, after all; ol' Fitz—Presner didn't want to be there when Fitz called either, despite promising Roxie that he'd bring the renegade to account.

"I don't know what I'll say," he confided to Lisa Caner. "But I know what I'll *do*. I'll reach my hands through the phone lines and strangle the renegade. You've heard of phone sex?"

"No, I haven't," Lisa said.

"This will be phone strangulation. The second before his last gasp he'll promise to return the money. At that point I may not think to release my hands. Do I care?"

Lisa wondered, "Did you ever see these antisocial tendencies in your friend?"

"No way. He's always been bipolar, I guess. But those are his moods, not his values."

Presner called Henrietta and Pepe, leaving identical messages on their machines. "Anyway, I heard about the alleged swindle. Roxie told me. I want you to know I plan to talk to Fitzhugh. I'll see what I can do. Perhaps it's all a misunderstanding. Hope springs eternal, I guess. See you at the wedding if not before."

Presner dialed Gary Marx and told the machine. "Anyway—"

"Oh, it's you," Marx picked up.

'Don't talk to Marx in two years and he recognizes my voice *by the first word*,' Presner thought, flattered. 'The guy's good.' Also, 'Just like Marx to be home at noon—bustling lawyer though he claims to be—when a guy tries to sneak in a call for the machine.'

"That's right. Congratulations."

"Yup. I'm attending to some details right now."

"I won't keep you, Gary. Roxie told me about the Fitz Fund fiasco."

"Oh, that's nothing," Marx said.

Presner imagined the immaculate attorney filing his nails. "That's the problem, I understand. It was nothing. Well, I'll talk to Fitz. I'll see what I can do."

"Now I can sleep nights. Presner's on the job. Straight from his throne at the smokeshop."

Presner thought of thanking Marx for reminding him of why they didn't talk anymore—plus stealing Hankie—but imagined that the first 10,000 barbs were slung by him. Eventually Gary forgot they were all *deserved*. "I wanted you to know, that's all. I'll take care of Fitz. Also, Gary, I look forward to the wedding."

"Roxie tells me that you've been shaping up. You're a bruiser now."

"You know how it goes. Healthy body, healthy mind."

"How's the playwright business?"

"I've got some stuff in the hopper. But you know me, I'm just a news clerk. Hope springs eternal but I'm whistling in the wind, searching for four-leaf clovers."

"You don't fool anybody with your Sad Sack routine," Marx said, hanging up.

Everybody always assumed the bruiser was looking for sympathy.

Afterward, Presner thought about writing a play dramatizing a news clerk's lonely vigil, waiting by the phone not for news of armistice or the forlorn voice of a damsel in need calling him over for emergency service or the family back home, though all these calls would come in as the bruiser waited, but a friend abroad who probably was never a friend, to read him the riot act for a crime he'd claim was imagined.

The news clerk, a bruiser, sits by the phone in his palatial apartment. His feet are kicked up on the couch. His boom box plays softly, though he

can't identify the song. He looks through the living room to the copper pot
on the stove. He looks to the small hallway between the living room and the
kitchen, at the posters on the wall, then looks away, then looks back at the
Bellows, though who landed the punch and who's flying through the ropes
he also couldn't tell you. His expression is fixed in contemplation, as if he's
willing the phone to ring, or willing it not to.

The phone rang. Still not Fitz. Henrietta, calling Presner for the first
time since law school, other than a condolence call several days after Sara
died. Another time she'd called his place looking for Fitz.

"Hi. I got your message about taking care of Fitz and I'm returning
your call."

"Is this the message I left last week?"

Henrietta paused. "Sorry. How have you been? Has Fitzhugh
called?"

"No, not yet. Roxie gave me the general outline. I understand that he
threw you for a loop. I'm sorry, Henrietta. It was a misunderstanding."

"Your basis for that conclusion?"

"Knowing Fitz," Presner said.

"He didn't throw me for a loop. He defrauded me."

"I'm not insensitive to the distinction, Henrietta." Fifteen years ago,
Presner remembered, a group went out to a bar after an orientation
session, "Coping with First-Year Stress." The group converging at Scotty's was large, spreading out over several tables. Across the table sat a
pretty, plumpish girl who introduced herself as Roxanne, seated beside a
beefy, towering guy—Norman Fitzhugh, by the name tag—who looked
at Presner with an amused, slightly baffled expression which didn't leave
his face until they were out of law school. At the moment, he'd considered the expression suggestive: 'Here we are, friend, strangers previously
unknown to each other, quarantined at a table beside two pretty girls
and a pitcher of beer.' Presner thought he was expected to wink back,
'I get it, we're a *team*,' and did. The girl beside him was thin and had

mounds of curly black hair, some of which fell onto Presner's shoulder by the second pitcher. To everything he said—an unaccountable series of inanities relating to stress reduction mechanisms, "For the first year." "And then the kid turns two!" Norm Fitzhugh, his brother in conspiracy, bellowed across the table—the pretty aspiring lawyer's shoulder leaned closer to Presner without listing back upon completion of his locution. By then the amusement on Norm Fitzhugh's glowing red face across the table magnified. Roxie was doing most of the talking, gesturing with extreme animation—the barroom noise deafening, he couldn't take in most of it—couldn't even if he could, with the pretty girl's black ringlets tickling his shoulder, her elbow touching his, their knees and thighs tapping by the third pitcher—though still, when the expectation on Roxie's face intensified and Fitzhugh's amusement elevated another notch, both looking at him across the table, Presner offering the occasional locution, the girl beside him—Henrietta—tilting yet closer until it seemed that they shared respirations—How much of this was she aware of? Presner found himself wondering. How much was the deafening noise and the beer and knowing that he was in the club, too, his orientation nametag dangling at 45 degrees from his shirt pocket? How much the good student practicing stress reduction technique? Presner knew he was a born second fiddle, but wasn't second fiddle also in the orchestra? Don't they turn the sheet over when the last note on the page is played, and rise with the others and bow to the ovation? Aren't they every bit the fiddler to the undiscerning ear? Then Roxie and Henrietta were standing beside the table, both smiling maniacally—there was the incident of the two leaving the table together for a trip to the restroom—and announcing, "We'll see you guys tomorrow! Back here? After the session? That's if we don't see you before." "Later alligator." Presner and Fitzhugh turned to watch them leave, filing out with others from the larger group. Norm Fitzhugh turned back to Presner, the amusement on his large face taut to the point of snapping, extending his hand. "Tomorrow after the session then?"

"If not sooner," Presner said.

During the next day's orientation sessions, he'd looked for Henrietta—Roxanne and Norman, too—but the first-year class was large, almost 200, and from Presner's perch in the back row of the auditorium, half the young women in the preceding rows had curly black hair bobbing up and down to the advice from the podium. They, too, might list toward him when they talked, elbows and knees tapping. 'If she's not there tonight others will be,' Presner *promised* himself. He kept his eyes peeled, though thinking it might be better not to be disabused by daylight—a two-way street. After the evening session, Presner walked to Scotty's. The place was already filled with law students. "Presner!" he heard when he walked in. It was Norm Fitzhugh, waving from a corner table. Henrietta was at the table staring up at Presner, smiling through her black ringlets, moving over and patting the spot she'd instantly slid over from as if she'd been warming the cushion for his arrival. He felt like he'd arrived. On the other side of Henrietta was a lean guy with thick coiffured hair—about as tall as Fitzhugh—off the pages of *Esquire*, Presner thought—"Gary Marx," he said, extending his hand. Beside Marx was Pepe, it turned out, looking distracted, uncomfortable, antsy, poised perpetually on the verge of popping up from the table to make a beeline for the cigarette machine, knocking over small children en route. Roxanne had met Gary and Pepe in the afternoon session, which broke into small brainstorming groups, then asked them along. That's how they began. Sometimes the bruiser wondered if Roxie hadn't found herself in the breakout group with Marx and Pepe and been Roxie the Mother Hen, or if Fitz hadn't called him over when he walked through the door and instead he'd seen Henrietta first, beside the guy from the pages of *Esquire*, and walked out in despair, well, isn't fate the expression of a million arbitrary circumstances, modified by a thousand decisions, be they cause or effect? If not this, then that. Chaos Theory. A butterfly flaps its wings and everything changes. Still, it's Presner and Henrietta. Though he knew the Henrietta he talked to now over the phone found him slightly distasteful and was in a thousand other ways far from the Henrietta who looked up at him with what Presner swore was sheer *relief* at seeing him as he walked toward the table at Scotty's; Presner knew if some dark angel had taken him aside at that moment, saying, 'Look stranger, what's that name on your tag? Presner? Here's the deal. In fifteen years you'll be talking to that girl, Henrietta, *boychik*, so relax,' he would have done just that, relaxed, even knowing it was the dark angel who gripped him by the lapel.

"I'm so furious with him," Henrietta said. "That's why it took me a few days to get back to you. I wanted to talk to you rationally."

"I understand."

"Do you?"

"Sure," Presner said, "I react emotionally all the time too, shooting from the hip, blowing off steam, flipping my lid when the rational, considered response is called for—and that's when people don't say 'Thanks' when I hand them back their change!"

"The question was rhetorical," Henrietta said, "but thank you for the answer."

"Sorry."

"We've been talking for five minutes and how many times have both of us already apologized?"

"Is that one rhetorical, too?"

"You really do hate me, don't you?"

Presner sighed and wished he could reach into the receiver to retrieve the sigh. "Of course I don't."

"Do you think I owe you an explanation?"

'For sleeping with Fitz and giving him Chrissie's college fund to invest?' Presner wanted to say, as if she'd believe so much had transpired at such breakneck pace that his disappointment of fifteen years back—may as well be thirty—was forgotten or, better yet, not a disappointment to begin with, the misunderstanding Henrietta's, the poor woman still cultivating those myths. There was that about Presner, a paltriness of spirit. Who would deny it? Or worse yet, saying to her, 'An explanation for not calling until a week after Sara died? My sister cold and decomposing by then? That one?' Or, 'I'm not certain how objective people are about their experiences, Henrietta, or what explanations really clarify beyond that somebody wants to feel better or thinks somebody would feel better for hearing,' the unburdening a Chekhovian comedy where there was plenty of meaning, though not necessarily in what the words directly said but somewhere inside or beyond.

"You already explained. Anyway, we were kids. Hard to see that it matters now."

"Don't pretend you don't care. Your feelings come out in your hostility."

"I don't altogether deny it, but here's my theory, okay? People do things, like falling in love or choosing somebody for a job when there are a dozen lined up, similarly qualified, because it *feels* right. Intuition, too. If demanded by the losers to justify the choice—why did you pick the other guy? Why didn't I get the job?—they can draw up *reasons*, but those proofs never add up, haven't you noticed? Just because you can win a debate doesn't mean you win her heart."

"Fine theory," Henrietta said.

"You liked Gary better back then than you liked me. He looked like he walked off the pages of *Esquire*. I don't mean that in a shallow way," Presner added.

"Not likely," Henrietta said.

"Also, he was a nicer guy, and probably a lot more amusing. I imagine that to everybody but me it was self-explanatory."

"You don't have to be so nice about it all of a sudden."

"You thought I was about to sell out, Roxie said."

"You let me know you had money."

Presner didn't say anything. He wondered if when Fitz called, the confrontation would go like this. He'd say what he was going to say, or a version of it, while backing off, 'It's mostly my fault you took the money, Fitz,' he'd probably offer, then Fitz would say what he'd say, another version while backing off—if he knew Fitz, Fitz wouldn't let Presner have it, toe-to-toe—and then there'd be a similar silence over the line, each wondering what would happen if they dropped their controls altogether and said the one thing too many, the one thing you can't take back, the thing they'd meant to say when they rehearsed the conversation, not the softer, backing-off version; wondering, too, if that would be better than this comfortable silence where both could forget for a moment that they were having this confrontation for a reason.

Henrietta read his mind. "I hope you'll be more steadfast when you have it out with Fitzhugh."

"You're a woman, Henrietta; with women I look away. But grown men cower when I enter a room. Their knees shake like cheap maracas."

Henrietta didn't say anything.

"Admit you're impressed," Presner said.

"Before you shoot Fitz, tell him that he hurt me."

"I'm sorry he hurt you, Henrietta."

"Presner, I am too," Henrietta said.

Soon he found himself leaving the Pleasure Palace for longer periods of time, not checking the messages immediately upon returning. After talking to Roxie, he'd been fired up about confronting Fitz, playing the hero, making the calls to let everybody know that *Presner* was in charge, getting everybody's money back. (Fitz, too, would defer.) But in the days that followed, no call from Fitz, he'd lost the fire for the spectacle of accusing his oldest friend. That was by nature and inclination. By circumstance—looking back—he could see he'd often been confrontational. He *looked* confrontational. People crossed the street when they saw the bruiser approaching. 'What comes to mind when I say "Presner"? *Confrontational*!—that's the report from parlor games all across the Front Range,' he'd tell Lisa Caner. People saw him as edgy, driving a hard bargain, though the bruiser knew himself as soft, compromising, a door mat. 'Let *them* have the satisfaction, not me,' was his other motto.

While running along the Platte, he imagined that he still had a portion of his inheritance left, which he distributed among Roxie, Henrietta, Pepe and Marx to offset their losses. 'Fitz mailed this in,' he'd tell them after gathering the group together. 'No return address.'

One day he ran his route in thirty-nine minutes, eight minutes faster than the last time he'd timed himself several months before. Back at his place—the phone not ringing, no messages—he did 140 pushups, holding strict form, the all-time apartment record. 'Pointless to try for the crunch record,' Presner thought.

When you wait for something long enough people look at you differently. They turn away as if glimpsing your secret shame.

At Tyson's the regulars lining up with their magazines and newspapers and smokes and candies looked at him differently as he made change and answered their questions and talked when they wanted and didn't make a maniacal fuss if they weren't buying but merely standing around to kill time under a warm roof, bothering nobody. They didn't think too much about him, for all the warmth they sometimes generated. Whether this was the bottom or the top of his arc, whether he had a woman, whether he ran his route in thirty-nine or forty-two, backwards or forwards, and was supposed to talk Fitz into returning the money, his mind back at his place, fixed on the telephone, didn't cross their minds. They didn't want particulars; the bruiser's expression was enough. Still, some were happy to see him, he was sure of that, and there were times, his mind back at the phone un-ringing at the Pleasure Palace, when he nonetheless tried to imagine their lives with the same sympathy and admiration he'd hope they'd apply to his.

"Indiscriminate attacks of compassion," he described it to Lisa Caner. "'We're in this together.' 'Love one another or die,' that kind of thing, when I run somebody's charge card through the machine, or point them toward the adult enclosure at the back of the shop."

"You're a romantic."

"It'll pass," he assured her.

When he got back from Lisa Caner's, no message from Fitz was on the machine. I'm not cut out for this, Presner thought.

By the sixth day of the vigil ("Sixth day post-bombshell," the guy in his play scratches on the wall) he found himself waking up rolling snake eyes. One morning Presner lost $100 out of his wallet. Not the wallet, just the jack. For two days he retraced his steps, finding nothing. It's not the money but the principle, he told himself as he re-walked his routes, studying the asphalt and cement, hoping to at least find one of his combs. Suddenly Presner couldn't buy a comb that would stay in his back pocket. Later, he'd sit at his desk for hours under the guise of working on his play, scribbling lines on paper and inventing number games he'd forget the purpose of midway through. As for the lines? Dead on the page.

After work he'd walk back in a daze. Curiously, during the twenty-minute walk until he'd get back and find the answering machine unblinking, he'd feel invincible, insulated from the bump and grind, as if he were wearing a steel helmet. Another morning, though, he saw the world differently. The freezing morning post-dawn air blistered his ears; halfway back, the walk became murder. He closed his eyes and stumbled down curbs and brushed light posts and bus benches. A few bums were out, beckoning Presner to join their club. Years later he made it through his door, checked the unblinking machine, dove head-first onto his bed, and dreamed he was walking through green fields toward the sound of quiet water. A fishing pole was slanted on the bruiser's shoulder. Eagles and cardinals and robin redbreasts flew overhead circling back at the edge of the red sky. Then he was at the water. Then—same dream—it was dusk, and he was standing and leaning against a corral of wild horses running with the wind within the freedom of the corral. The corral was a green field miles in circumference. Even dreaming, Presner saw that everything was invisible, that he was leaning on nothing though still the horses circled freely. Suddenly he looked for the corral and couldn't see it anywhere on the ground or at the edge of the red sky. The bruiser had the idea that it was all in their horse minds, where they never broke down in creeks or drowned in mud or knew a bridle yanking at their mouths or the crack of a sharp whip breaking on their flanks. Within the circumference they were everything they could be within everything they were within everything they would ever be, spinning smaller circles in his mind as they ran. Still, he watched the horses, leaning. Then—same dream—Presner was traveling lightly through loose green woods and then was swimming across peaceful lakes never tiring, loping back into the woods, swimming easily across the lake but never knowing shore, thinking yes yes tree water tree water tree water, as in a clearing in the woods he was making love to a beautiful woman, blind to all but the beauty alive within her where he lived among the quiet sounds of great birds swooping to softly stirring lakes.

He *wanted* to be walking over green hills. He wanted the rustling of a creek and the bleating of sheep in the distance as he walked the green hills smoking Parodis and thinking and being happy about something—always a memory. He wanted to look down the hills over more hills and small farms and herds and a cozy little town where he was well known as a great man. In this town nobody bothered him, but everybody was pleased to see him and gathered around and fired friendly questions when he walked into town for supplies. They sensed something about Presner, perhaps a romantic loneliness without hunger in the deep lines on his roughhewn face. He'd walk through the green hills and at night beside a fire he'd write secret memoirs—full of aphorisms useful and profound—of his serious life.

Occasionally a chauffeured limo arrived in the little town. A beautiful woman dressed in red would step out of the back seat. In the general store she'd ask where a man called Presner lived. Is he here? In the green hills, they'd tell her, you can find him.

In the dream the earth moved an extra length. It was a spring day. The beautiful woman had arrived to talk pointlessly, as if she were talking to a child who understood words here or there but lacked the concentration to fuse sentences together. Still, she smiled at him: Presner couldn't help himself. She wore a long red dress and sandals and held his arm as they walked along the lake in the spring sun.

Inspired, he took a white flower from a bush and hooked the stem into Lisa Caner's hair.

A week before the wedding, still no call from Fitzhugh, Presner went over to Lisa Caner's unannounced.

"It's you," Caner said when she opened the door, peering over the chain into the hallway where the unshaven bruiser stood with a bouquet of roses.

"May I come in?"

He understood he was making a mistake. His sentimental dreams? Malarkey! Rigamarole! Shtusss! Bubbamagumba! But also there were his tendencies since he'd first tried to woo a girl. He'd miscalculate, overloading the mechanism with data. Even when the numbers were accurate, short circuits were inevitable, Presner hemming and hawing, shifting his weight from foot to foot, his beard growing darker by the half-second, pearls of spit bubbling on his lip. Presner figured he wasn't an easy man to love, but perhaps you could love him if you *already* loved him? Take Fitz as a counterpoint. Fitz—even now? he wondered, and bet *yes*—even now Henrietta, for example, would lift her skirt for Fitz. Women *found* ways to fall in love with Fitz. They talked themselves into it. They saw what they wanted to see—which was Fitz standing beside her—oh Fitz, Fitz—Presner thought 'the eye of the beholder' was coined with Fitz in mind—"He's no beauty but *I* think he's beautiful," a thousand women had scribbled pensively in their diaries; Fitz himself was the source for the speculations. He had the roughhewn looks that knocked women off balance. They always thought they were the only ones even when—like Hankie—they knew there were hundreds. Fitz *counted* on it. But this isn't about Fitz, the bruiser thought, standing in the hallway with the bouquet, Lisa Caner staring at him over the chain as if a muskrat had snuck up the garbage chute. Presner? An acquired taste. 'In the eye of the beholder' his best card.

"Sorry I didn't call first. I hate it when people don't call first. If it were me, I wouldn't open that door. No way, Jose. 'Come back after you call first,' I'd say. Pardon me."

"Are those for me?" Lisa nodded at the bouquet.

The question was genuine. "Sure," he handed the bouquet toward her. She unlocked the door, took the long stem roses, and he followed Lisa Caner through the door and her living room into the kitchen, where he sat in his usual chair facing the play poster. The chair was an upholstered rocker; Presner liked leaning back into it as he pontificated on Strasberg and other theatrical matters. Lisa pulled a vase out of the cabinet and filled it with water, then placed the flowers in the vase as if sweeping glass from the floor. "Coffee?" she looked at Presner, who nodded.

"What are you doing?"

"What am I ever doing? I'm working on an audition piece. Nora's parting shot. Can you believe it?"

Presner stared at her blankly.

"How's the waiting going?"

"Fine."

"*People are bloody ignorant apes,*" Lisa said in her breathy actress voice.

"I'm a bloody ape," Presner admitted.

"It's a line from *Waiting for Godot,* you know that. It's a *pun.* How's the waiting going? *Waiting for Godot*?"

Defeated, Presner nodded.

Was it two weeks ago that he was Batman? 'The undiscovered Arthur Miller of Lodo?' It may as well be two years, or twenty, or never; the chronology was for other times, when he lay back on his couch listening to the boom box and contemplated and discerned, as if inventing language itself. Presner was surprised the coffee cup didn't rattle in his hands, or the chair break beneath his bruiser's bulk.

"Thanks for the flowers. You look awful, by the way. Out of sorts. Something's bothering you. What's the special occasion?"

Presner shrugged. "No special occasion."

Lisa looked at the roses. "Those are beautiful. Thanks."

"You're welcome."

"Why do I have the impression that you're trying to prove something? I'm sorry that Fitzhugh hasn't called you back."

Presner nodded. "Can I ask you something?"

"Please don't ask. Okay?" Lisa looked at the flowers, then looked away the way she looked away in the poster behind her, as if considering dimensions that the audience couldn't yet fathom.

"I can't ask?"

"Please don't."

He stood up and lifted a stem from the vase, then walked around the table and stood above her and placed the stem in Lisa's moppish red hair, briefly brushing her ear—she didn't recoil, but turned and looked up, her huge eyes opening in bafflement or censure, he couldn't tell, and a degree of pity that snapped Presner to attention—Presner thinking of lowering his lips to those lips, the spasm of melodrama appealing to Lisa Caner by relegating the gesture to further remove—the only way he could salvage the friendship—Presner here not as Presner with romantic designs but ironic *commentary* on one hundred years of modern theater—Lisa waited, holding her ground despite the pity and bafflement and censure, lowering her eyes.

Presner walked out of the kitchen, through the living room to the chained door where he paused a moment, then a moment longer, waiting for Lisa to call him back as she sat at the table staring at her coffee cup.

Presner walked back along the Platte, then circled to the 16th Street Mall. He sat on a bench, staring at his hands. A group of runaways passed his hulking pose. "Do you have a smoke, Mister? Can you spare a quarter?" Presner thought of a lot of images of Lisa Caner, from the first time he'd met her in Continuing Ed, the first time he'd heard her disembodied voice reading the script, and then the muted affair when he would walk her to the door and walk back to his car, meeting her a year later in the Post Office and beginning it all again—and these preposterous fantasies which had sustained him—Presner the ringer, Presner the brilliant intellectual, Presner the sufferer, Presner the last loyal friend, the bruiser; even Presner the news clerk—even *that* sounded wrong—the everyday guy without pretensions, accepting himself as others saw him—all his life was a costume drama.

Throw an accusation at the playwright, and already he's confessed. 'I never bought into any of that stuff with more than half a heart,' Presner thought, though if he'd never done anything all the way, without a net, it wasn't as if there was anybody out there watching his back. You couldn't expect but that it would show. But how strange that he'd expected more of himself than the numerous dumbshows.

'The grandeur and the pity both,' Chekhov called it, or should have, referring to the sense of things, the consciousness that one has. Presner leaned back onto the bench, breathed in a mouthful of air, breathed out, breathed in—this he could do—out, in, out, in, as if chanting her name.

An hour later Lisa Caner talked into his machine as Presner walked into his place. "You're not a bad guy, Presner, but you're looking for your sister. You can't get past that. Sometimes when I'm with you I wish I wasn't an actress at all. Then we'd have a chance. But then you wouldn't want me."

Presner prowled back and forth across his living room as he listened. He understood that she was relieved he didn't pick up the receiver, then wondered if he was wrong again, that what she *wanted* was for him to pick up the receiver to talk her out of what she was saying, or into something else.

As much as he wanted to try, the bruiser was heartened by his restraint. He was a guy who could take it without blabbering desperately into the phone, yammering about misunderstandings, second chances. Not just a bruiser but a stoic. There was such a dignity about that, he wasn't even inclined to grab the phone, blurting, 'Oh, it's *you*. By the way, that question I was going to ask? It was about Turgenev and Chekhov. Did they ever meet? Why didn't you want to hear? I don't get it. Gee.'

Perhaps Lisa was opening up a new avenue with her message, placing items on the table for further discussion and scrutiny, setting the new agenda for the new Presner and the new Caner? 'How can two people who frame their experiences in terms of what they'll be able to tell each other'—Presner had found himself doing this—'throw that away because somebody wants to ask a question? Even assuming you're right about that question?' She'd say, 'You've betrayed me.' 'I thought you'd be flattered.' 'That's not the point. You've been positioning me all along with your Chekhov this's and observations about the grandeur and the pity.' 'You've been positioning *me*,' Presner would say plaintively.

"Enough of this. Call me if you want to talk," she said. "That would be okay. I want you to understand."

Presner prowled his living room, picking up the pace to a virtual trot, talking himself into and out of a thousand contortions. He tore into a half-gallon of Pralines and Cream that he kept for special occasions, pronounced himself cowardly for not picking up the phone, and finished the carton by the time the phone rang again, the bruiser's news clerk heart leaping with impossible optimism as he picked up the instrument. But no Caner. Fitz.

"You sound out of breath. Hope I'm not interrupting anything. On the other hand, you didn't have to answer, did you, Counselor? If you were in the middle of something, you could have let it ring. Though knowing you, Presner, you'd pick up anyway. It's the bar mitzvah boy in you. You know who this is, I trust."

"I was finishing a half-gallon of Pralines and Cream. Practicing for Gary Marx's wedding reception, I may add, where I contemplate consuming my body weight in mint juleps, barbecue ribs and French fries. I may not stop there, Fitz. If this is Fitz. I may consume *your* body weight."

"That's some tough talk."

As usual, Presner wondered where Fitz was. "Remember that woman you advised me to *shtup*, one Lisa Caner? The woman I go—went—running to when I scratch—scratched—my pinky? The one who finishes—finished—my sentences. The one—"

"I get the picture," Fitz said. "Or got it."

Presner didn't say anything. All the existential points he won with his stoicism when Lisa Caner spoke to his answering machine and he didn't whine, shamefully begging Presner-style for a second—third—chance, he was about to relinquish with shameful whining to Fitzhugh—double whining, since his lament was more impressionistic than literal, having never run to Lisa Caner with a bleeding pinky—would that he had!—that he'd brought his heart to her on a shield—or begun a sentence she'd finished, or at least the way Presner would have finished it—'Anyway, since they're existential points, who's keeping score?' Presner thought. He could *triple* relinquish with impunity—this the very kind of observation Lisa Caner would find amusing; he'd never really let her know the real Presner, the funny man, the punster; just the Chekhovian version. Looking back—Presner knowing this for the melodramatic posturing it was—nonetheless posturing—there were few things that he'd done right that he hadn't shortly thereafter double-relinquished, if not triple.

"You called her bluff, I take it," Fitz said.

"Called and doubled. It's the Presnerian way."

"Nothing that hasn't happened to me a thousand times," Fitz consoled.

"Thanks," Presner said, genuinely.

"What did you do, anyway? Take her out for dinner and a movie, then back to her kitchen for mint juleps, then surreptitiously slip your hand on her knee and breathe in her ear?"

"Nothing so suave," Presner admitted. "I knocked on her door unannounced then asked if I could ask her a question."

"*You asked if you could ask her a question.*" Presner envisioned Fitzhugh on the other end in Argentina somewhere, shaking his head dismally.

"That's right."

Fitz hesitated, *still* shaking his head, Presner imagined. "Presner, the answer to that question is always 'No!' I thought you went to law school. You *need* the mint julep, hand on the knee, breath in the ear. They're called 'tools of persuasion.' Here's what you did: You went over there without any tools of persuasion in order to persuade her."

It was too late to mention the long-stem roses. The point was made. "I didn't plan well."

Fitz mused, still incredulous as if he'd never recover from the bruiser's dimwitted miscalculation. "By the time you—"

"Me?"

"Anybody brings the issue up as an item for discussion, it's too late. If you have to discuss it, that only means you've missed a hundred opportunities to do it without discussing it first. The time for discussion's *later*. Though I wouldn't advise that either."

"This is straight from Fitzhugh's *Rules of Seduction*, I take it. Chapter one?"

"It's from the preface," Fitzhugh said.

Presner enjoyed everything about this. Pending the next turn in the conversation, where he was set to accuse his best friend of feloniously and immorally defrauding the old law school gang, then threaten to press charges if restitution wasn't forthcoming by the end of the conversation—Presner figured he'd also call him a *nudnick*, for emphasis. Fitzhugh knew it was coming, too, but now they were discussing the latest unpleasant turn in Presner's love life with rapt attention, and Fitzhugh's solicitousness was genuine. Later was for later. For now, Fitz felt for his old pal. "You never liked her."

"I never liked *it*," Fitz amended. "All that going to the kitchen and discussing Shakespeare. It was a time drain."

'After I already called her bluff last year,' Presner added to himself.

"You needed a more appreciative audience," Fitz added.

"Give me points for optimism, though."

"As long as you're working the past with your chin up, why not try Henrietta next? Better, there must be a few gals from middle school you haven't gotten over."

"Lisa thought I was looking for Sara."

Fitzhugh didn't say anything right away. His friend wasn't above levying a joke at Presner's expense, even at sacred times like this—Fitz was known to work a joke in during his *summations*, back before he became an impresario, according to Roxie—stuff that looked sarcastic in the transcript, though the jurors knew better, just as Presner knew better now—Fitz took it all in, two steps ahead. Wherever you walked around Fitz you walked into a trap, though for the sake of your own interests, according to Fitz. He reminded Presner of a guy he played football with in high school who (so it seemed to Presner from the bench, where he could barely see beyond his face guard) could take in the whole field at a glance as if there were a wide angle camera perched behind *his* face guard, extending from his eyes.

"Everybody's looking for somebody," Fitz said softly.

"Why'd you do it?" Presner asked. This was later in the conversation. The unpleasant turn in Presner's love life was two steps ago. Since then they'd covered the old gang's activities—everything but the elephant in the room—and, vaguely, Fitz's latest scheme, which involved clearing some hurdles for a firm dealing in a balsa wood product, possibly perfume; whether on the import or export end, Presner couldn't decipher. When he finally asked, Fitz was in mid-pontification.

"You don't beat around the bush, do you?"

"I don't want to get into the deceit," Presner said. "I don't want to get into the way you played on Hankie's dreams, romantic and material—that's all you've ever done—and stole her life savings for the 'Fitzhugh Fund.' *Shtuss.* Bubbamagumba. Was there ever a 'Fitzhugh Fund'?"

"Yes."

"I don't want to get into the way you played on Roxie's trust to bail yourself out of whatever and if it cost Roxie her savings as well as what little faith she had left—you took her *past*, Fitz, that's all—all for the sake of your *sociopathic* convenience—or whether you really thought you were giving Marx and Pepe a windfall, a favor—but *caveat emptor*, after all; deals go south—is that it?—or they knew what was what, they knew the risks, they're big boys—I don't want to know why you didn't think to *ask* for the money—gee, Fitz, they'd think you weren't the *macher*—'What a pathetic spectacle, Fitzhugh asking for help'—pitiable, phony Fitzhugh—I don't want to hear how you were momentarily blinded by greed—and all it took was a couple of hundred grand—'takes money to make money'—so you didn't think through the implications—'But they were blinded by greed, too.' Is that your line? The big chance everybody else is getting, why not us?—'We're just Fitzes too, deep down'—I don't want to hear about how you'll pay back every red cent if Roxie and Hankie and Pepe and Marx don't press charges," Presner cautioned.

Fitz didn't say anything. Presner heard him breathing heavily into the other end in Bolivia or wherever. He felt momentarily as if he'd landed a sucker punch to the gut of a friend who was just calling to say hello, all because he thought the riff sounded right. 'Words have consequences,' Presner reminded himself. You say things to people and it's not always going to roll off their backs or bounce off the rim. Ninety-nine percent of the stuff you say to people you can take back. That's if they even notice—if *you* even notice—that you said it in the first place, Presner thought. Take every last exchange down at the shop. But the other one percent wrenches your soul with its syllables. People taking the sucker punch, breathing labored on the other end. Presner was happy that he didn't go around all day saying more, sucker punching people right and left until half the air was gone from the universe. Though you could say good things, too, that puts the air back in their lungs and puffs out their chests. Presner figured the same ninety-nine percent principle was at work, whether you said good stuff and inflated the target, or bad and deflated. That was worth reminding himself now. All stuff he was feeling momentarily. Could you put the same air back in after pushing it out? He was doing a job for Roxie and Hankie and even Marx and Pepe, he didn't lose sight of that. Presner hyperventilated too, out of breath, Fitz's doing.

Fitz said, "It doesn't sound like there's too much left that you want to hear about."

"Maybe we can set up a payment schedule," Presner suggested. Fitzhugh told Presner he was flying in tomorrow for the wedding. They'd attend to details then.

"Better wear your suit of armor if you can find it."

"I'm wearing it now after talking to you. Are you still the monster?"

"*Was* the monster," Presner commented. "'Guy with the athletic build' is another way to put it."

"Whom are you going with?"

"Nobody."

"I'll make some calls," Fitz promised.

That wasn't so bad, he thought, spirits lifting for the first time since he'd had the dinner with Roxie under the false pretenses, Presner the Personal Trainer, when all she wanted was to get him to do the dirty work, all the unpleasantries, so they wouldn't have to press charges, though with Fitz in Bolivia or wherever, who'd know if they'd ever reach him? Probably asking the bruiser was the last resort. Still, it stood to reason that Roxie trusted him to do the job, to track Fitz down, because they were all at wit's end. It made Presner feel better about himself, though after the Caner debacle he was already casting about for ways. Maybe nobody *liked* him, but when something important needed to be done, when the chips were down, little ol' Presner's the one they called, tiny wee Presner, small-picture Presner, trumping up false pretenses if necessary.

The lid lifted, Presner thought of what he might say to Fitz, once he arrived in town and they attended to those "details." He felt like he was a heavyweight contender who'd prepared for a big fight and come out the other side. Win, lose, draw, who could say? But there was Fitz agreeing to the payment schedule, making good. There was Fitz ending the call by promising to call some women, Presner being Presner drawing blanks. The old arrangement, still.

He walked around the living room. He felt like taking a long run, maybe double, to make up for the last several days. All that had changed really, he thought, was that when they went to the wedding, the old gang together again, for once Presner wouldn't be the black sheep, the tragic figure, the dark underbelly.

Honors went to Fitz this time, the unofficial felon.

When the phone rang again the bruiser knew it was Caner.

Fitz.

"Presner," Fitz roared into the machine. "I've been thinking about you. I have a *better* idea."

Part Four

Presner on the 747, his ticket *arranged*, courtesy of Fitzhugh. He'd been a pisher in short pants the last time he'd had a ticket arranged. On the flight, Presner tried to remember when, though he was distracted from the reverie by the guy next to him, whose head had fallen to his lap and bobbed up and down as he snored. Something about his grandmother back east, a beauty in her day, though Presner remembered her as a sickly, white-haired matron. Sara had visited the year before, her first trip alone; then it was Presner's turn. Their parents made a big deal about it by baking a cake and setting up streamers the night before, though as Presner thought about it, the celebration may have occurred after he'd returned intact. He remembered his mom crying at the rite of passage. It was—this is what Presner imagined got to people—almost always a pleasure to think about his sister and parents. What *defined* them—at least to most people he knew in recent years—is that they were dead. Presner perhaps contributed to the impression. "What about your parents?" somebody might ask him, usually after the news clerk had inquired after theirs. "Oh, they were killed in a plane crash a long time ago."

"Do you believe you'll die in a plane crash too?" This Lisa Caner had asked him not long after he'd started coming over. Her look of intense curiosity startled Presner.

"I'm not *that* sentimental," Presner assured her.

The snoring next to him didn't encourage indulgence. You can't meditate next to a furnace. Nine hours from Denver to London. The playwright had eyed every pretty woman walking down the aisle with her carry-on, some dressed like teenagers on a hayride, though many (this was British Airlines) well-coiffed despite the long hours ahead in cramped quarters—sometimes the bruiser, though tending toward t-shirts and sweatshirts, imagined that if an airline required a dress code, same fare, there'd seldom be an empty seat—their mistake, as always, was *lowering* the common denominator—as it happens, this was a big theme of Fitz's back when—when a well-dressed guy the size of two Fitzes wallowed down the aisle and hovered above the oblivious playwright. "That one's mine."

'Figures,' Presner almost said, but smiled pleasantly. "Let me move out of your way."

"I'll arrange the ticket," Fitzhugh had suggested when he called Presner back the night before. "Bring your play along too. I know some guys out here."

"I couldn't," Presner allowed.

He knew what Fitz was up to. You could practically call Fitz a thief and a betrayer—a shnook, too, Presner may have added—but let on that your heart's been broken by a woman he'd warned you about, and he arranges a ticket. "You don't have to turn away from every opportunity," Fitz said impatiently. "These guys aren't assholes."

"There are no 'these guys,' Norm."

"And no Santa Claus, too, is that it? I see you've been reading your Carnap. Your Kant. Suit yourself."

"I already know the drill," Presner sighed. "You'll have a driver waiting to take me blindfolded to a neutral destination, where an armored limo will transport me to a fortress hidden in the woods. I mean, Fitz, I don't know where you are. What'll I tell customs when they ask? 'I'm meetin' a guy but it's all hush hush. He likes his, uh, autonomy?' What customs, anyway, now that we're talking? Timbuktu? I mean, c'mon, Fitz."

"I'm in Oxford," Fitzhugh said.

"Oxford?"

Fitz left instructions for the playwright to take the bus from Heathrow. Two copies of the play were in a briefcase under his footrest. The huge man next to him leaned away and Presner claimed the armrest, a pyrrhic victory—the guy would certainly lean back, and unless he moved it again they'd be arm against arm, an intimacy, come to think of it, on par with what he'd achieved with Henrietta back in law school, or Lisa Caner now, whom he was determined not to think about again in order to preserve his sanity—'This is something I'll never think about again,' the playwright resolved as he walked home from Caner's, hat in hand—though intention was everything (as they say in the law), which he wasn't going to think about either. For a while, Presner watched the little screen above the tray in front of him, a caper flick celebrating two guys doing a last heist—and this his last heist with Fitz? Gee, he wasn't that sentimental either—nonetheless he turned it off and switched to easy listening, enjoyed his free drink, again switched from easy listening to the movie channels, then stood up and roamed the aisle back to the last row by the restrooms, where he did some knee bends as he waited, anticipating the "guys" Fitz lined up—even worked himself up about these guys, producers with deep pockets—but a heaviness overcame Presner's heart. Ah, Fitz.

At the terminal, Presner followed Fitz's directions, exchanged his money, waited in line for the express, then bought the return ducat. He had the bus seat to himself and tried to summon the sleep he didn't get on the plane but was too tired to give it a real go so ended up passively watching the English countryside through the window. Pleasant, Presner thought. The rolling hills of sheep led to more rolling hills of sheep—more sheep per square foot than the playwright had ever seen—but they didn't help him sleep despite a halfhearted count or two. Presner couldn't think of the last time he'd been this groggy and wondered if—assumed that—this might be Fitz's strategy. 'Can't put one over on Norm,' Presner thought. Not when he was like this, all groggy languid torpor. 'Might have told him off and put him in his place from across the Atlantic, but now Fitz has nothing to fear.' The *sheep* would have the drop on him in a battle of wits.

Fitzy was waiting at the stop in front of the Queen's Coffeehouse, saying, "You look exhausted," as if Presner had committed an indiscretion. Immediately Fitz bear-hugged the playwright American-style and patted him on the back as if stomping out a brush fire.

"Good to see you, Fitz." It was true. He may have been groggier than he'd ever been, his heart heavy over his friend's indiscretions, chicanery, treachery, but two minutes around Fitz and the lid blew off. Presner even wondered if they all hadn't overreacted, paranoia run amok, 'cause Fitz was overseas, unavailable to instantly address their concerns face-to-face, so their imaginations ran free with neurotic implications. When they talked among themselves, they encouraged the paranoia. Fitz could light up a mausoleum, though he could darken a place, too.

They walked side-by-side, Presner adjusting his backpack, big Fitz striding purposefully—two guys from Denver adrift in Oxford, Presner liked thinking—for ten feet, whereupon Fitz pointed at a sign: "City Tours. Get off anywhere. *All day.*"

"The tour takes an hour. You can see the sights, take your pictures. That'll clear the decks for pushing your play."

"That's okay. Thanks. But I don't need to see the sights. I'm not here to see the sights."

Fitz smiled indulgently and exhaled, "But as long as you're here," and slipped ten quid into Presner's pack, then pushed the groggy American toward the curb. The bus had just pulled into the stop lane.

Fitzhugh smiled. "I'll be here in an hour waiting."

Presner accepted a headset from the driver and trudged up the steps to the upper level. Presner lay back in his seat in the open air, pulled on his knit cap and the headset, then closed his eyes for the tour.

It wasn't a bad way to take in the lay of the land, though, and from the open-air upper deck he imagined he was sailing on the high seas. Why hadn't he done that in his youth? Could you do something like that in middle age and cut anything other than a pathetic figure? Other than what he took to be an Indian couple toward the front, he had the deck to himself. From his bird's eye level the city was medieval, with castle walls carved with secret entrances and ancient cathedrals with names—"All Souls," "St. Thomas the Martyr"—as foreboding as a horse whip, but enchanting greens as well—it was like taking a bus ride through an elaborate movie set—interspersed with what could have been blocks of downtown Denver. Presner dozed off in comfort, listening to tales of the pub—"short for public house," Fitz later informed Presner—where Tolkien and C.S. Lewis used to meet after tutorials. 'Wherever you walk in this burgh, you walk through history,' Presner took in. You didn't get that in Denver, at least not a history anybody wanted to hear about. He slept, and when he came to, the Indian couple was staring at him. The tour? Well, Fitzhugh, Presner thought. Just like Fitz to give him a chance to catch up on his rest.

As promised, Fitzhugh was waiting by the stop when Presner got off. "How were the sights?"

"Swell."

"You're probably hungry."

Presner grunted. "Thanks for arranging the ticket."

"You're doing me the favor," Fitzhugh insisted.

They stepped into an Indian restaurant, where Presner slumped in his seat and Fitzhugh disquisitioned on the English class system and the burgeoning anger of the proletariat.

"Can't blame them," Presner yawned.

"Just don't think the English are all repressed and socially correct and go daft over Benny Hill. You should see the second page of the *Mirror*."

"I plan to."

"It's the lifetime dream of some of these girls to appear topless in the tabloids, to be drooled over by commuters in the underground. You think it's all lascivious, Presner? They're spitting in the face of the upper classes! That's right, they're boogering the stereotypes that guys like you have back in Denver."

"Hmm," Presner said over the lamb and chutney, which had arrived ten seconds before he was sure he'd be down for the count.

Fitz assessed him. "Don't worry. We'll do the whole scene. We'll do the pubs, ancient to contemporary. You'll have your bitters."

"How long have you been here?" Presner wondered.

Fitz shrugged. "A few weeks."

"Business?"

"There's more to life, Pres. It's time you cultivated the finer things."

If there were a thousand ways that Presner could have answered that, there were a thousand ways he didn't. Fitz was staying in a hotel (which opened through a wall, it seemed to wide-eyed Presner) across from Radcliffe Square. There were two double beds in the room. Presner flopped on one bed. When he awoke his watch read 1:00. 'That would be 8, adjusting for the difference,' Presner thought. Morning or night, he couldn't say.

A few minutes after he awoke and calculated the time and closed his eyes again, Fitz came into the room and stood over Presner's bed. Fitz was dressed in a blue business suit—what he usually wore to court or when he was interviewed on TV, Presner remembered—and imagined that the effect might approximate elegance to anybody who hadn't seen him in overalls. "Morning or night?"

"Is that a question?"

"Yes."

"Night," Fitz said matter-of-factly, as if it were a query he answered regularly.

"Are we inside or outside?"

"Inside."

"On the air or ground?"

"Ground," Fitz said.

Presner nodded, collecting his bearings.

Fitz really tried to show him the place. Touched, the playwright tagged along in good spirit. Fitz imagined that all Presner's life all he'd wanted, really, was to do the pub crawl in Oxford, but was always too accommodating to insist upon it. "That's the Lion's Den." Fitz pointed at an insignia above a courtyard down the block after the third pub. "Tralawney's rumored to have gotten into a row there."

"A row? Gee."

"Want to try it?"

Presner didn't have the heart to say, 'This is our fourth pub, so I get the picture, Fitz, but I'm a zombie. What's more, there's only so much I can absorb about incipient fissures in the British class hierarchy.'

"Wouldn't miss it."

Presner thought that Fitz might open up with the fourth round of bitters. Sometimes liquor made Fitz boisterous so that, urgently waving his arms, loosening his collar, clearing his voice with a tumultuous cough, he'd pontificate to the room at large as if they'd purchased tickets for the spectacle. But at other times the liquor seemed to sober his pal as if reminding him of grave matters he'd been foolishly neglecting now urging him back to brass tacks. "Well, do you miss her?" Fitz said after his second pint at the Lion's Den, suddenly beholding the playwright/news clerk/attorney with more compassion than the man could bear.

"Who?"

"Don't be disingenuous."

Presner guessed. "Caner?"

"That's right. Do you miss her even now as we sit, for all we know, at the very table where Kit Marlowe composed *Dr. Faustus*?"

Fitzhugh knew better. He shook his head sadly with the weight of a thousand assumptions about Presner's broken heart. He too had been dumped by women. He knew the brutal impact, the damage to the psyche, Presner's resolve never to trust or love again. It was all there.

"Well, you told me," Presner said. "I should have listened. Fitzy Knows Best."

Fitz nodded.

"It wasn't anything. I'm not sure she wasn't just something good to talk about, really. Something good to keep 'em guessing."

Fitzhugh shook his head tragically again; there were horrors beyond speaking on the tip of Presner's tongue.

"And now, if you'll excuse me, I'll kill myself," Presner added.

Fitz smiled. "You act like it's nothing, but I know you. You don't fool me, Presner. Everything hurts you. You can pretend you're being melodramatic. You can pretend I'm being melodramatic. You make fun of yourself, you always do, but I know that you stand behind the counter at Tyson's counting the minutes, looking into the eyes of every woman who enters, then you walk home and twist your guts out."

There was nothing to say about something like that, so Presner said nothing.

"Ah, Pres, you'll notice—not now, not here in the Lion's Den—but we'll walk around the city center tomorrow, you'll see—that the women in Oxford are prettier than the women in Denver, and the women in Oxford are a dozen times smarter. Plenty of fish in the sea, as my mom used to say."

Presner nodded and sipped his bitters. "You'll see," Fitz promised.

Fitz could go on like this forever and Presner almost wished he would, but he had to say it. "Be that as it may there are a few things we need to talk about. Such as how you're going to reimburse Roxie and Hankie. Marx and Pepe, too," ('Paternalistic asshole I am,' Presner thought in his languor, 'thinking of Roxie and Hankie first.') "The guys back in Denver? Not the whys and wherefores—those can wait. At you own speed, Fitz."

Fitz smiled indulgently: Fine lad, the bruiser, getting down to business! "Wait a second." Fitz stood up slowly. "We'll do it all, whatever you have in mind, but I want to show you something first." Fitz lifted his pint and walked out of the room to the adjacent room. Presner took his pint and followed. Although it was almost midnight—if three in the afternoon *my* time, Presner thought—every table but one was occupied. Perhaps it was Presner's preconception, but the drinkers seemed sedate and dignified—very British, the playwright thought—as if this were high tea. He assumed Fitz was angling for the free table—a minute change of scenery by which to adjust the awkward turn in conversation—Presner not above such maneuvering himself—but instead approached a corner table where two middle-aged women willfully ignored the large approaching Americans like the rumbling of a distant stampede.

"May we sit here?"

The women looked at each other. One—a heavyset redhead in a bright pattern dress—nodded reluctantly.

"I hope we're not imposing."

Presner was tempted to roll his eyes. It could have gone that way, Presner calling his old pal on the transparent maneuver, growing impatient, fuming, tugging at Fitz's sleeve like a sanctimonious whistleblower, or a reluctant adolescent. But instead, the playwright sat down next to the large redhead, Fitz getting the slimmer, heavily mascaraed brunette who had so much powder packed on her face she could have arrived straight from the BBC. But the women were Americans, it turned out, on tour from Ohio—"*Been there*," Fitz said. "*Been there*," Presner added; they were a team and rose to the challenge—the two Ohioans a team themselves? Presner wondered—four middle-aged Americans sitting around a table in England, refusing to be dispirited—that's what it was, Fitz winking at Presner the way he had across the table the first night of law school orientation. The women were nothing special—but look who's talking, the bruiser thought. The sea was large. Presner thinking, 'Gee, this is nice, two American males sizing up an opportunity, playing the eternal game, reading each other with the instincts of jazz professionals at a jam session,' though the redhead kept her distance from Presner, tilting away as Presner tilted toward her, wary. She'd seen his kind too often.

"We can have a picnic tomorrow," Fitz proposed after a smattering of observations. "Have you been to the British Museum? We can rent a car for the drive to London Town, then gape at the monoliths or sit in the Reading Room where Marx wrote the Communist Manifesto, then purchase sandwiches with the crust trimmed and a slab of baloney postured in the middle. A scrumptious lunch!"

"English style," Presner said.

"Then there's dinner. We'll have you back in time so you can rejoin the tour group."

The brunette, Tracy, asked what else they might do. "Or are you boys out of ideas?"

"We can see what's playing in the West End."

Peg, the redhead, looked at her friend and smiled painfully.

"He's a playwright, a man of the theater," Fitz explained. "Naturally, we'll go to the West End."

"He's an international entrepreneur," Presner said. "A scion of the markets. We'll stop off at Broad Street."

"Have you written anything we might have seen?" This was Tracy, looking openly at the playwright.

"It's a state of the spirit mostly," Presner admitted.

"We're seeing a couple of guys tomorrow," Fitz said, "about staging a production of his latest."

They all looked at the bruiser, who shrugged modestly.

The women were secretaries from Youngstown. ("Been there," Fitz said again. "Been there," Presner said.) At first, they'd exchanged impatient looks at everything Presner said, as if he were the bad apple they'd been warned to avoid; not Fitz, the straight shooter. But soon they exchanged looks after everything Fitz said as well, as if Presner were contagious.

"We're staying near Radcliffe Square," Fitz posed. "Have you seen Radcliffe Square at twilight?"

"They say you haven't lived until you do!" Presner said.

They really are beautiful, Presner thought. At first blush he could see himself working his hands, Peg moaning, softly giving in, the decision made and not yet regretted. Two guys, two gals, life short, the ancient formula. But there was something beautiful about them beyond the dumbshow they were performing, something he thought that he could express if he really were a playwright. That's once you got past Tracy's powder and Peg's disdain, though they'd be swapping tales later about the two drunken Yanks. ('Go all the way to Oxford and it may as well be Youngstown,' Tracy saying. 'Drunken horny shits,' Peg saying. 'Could you believe those corny lines?') Talking to them was like watching a Chekhovian play where what moved you weren't the people themselves—who could be as vexing as anybody Presner knew—but something essential in their situations that made them just so. Presner had to be a human being to like these women; battered, a history of coming in second best; and the bruiser wondered if you had to be that way to like him, too.

"Care to join us for a stroll?" Fitz said, smiling graciously.

"I don't think so," Peg said. "You boys go ahead."

"Thanks for asking," Tracy said curtly, turning back toward Peg.

"I have seen the Master at work!"

This was Presner, regaling at the wind as they walked back. Shuffling, stumbling. Fitz belching. Presner belching.

"They'll be waiting for us back at the hotel, that's for sure."

"That Peg was stacked, as we used to say back in high school! Did you say that back in high school?" Fitz asked. "I think she *liked* you."

"You and Tracy had that body language going. Won't surprise me if you arranged an assignation, exclusively communicated through soulful glances."

"Hmm," Fitz considered. "Here we are, two guys in the throes of drunken revelry, at large in Oxford, England."

"Nobody better look at us sideways or we'll clean their clocks."

"Oxford, England," Fitz repeated, as if he were the one who flew in yesterday and still lacked sea legs.

"Can't imagine getting over the novelty," Presner said sincerely. He had the pleasant sensation of walking through the rest of his life in drunken revelry. He'd have more women than he'd had in the past, he was pretty sure of that. And he'd never have to call guys like Fitz to account if calling them to account was necessary. He'd lose muscle tone, but when you were in the midst of drunken revelry you didn't especially care if you lost muscle tone, or gained it, Presner guessed.

Twenty minutes later—Presner thinking it was a good hour—where was the damn hotel?—was Fitz setting him up?—Presner stopped to rest on the steps of a cathedral. Or a college? He brought up the matter with Fitz.

"It's a cathedral," Fitz said.

"Fuck no."

"Does it *look* like a college?"

"Yes!"

"A seminary, maybe," Fitz allowed.

They made their way back to the hotel by Radcliffe Square, where Fitz made a show of searching the wall for the door.

If Wednesday night was for lady killing, Thursday would be for conquering the world of theater. Presner slept deeply, then at first light slipped on his running shorts and t-shirt and stretched on the hotel floor: a set of crunches, a set of pushups, performed as softly as he could manage. Presner never liked doing pushups while others were within earshot, for fear they'd confuse his heavy breathing with self-gratification, or criticize his form.

"There's the bruiser," Fitz said groggily, looking up as the t-shirted Presner fumbled through his pockets for his hotel key. "Going for a run?"

"I'm considering it."

"There's a trail over by St. Catherine's. You might try that."

Fifteen hours in a town, and Fitz assumed Presner knew every nook and cranny. "That's fine, but I'll just run the streets."

"Wait a second."

The second turned into a minute, and the minutes into a dozen. Then Fitz was dressed in sweats, bounding up and down ostentatiously like a boxer, leading Presner to the street. The bellboy looked at the pair as if they'd escaped from the circus, and Presner wasn't sure that they hadn't.

Fitz ran like somebody who hadn't run in years other than out of the way of cars. He stood straight up and pumped his legs like he was riding a bicycle. 'Roxie runs better than Fitz,' Presner thought not to mention, then thought that he should voice the observation; that's why he was here after all, to connect the guy with the old gang back home, then to bring the guy back, or at least his money.

"In shape, Roxie'd be even more imposing," Fitz said. By now—they'd gone three blocks—Fitz was steadily breathing more heavily, though Presner, savvy to his ways, wasn't sure that Fitz wasn't feigning the furious huffing to forestall conversation or to mock Presner's own pretensions. Fitz had a bag of tricks he'd reach into any time; he'd made a career of pulling rabbits out of hats.

"You're right about that."

"That Caner gal must seem like a long way away," Fitz said, changing the subject.

Sure, Fitz. Four days, 10,000 miles on the 747, five pubs, twelve pints, a couple of women we pretended to pick up, Fitz & Pres, a team again, a good night's sleep, and six blocks of a run at a snail's pace.

"Here it is, St. Catherine's," Fitz said at last, the moment before Presner was set to drop the laggard and surge forward in a sprint. They were barely moving by now—Presner surprised to see they'd gained on pedestrians—when Fitz stopped at the mouth of a parking lot. The sun was rising, and big Fitz was sweating much more than Presner—who typically sweated a lot when more than barely moving—and couldn't catch his breath.

"Keep moving. Wind down. That's what you're supposed to do when you stop," Presner said.

Fitz placed his hand on Presner's shoulder, as if to brace himself, and walked slowly. Still, he had enough in the tank to smile at Presner. "You inspire me, Presner. You should be my Personal Trainer, too. I didn't realize I was so out of shape."

"I take it that globetrotting's a figurative term."

"That's right, Presner, *needle* me." Fitz pointed at some tennis courts at the end of the parking lot, behind which was the path to University Trails.

Presner ran slowly. The trails were narrow, cutting through dense brush. Occasionally he'd pass bridges over the Thames tributary. Presner tried to cross, but the bridges were closed, access cut off by locked gates that he imagined were centuries old. 'You don't find that in Denver,' the playwright thought. Sometimes he'd hear footsteps up the narrow trail and encounter small dogs running ahead of their masters. In what he took to be expressions of common courtesy, they wouldn't look at Presner as they passed. Over here you gave a man in jogging shorts his privacy. 'Snobs, or else considerate two times over,' Presner thought. At first, looking up, he'd nod, but soon dropped the expectation, and tried to imagine the famous personages who may have walked along this trail. Nobel chemistry laureates, charismatic knights, famous poets he could track down in the *Norton Anthology*. Stuff you never thought about in Denver, even though objectively he'd crossed paths with some pretty famous types there, too. But there'd never been anything exotic about Denver. If he passed a locked gate in Denver, he didn't wonder what was behind it. 'Probably an angry dog,' Presner thought. Here: buried treasures or damsels. Why wouldn't there be? When you passed a stone around here you didn't think to pick it up to test your arm, Presner thought. You wanted to get it inspected by experts. It could be the Rosetta.

Presner liked himself, running in Oxford. He may have liked himself running in Denver, but if so, back there the observation seldom emerged through the reveries and fog. It wouldn't occur to the runner, one way or the other.

Fitzhugh, off on business, left a note that he'd be back by late afternoon. "We need to prep before seeing the two guys about the play. Fend for yourself, Bruiser."

After showering, Presner dressed in his shorts and jacket. By the time he stepped outside, the sun had disappeared. He pulled on his knit cap and considered whether he should buy a slicker. Rain could torrent here at any moment. Did the immense precipitation weather the spirit as well? All joy, all optimism highly qualified, conditional? Nobody else wore a knit cap and nobody else wore shorts. As he walked, Presner looked in the faces of everybody he passed for clues. Nobody looked back at the amateur ethnographer, out of terror or courtesy or envy he couldn't say, but quickly nosed out the envy.

He walked for an hour. Whatever direction Presner went, the streets circled back to the city center as if the place were modeled after a gyroscope. Still, he liked the idea of walking through a small slice of history. Presner liked the ancient pedigree. With the gothic walls and castles, the moment calcified. He could readily imagine what the place looked like in the Renaissance or the Middle Ages—it looked like *now*—to guys like himself, killing time before their appointments with the senate council or the courts. He felt like the latest issue of an archetype, guys like Presner a dime a dozen, wandering around, awaiting the kindnesses and patronage of friends and the guys their friends knew.

Back in town the playwright bought a frappe at Starbucks, then wandered down the street to buy the *International Herald* at a newsstand. Busman's holiday? He walked back to Radcliffe Square, the newspaper curled under his arm, safe from the mist. He sat down by the gates across from the cathedral and tackled the crossword puzzle, waiting for Fitz.

The two guys they were going to meet about the play would meet them after dinner. "At the club," Fitz said, pulling off his shoes.

Presner looked away and nodded. Since he'd been getting in shape, he found himself judgmental about those who hadn't launched similar campaigns. "Who are these guys?"

"They're pockets," Fitz said, surveying the closet. "They're producers. They're investors in talent. You're the talent, *boychik*."

"What have they produced?"

"Capital," Fitz said.

"What have I produced?" Presner said.

The two prepped. First, Fitzhugh got the instant coffee going in the plug-in and they sat across the table by the latticed window, looking over Radcliffe Square. Two copies of Presner's play lay on the table. Fitz ran his hands through his thick hair, leaning forward in the overstuffed easy chair. Presner—the talent—leaned forward in the hardwood desk chair.

Suddenly Fitz looked up from massaging his skull. "Art or commerce?"

Presner had no pretensions. Still. "It's a play, Fitzhugh, not a dildo."

"Don't get defensive, Presner."

"Don't *you* get defensive."

Fitz stood up slowly and walked around the room. For a moment he lay down on his bed and apprehended the ceiling, then sat up and walked back to the easy chair by the coffee table, running his hands through his hair again. He sat down and faced Presner. "Sorry," he said.

"Sorry, you're right. I'm defensive," Presner admitted.

"Reluctant to unleash your baby on the world?"

Presner played along. "That's it."

Fitzhugh nodded. A look of such concern seemed to overcome his face that Presner feared Fitz was spiraling into one of his bottomless pits, as if it were dawning on Fitz—he really hadn't previously entertained the perspective—that he'd robbed his best friends blind, that his fraudulence was common knowledge, and that his good memories were turned to shit—plus the brain chemistry was skewed, Presner imagined, which could thrust you into the doldrums without cause—and now, looking up at Presner, Fitz was suddenly realizing as well that the guy across the table wasn't the same good ol' Presner of bygone days and adventures but his jailer.

What's more, he was about to stake it *all* on an unread play that, as fate would have it, wasn't a dildo.

Fitz emerged suddenly from the spiral and smiled across the table. "I got it," he said. "We don't sell the play."

Presner was disappointed.

Fitz walked over and jabbed him playfully in the arm. "We sell you!"

Selling Presner. Better to sell Big Ben or the London Bridge, the playwright thought. There was swampland and costume jewelry, and then there was Presner, a level below. Still, Presner found something so ingratiating in the suggestion—at this late hour—that it was hard not to be moved. And why not sell Presner? You could look at it that way, too. The playwright was about art, but Fitz was commerce, he knew sales. You don't defraud your best friends, each of them attorneys, if you can't sell. When you're around a genius, you bow to genius. It was unreasonable not to defer to Fitz's judgment, even if he had a choice. And if Fitz was working his sales con on Presner—buttering up ol' Pres, flattering his pal, gilding the lily so Presner wouldn't strangle him to death on orders from the gang back home—possibly Fitz valued their friendship, too; they were a team again, as always, Fitz and Pres—well, commerce and art—he wouldn't work the dodge if he didn't also believe it. Presner was convinced that Fitz believed it. That was touching too. What's 90% of a con? It's believing the pitch yourself. 'That's the secret to sales, along with customer service,' he could practically hear Fitz expostulate. 'It's like being a method actor—not unlike your dodge, Presner.'

Presner relaxed.

Fitz relaxed too. He rolled his eyes in self-mockery, as if he'd just forgotten the multiplication tables, or misplaced his watch only to find it right there all along, fastened around his wrist.

"We sell you," he repeated.

"Naturally," Presner said.

Still. "Do you want to know what the play's about?" Presner wondered. This was an hour later. They were walking along George Street toward the King James, smoking Montecristos provided by Fitz. Presner himself liked a cigar, pacing the streets in Denver. It reminded him of his youth, before his mom made his dad quit. Presner wore his jeans and a sweatshirt under his jacket. He hadn't shaved, Fitz advised against it. "You're about art, not grooming."

"Got it," Presner said.

Some people passing the two smiled tentatively at Fitz in his blue business suit. Fitz couldn't wear clothes, his shirts wouldn't stay tucked, his ties were always unknotted, but he managed to look official. Shabby gentility with the Montecristo, or a well-heeled guy too focused to care. Perhaps he was with Scotland Yard, escorting a prisoner back to custody? "In case it comes up, I mean. The characters? The plot?" Presner insisted.

Fitz stopped and turned toward Presner, waving his cigar and smiling patiently as if counting to ten before unleashing a treatise on Sales 101: Sales for Poets, as they called it in the universities. Presner could see it, guys studying Fitz for credit. Fitz didn't unleash but chuckled philosophically and resumed his long stride down George, Presner in tow.

So what happens? At first glance the two heavyset guys waiting in the King James lounge didn't strike Presner as producers. More like a father-son tag team on the wrestling circuit. The older guy was about forty or fifty, the younger twenty, both wearing brown herringbone sport coats to exaggerate the tag team effect. Guys you don't mess with if you can help it. Presner tended to glance uneasily at the door. But people *never* look like you expect, Presner thought. Probably movie stars only looked that way on the silver screen. In true life you confused them with their personal assistants. Who would take Roxie for a judge? Presner looked more like a playwright than Roxie looked like a judge. If you looked the role, you *weren't*, Presner thought. Both guys had what in Presner's youth was called a crew cut, the look fashioned by athletes and thugs, shorn brutally to the stubble. Were they producers? They *were*, Presner thought, Fitz-style producers—who was he expecting, David O. Selznick?—and on second glance resolved to call their bluff in case they weren't.

"Here's the guy!" Fitzhugh slapped Presner ceremoniously on the back, then offered the two producers—Cecil and Richard, as they were introduced—Montecristos from his briefcase. Presner glanced inside when he opened the briefcase. Next to the box of Montecristos was his play. Cecil looked at Richard, who nodded, then Cecil nodded at Fitzhugh who smiled at Presner then produced the two Montecristos.

Richard lit the cigar then held it menacingly in the air. "Foul piece of crap."

Cecil scowled. "Shit. That's why we like 'em."

In fairness, Presner thought, Richard may have said, "Find your piece of cake?" and Cecil responded with, "Sholom Aleichem," in a particularly British cigar-smoking ritual.

The waiter came by. Individually, Cecil, Richard and Fitz ordered scotch and sodas. "Scotch and soda," Presner said, keeping it simple.

The waiter appraised him.

"He'll have a Scotch and soda," Fitz said.

"Right away," the waiter said.

Cecil smiled at Fitz. Richard smiled at Fitz. Once in a while Cecil looked at Presner and smiled.

"Now tell me about this opportunity," Richard said when the waiter returned with the scotches, though in fairness it may have been, "Terrible about the tutus."

"Shit taken shaman," Cecil said. Presner didn't bother to translate.

"You know what I've told you," Fitz began. "The artistic merit's unquestionable. First rate. We'll be the envy of the aficionados! But that won't play in Hackensack. That's not why we're here." Fitz coughed. Presner had the impression that he was only warming up, getting his footing. It was possible that the producers understood this, too. They sat back placidly, and Fitzhugh stood up and paced, circling the table as he talked, then sitting down abruptly and nodding to himself by way of exclamation point. "It might get us the Pulitzer, it might get us the Drama Circle award, but I'm not coming to you guys because you need prestige. Leave the snob appeal to the snobs, that's what I say! It's about the guy in the street. It's about the hunger in the heart, the love that never happened or possibly happened once while we looked the other way. The one thing we said when we shouldn't have, or the thing we meant to say that would have changed everything. Capeesh? It's about knowing what we can never know—the knowledge of the soul, for example—made flesh, and what happened the one time we looked the other way. It's about that, too. Everything that should have been but wasn't and all that was that shouldn't have been, that's what it is, I won't kid you, wrapped together on the head of a pin. It's guys like us."

"Fagadan," Richard said, though pleasantly.

"Fuck a shaman shit," Cecil added.

Fitz paused, nodding to himself indulgently, then looked at Presner and nodded discreetly, whether to offer reassurance or summon it, the playwright couldn't tell. "But who doesn't know it's true?" Fitz said. Suddenly his old pal seemed winded. Presner wished he could help him out, perhaps offer an amplifying comment or two, a subtle suggestion to steer Fitz on course. "Richard, Cecil, you hear guys all the time holding out their hands to you as if in supplication: 'You'll laugh while you cry, you'll cry while you laugh.'" Fitz said this in falsetto but with such authority Presner could picture guys—perhaps Italian altos—saying it all the time to Richard and Cecil. "To quote William Shakespeare, 'The play's the thing.' Did I get that right, Scholar?" Fitz looked at Presner.

"As rain," Presner nodded.

"But it's the myth that sells the play, that brings us through the turnstiles and rattles and soothes the imagination until the very meaning makes us weep—cringe too, perhaps, knowing how we are—then makes us laugh. The myth of us. Behold here a man, one of the great *artistes* of our time but nobody knows—a store clerk by trade, eating shit by day—polishing his masterwork for years, that dream in the shoebox under the bed that everybody has—everybody with a pulse—behold the guy who at a glance doesn't know shit from Shinola, who walks about with his fly down, toilet paper stuck to his shoe, whose shirt could stand dry cleaning—"

"Now now," Presner said.

"He could be the one who tells us the words we've always ached to hear without quite knowing, that word truest to the image we glimpse in odd moments when we behold ourselves in the mirror, or when we stare down at the reflection in the puddle only to find, as if by surprise: yes. Yes, yes!" Fitz's voice was rising now, and he looked to Presner as if he might stand up again, braying, gesticulating, and throw his arms around Cecil and Richard, bringing Presner into the mix, in an obligatory huddle like the ones Presner remembered after Little League games; win or lose, they'd cheer "Hooray, hooray, hooray! Chiefs, Chiefs, Chiefs!" for the other team. But the salesman stopped suddenly—Presner sensed his voice would break if he said another word—and instead of rising slumped feebly into his chair, breathing heavily, Big Picture draining from his face.

"We'll take a look if you have a copy," Richard said.

"I feel that went rather well," Fitz suggested. They were walking back to Radcliffe Square from the King James, puffing two more Monte-cristos. Presner was feeling the second scotch, the celebratory one they had once Richard and Cecil left with the play amidst a torrent of hand-shakes, backslaps, and contact information covering the next several years. "Wouldn't you say?"

"I'm not counting my chickens yet," Presner said.

Still, his heart racing as if the fight or flight reflex had kicked in, he felt like celebrating. It was as if a taut cable within him snapped and for the moment, anyway, gushes of oxygen swamped his heart and brain. Fitz came through. The producers left with the play. For the moment, he saw things he hadn't seen before, felt things he hadn't felt. He thought, if it's not too late, the old team might track down Peg and Tracy from last night, prying them from the tour group, giving them something to remember back in Youngstown.

Fitz was exhausted.

Back at the hotel his friend looked malarial as he sat on the edge of his bed, too spent to pull off his wingtips. Presner went to relieve himself in the bathroom, tricked the toilet to flush. When he returned, Fitzhugh was curled in his business suit, snoring loudly. The bruiser pried off his wingtips and placed them carefully in the closet. If it were Presner, he could sleep in his shoes, and nobody would notice. Sad Sack. If they gave it a thought, they *assumed* Presner slept in his shoes. But this was Fitzhugh, the salesman, the entrepreneur easing back from the ledge where he'd taken the deep breath and roared.

He slid a pillow under Fitz's head and pulled the sheets over him.

"Will you go back with me?" Presner said to the sleeping Fitzhugh.

The next morning the two caught the bus to Heathrow and flew back to Denver.

They managed to get seats across the aisle, which pleased Presner. It beat having Fitzhugh stuffed between him and another seat, leaning on Presner the entire nine hours out of courtesy to the guy in the other seat, or elbowing him every five seconds to offer spontaneous pontifications on legal matters, women, or the state of Presner's soul. The bruiser welcomed the pontifications but not the flying elbows. "I'm surprised you didn't get a first-class ticket," Presner said across the aisle. It might have been inappropriate, considering Fitz was flying back to confront the old gang whom he'd defrauded, but the seats were larger.

Fitz raised his eyebrows and yawned. "I didn't want you to get lonely back here."

Fitz probably meant it.

The 747 filled up. Presner was seized by a certainty that Peg and Tracy would show up with their tour group, but if so, they were in first class with the larger seats and portions. He tried to will half a dozen young women to proceed down the aisle, not to sit beside him—nine hours was nine hours—but beside Fitz, so he could hear Fitzhugh working her as if reading a postcard from his youth. But nobody sat beside Presner until a college-age kid took the window seat. Immediately the kid leaned back and pulled down his ball cap visor, where it remained for the next nine hours. He looked across the aisle at his traveling buddy, who was also leaning back into his seat, eyes closed as the flight attendants went through their protocols. By the time the plane took off Fitzhugh was sleeping. Presner closed his eyes to envision Richard and Cecil reading his play, passing it back and forth in near euphoria. "Fabinga!" Richard would say. "Racalla!" Cecil would agree. If he were a fly on the wall, he wouldn't understand a word but imagined that they were debating art and commerce.

Presner stared at the frozen dinner-sized screen in front of him, clicking from movie to movie. None were movies he'd been moved to see in theaters, and nothing he saw now compelled him to revise the judgment. When the flight attendant took drink orders, the kid in the ball cap didn't stir, but Fitzhugh sat up instantly to order a Seven and Seven. "The same," Presner ordered.

"To international travel," Fitz proposed after the flight attendant served the drinks.

"How is it that it never takes you more than ten seconds to fall asleep?" Presner asked.

"Clean living."

Presner nodded. "Thanks for pitching my play, by the way. I don't know anybody else who could have pitched it that way, or at all, or would even think of guys like Richard and Cecil to pitch it to, or know them in the first place."

Fitzhugh winced, as if Presner's acknowledgment was an exercise in sheer gaucherie submerged beneath a dozen levels of banality, and shrugged.

Later, as the bruiser tackled his miniscule portion of chicken casserole, mashed potatoes, carrots, and dinner roll, Fitz said, "We'll have to talk about the numbers later. Richard and Cecil aren't cheap."

"I'm sure, as I look over the royalty and box office statements, that I'll rue the day you pitched the thing."

"That's what you don't understand. There's risk everywhere. You think guys like me are crass and materialistic and unethical, pushing the envelope where the rules are hazy—that's how you've seen me for years—but how else does anything happen? You think that what you do takes courage because you expressed your innermost thoughts? Nobody's going to chase after *you* if the thing bombs. Richard and Cecil wouldn't know Shakespeare from Robespierre, but if it bombs, they're going to forget that they met the playwright for cocktails and read the thing themselves and swam in the possibilities. All they'll know is that I'm the one who talked them into this thing. Not to mention the guys they'll squeeze for the real capital, who aren't going to be as equanimous as the old gang back home. They're going to squeeze back. But you're right, you could have kept it home in your drawer and circulated it among the other artsy farts, and I could have patted you on the shoulder and wished you luck."

Presner closed his eyes. "How well do you know these guys?"

"Enough to make a deal. Enough to know that Richard and Cecil aren't doing me any favors, and I'm not going to pretend that I'm doing them any favors. That's the problem with Roxie and Marx and those guys. They have to dress everything up with sentiment in order to live with themselves, they have to believe that their motives are pure, that what they're really doing isn't looking for a killing but helping out a friend. If the deal sinks and they take a bath, their hands are still clean. They need to point the finger at somebody, and you know it won't be at themselves. It's the greedy guys like me who made them drink the poison and act crazy. Roxie and Marx may be more presentable, but Richard and Cecil don't require the illusion; at least they have the courage to be honest. They don't pretend that anybody's doing anybody any favors."

"You took Hankie's life savings," Presner said.

Fitzhugh looked at Presner and refrained from rolling his eyes. He'd ordered another Seven and Seven and mixed it neatly over the two cubes of ice. "I took it?"

"She may have known there was a risk, but you sold her on the dream so that she'd take the risk. She's not Richard and Cecil, but you're not either. At least with Richard and Cecil, she'd put up her guard. She trusted you."

"Ah trust," Fitz said, leaning back into his seat. He seemed bored already; he'd made his point. It wasn't his fault if the bruiser was obtuse. "Yes, trust. Do you think if there was any chance the deal would sink that I would have talked to her about it? Maybe it sank, but she thought it was a sure thing, not because I played on her dreams, but because *I* thought it was a sure thing. And I did. What would you have me do, not give her the chance because we're involved in market laws, where there are no sure things, and not physical laws, where you can have your absolutes. You can call that playing on their dreams, but what they wanted to know is if it looked good, and it looked good."

Presner didn't say anything for a while, but then he looked at Fitzhugh and waited until Fitzhugh looked back. "I'm sure that's what you tell yourself."

Fitz trembled and breathed in and out, as if exhaling everything Presner meant to him, if he still meant anything. He'd never seen him that way. It wasn't *what* he'd said to his friend, but the contempt with which he'd bathed each syllable in acid. But it was also *what* he said: Is there anything worse you can say to somebody than to accuse them of self-denial, not out of fear—Presner's domain—but avarice? By now Presner had the impression that half the cabin was watching them; some were giving them dirty looks because their voices had been raised as if they were naughty toddlers acting out, or the parents who let them, and the bruiser gave them dirty looks back. The other passengers looked away. If they wanted to rescue Fitz from Presner's vitriol or scowl at them or tell them to shut up, suddenly they didn't want to that badly. Presner looked at Fitz again. He still looked like he was going to hyperventilate and wondered what he looked like to Fitz. He thought that Fitz was going to throw over his tray, or throw the vitriol back and say something like, 'And what do you tell yourself, Bruiser?' then remind him, point by point, of every time that Presner was down and Fitz was right there with a good word—helped him with his sister, offered romantic counsel, provided him with vicarious triumphs and disasters that Presner enjoyed through the safe prism of aesthetic distance, flew him to Europe, pitched his play the way nobody in world history could—Presner wished Fitz *would* let him have it—'What's your deal, Bruiser? Nothing ventured, nothing lost?'—but instead of reciting the litany Fitz took another deep breath and closed his eyes. "Maybe so," he whispered.

Every few minutes after that, Presner eyed Fitzhugh across the aisle, Fitz eyeing the bruiser back, like two unmarried sisters ever on the verge of betrayal, scared to let each other out of sight.

Part Five

O nce they got past customs, the impresario and the bruiser shared a cab back from Denver International, Fitzhugh paying. During the ride, Fitz was out cold, or pretended that he was—the bruiser didn't fault him for the hard feelings—but came to as Presner was dropped off. "Thanks," Fitz yawned when Presner eased open the door.

"Well, thank you," Presner said.

"For the cab ride and everything?"

Presner nodded. "England too."

Fitz extended his hand. "You can lay it on thick. I like that about you."

"You're not so bad yourself."

"Don't take any wooden nickels. Watch out for the jet lag."

It had been three days since he'd left Denver. "I'm still waiting for the jet lag to hit from the flight over."

"You'll see."

"No hard feelings?"

"None here."

No hard feelings from Fitz? The sentiment was liberating. The next morning on his run the bruiser required fine-tuning, that's all. There was an extra bounce to his step, an extra snap to his stride. Mostly—in bygone days—when he'd run, he'd strap on the headphones and fantasize that he was a rock star, but the next morning he wondered instead if he'd felt sorry for himself for years, a tragic figure keeping his distance, or just—during times like now—*liked* thinking he'd felt sorry for himself so he could think he'd turned a subtle corner.

After his run, he lifted weights for twenty minutes, then called Roxie.

"How was England?"

"Saw all the sights—St. Catherine's, the Lion's Head, Radcliffe Square, the British Airways ticket line at Heathrow. Incidentally, Fitz came back with me."

Roxie didn't hesitate. "Thank you very much."

"*De nada*. We'll work out the details soon, but he's determined to pay you back, every red cent plus interest."

"Is that your phrase or his?"

"Mine."

"Did he happen to mention, in your discussions as you traveled England, why he did it?"

"'Just a deal like any other.' 'Bad luck.' 'Market laws.' Like that. Fitz thinks he was giving you guys a big break."

"You know the old expression, 'Denial is not just a river in Egypt.'"

"Well, he doesn't see it the way you guys do."

Roxie sighed. "Presner, I know it couldn't have been an easy conversation, whatever you said. I'll have to take you out to dinner to show my proper appreciation. Furthermore, I doubt Gary will expect a wedding gift. You've already given him one."

"Is that Gary's view, too?"

Roxie laughed as if it weren't an honest question. "You'll be everybody's hero for the day. How's Lisa Caner?"

"I called her bluff."

"About time."

Roxie said she'd tell Marx and Pepe the good news. Presner envisioned it: 'He's agreed to the payment schedule. Every red cent plus interest,' and wondered if the euphoria lifting the lid distorted his judgment. Fitz's *word*, bankable to Presner, wouldn't even be an oral contract to these guys. They were attorneys; a contract was barely a contract. 'Great, he got Fitzhugh to *say* he'd make good eventually,' Marx would whine.

Pepe, incredulous, would hang up when Roxie told him, then immediately call the federal marshal to do the job right.

'We took Fitz's word before; Presner thinks we should take his word again?' Marx would squawk. 'Presner better bring a gift.'

'Fitz wouldn't lie to Presner, though,' Roxie would counter, and that would be that.

'You're right. It would be like lying to a Labrador. Or a nephew.'

He called up Henrietta and told her he'd brought Fitz back. "We'll set up a schedule. Every red cent plus."

"Did he say that?"

"No," Presner conceded.

Henrietta sighed impatiently. "Well, it's a step in the right direction. Did he say why?"

"I'm sure he'll tell you to your face."

"He left a message last night," Henrietta told Presner. "I wasn't in."

They just got back last night. Fitz never wasted a minute when he was in town. Jet lag? For shmucks. "Where were you?"

"I don't know if that's a question you're entitled to ask me."

"What movies do you recommend?"

"Oh, Presner," Henrietta said.

You call the bluff of a girl you didn't realize you were in love with, you read the riot act to your best friend (sucker punching the guy in the gut, then eliciting promises of payment schedules and dates to the wedding, then you drag him back from England and bully him on the plane), place your play with a couple of producers (better yet, rough-hewn types of questionable pedigree), make a couple of calls to bask in the gratitude, suggest inadvertently to a lonely former infatuate that you carry a torch for her yet—a full four days even by Fitzhugh standards—then you show up at work. Presner sensed a universal law at play. Instead of the red-carpet treatment punctuated by genuflection, you're still expected to stock the shelves with magazines, newspapers, paperbacks, candies, smokes. If lines form when you're behind the register, who cares if you've turned a subtle corner? Or whether you're just pretending again? *A brisk pace* is what they appreciate.

He still liked the shop. That wouldn't change. Perhaps someday he'd work a thousand miles away, in a different city, with an entirely different old gang, married to a woman who never knew Sara or heard of Fitz, and he'd think back to the shop fondly. Maybe he'd outstayed his need, but the place saved his life. 'The place saved my life,' he'd say to his wife, who—to the bruiser's relief—wouldn't ask too many questions.

If there were days the shop was desolate, Presner power-napping between customers, memorizing bulletins from the *US News and World Report*, further contemplating the incongruities of everyday life, considering with deep sentiment the lives of everybody he'd ever met, anticipating Fitz bursting through the door full of the old vitality, like old times, today the traffic *was* brisk. Time cantered, then galloped. Before the playwright could idly consider what it would be like to return to his second floor hallway to find a mop-haired strawberry-blonde waiting by his door, he was already walking down the hallway toting grocery bags. There she was.

"Presner."

"Lisa."

In the dim hallway light, Lisa Caner looked more exhausted than she ever had in her kitchen hearing him out or across the room in the Continuing Ed class at Metro. The actress was as tall as the bruiser and leaned forward slightly and squinted at him quizzically, though whether to inspect what she missed out on or to soak up his new gravitas, he couldn't say. "I was in the neighborhood. Do you still want me to go to the wedding? That wasn't clear."

"You don't have to."

"You've been looking forward to seeing the old gang. I thought it would be fun to meet them, I've heard so many stories. Are we still on? That wasn't clear from our last conversation."

Presner thought wistfully of the girls Fitz promised to line up, and the beautiful women who'd line up once the play hit in England.

Just his luck Caner couldn't let go.

"We're still on."

"I wanted to ask *you* something now. Can I ask you?"

"Here's how that particular question should be answered, in my view: 'Yes, you can *ask*. What's stopping you? Thanks for asking.' Did you get that?"

Lisa Caner stepped toward him again, then stepped back and asked—*this* he didn't see coming—if she could read his play. "I'd really like to. You must be crossing the t's and dotting and un-dotting the i's by now. It's time you abandoned it."

"Did I mention that a couple of producers are reading it? Fitz and I—Fitz, actually—pitched it in Oxford."

"*Oxford*?"

"Bare-knuckle guys, but Fitz pitched it like Sandy Koufax to Lew Burdette. Went an entire season without getting a hit. It's not art, it's business, so nobody reads the thing unless they have a stake. When?"

"Now."

Inside the Pleasure Palace, he set her up in the easy chair across the living room. If she pushed the easy chair forward, Caner could lean back and elevate her long legs on the couch arm. She'd only been over once, and that time with fair warning; the place cleaned and dusted, the kitchen counters visible. Now he bundled the newspapers for the recycling bin, bagged the garbage, and told her he'd be back. He walked his five-mile running route by the Platte—that took an hour—stopping off on the way back for coffee to go. He sipped the coffee on a bench on the 16th Street Mall, watching the RTD trains load and unload, the mix of well-dressed businessmen working late—he expected to see Gary Marx, crossing a few last t's before the wedding—and drunks stumbling off the RTD along with several couples on the town and hordes of teenagers who lit up cigarettes so quickly as they deboarded that it was hard to imagine they'd doused their cigs for the short lift up the mall. He didn't notice any attractive women walking off by themselves as if looking for a guy like Presner.

His conception of what was attractive had broadened now that he was middle-aged. No doubt there was a Darwinian dimension to the formulation, but today the bruiser understood it as a deepening. He'd often seen women more as statements about himself than as quantities of human protoplasm, behavioral conditioning, romantic delusion. But at forty he found women pretty whom he wouldn't have found pretty years ago, and all the time now—practically hourly—he made change and pleasant small talk with women who, in other circumstances, he knew would eat him alive. Nobody told you that when you were twenty; if you bothered to look that far ahead (like imagining what it would be like to colonize the moon, Presner guessed) you figured that you'd be so decrepit that you wouldn't care, or have so much money and be so famous that women would go nuts over you even if you *were* decrepit. More likely, you'd lower the bar profoundly. You'd go for qualities like personality and tell yourself that it's really better this way. But what really happened was the expansion, and when you saw those twenty-year-old girls who once would have turned you inside out, with most you found yourself thinking they could use another twenty years. Still, he didn't notice any attractive women out tonight, even considering his expanded concept. They were all off in some guy's apartment, leaning back in the easy chair, their long legs elevated on couch arms, reading plays that British producers were also considering, that's what Presner imagined.

Why was he thinking of this crap at forty? Presner couldn't decide if it was a disappointing quality to discover in himself, or invigorating. He didn't have a pot to piss in, most of his satisfactions he yielded from daydreams; he was an American in the early twenty-first century, healthy and free—so far—from torture and pogroms. But if you wanted to know what he was really about, at the core he was a leg man *and* a breast man. He closed his eyes and tried hard to summon England, write-ups in the newspapers featuring the latest sensation from America, or Richard and Cecil leaping up and calling Fitz, 'Let's do it!' ('Leap fadit!' but Fitz would know) but all that came to mind—with Caner in his apartment, long legs elevated—were Peg's breasts, which also, it was a fair bet, wouldn't have lived up to his standard at twenty.

Did the bruiser envision himself any better at twenty than the twenty-year-old Presner would envision himself twenty years later? What else didn't they tell you back then?—as if there were a box office you could storm and demand a refund. Presner himself wouldn't admit it, his upbeat mood, play being read, Caner in his apartment; today was different. Watching the thirteen or fourteen-year-old runaways huddled together smoking, and the panhandling homeless guys living off the pavement like smoke rising from the grates, *their* lives naked at the elemental nexus, he remembered a time when he'd see similar faces and feel a pity. Beyond that, the pity transformed into a desire to *do* something about it. This was back when he was twenty, also, at the U with the double major in theater and sosh. He'd wanted to help people, to be palpably useful, either defining the condition through drama or directly working the streets, shedding his sweat and blood on the front lines. He had a force in those days; nothing that anybody spotting him on the street would see, or nothing his friends and family might sense—who would think to wonder? It was a *secret*, but the twenty-year-old Presner couldn't pass faces like these without identifying a condition, even if he was mostly seeing himself magnified, and couldn't identify a condition without telling himself 'I *get* it, that's how it is for *now*,' but that he was going to change all this someday. He didn't pretend he knew much, but he wasn't going to leave this place without turning it upside down if that's what it took to make this world a paradise.

That's how it felt, *impressionistically*, to be the twenty-year-old Presner before his eureka moment on the theater steps. He couldn't live with anything meaning nothing, back then when he had the force. It amazed the bruiser now to think that at twenty he took the responsibility of being human so seriously, though perhaps it was as simple as that he had a future to sustain his waking moments with its prospects for grandeur. He wanted to protect that kid! To have him consult Chekhov for a prep course in the ways illusions both liberate and paralyze. To warn him that he's not immune, that the future's likely to be a straight line leading into the past like a stake into your heart—that same dumbshow with the same actors changing outfits between scenes—after enough of that you have your hands full keeping your own head above water—it's not a jadedness, not a callousness, but how it *feels*. Impressionistically. Presner knew what the kid would think of him, the overwhelming disappointment he'd feel to see himself twenty years later—'That's *all*? Where's the paradise?'—even knowing that it all led to Lisa Caner in his living room, reading his play, for all he knew waiting with a bottle of champagne, swearing she'd act in his play or bust. To grab the kid by the shoulders and shake him, 'It's not like I *wanted* to throw the future away. Let's see you look the wind in the eye when your energy's depleted, your nerve extinguished, pooling your resources for another go when you know all too well what's going to happen when you ascend the high wire.'

If his folks and his sis just wanted this kid to be *happy*, Presner too wanted to spare him every last thing he'd wished he'd been spared. But as the bruiser remembered, life is sweeter when you carry the force with you wherever you go.

When Presner returned to the Pleasure Palace, Fitzhugh's call was on the machine. Lisa was still in the easy chair. Then she walked around the room holding the script in the air, voicing words that sounded suspect even allowing that she was a great actress; but it was still a thrill hearing words he'd written coming out of somebody's mouth—even if the words were for a blustery male; Caner wasn't *that* great an actress—until, after a few moments, it wasn't the words he'd written or the corny novelty of Lisa Caner reading his words as if she were a male, but an entirely separate being he'd never seen before, who wouldn't have otherwise existed if Presner himself hadn't bothered, whom he bet—if this being *wasn't* saying these lines—would be off elsewhere eating cornflakes or switching on the TV or beating his chest, railing against the fates: 'Prick him and he bleeds,' Presner would bet.

Caner noticed him as she worked over the lines. He waved; she waved back. She walked to the easy chair, and Presner walked over to check his messages. "It's me, *boychik*, checking in with the marshal. I'm rested up from the trip, the jet lag, the languor of international travel. I'm back in the saddle. Ready to rumble and dance the light fantastic! Sorry you're off, but a guy like you's always in training. Call back."

The actress dropped the last page to the floor, then looked up at Presner.

"You don't have to say anything, of course. It was *enough* to hear you mouthing the lines. I could see why people write plays, even people like me. *Moi.* You got through the thing. *That's* amazing."

"You don't mean that." Her strawberry-blonde hair swayed forward as she looked at the floor, then up at Presner, contemplating—surprised—no, *she* wouldn't be surprised—by his vulnerability. In twenty seconds Presner would walk over and sit on the floor and she'd slide into his arms. He wasn't sure if it was the play or what he'd said afterward or that he'd been so anxious as she'd read it that he left for two hours—the kind of things she found *cute*—or that he'd let her off the hook. She may have had it in mind before she'd walked over and offered to read the thing, Presner thought. He was sure they'd be friends again and have conversations that had nothing to do with the way he felt then or when she'd walked across his living room taking the words seriously—just Presner again, just Lisa, with the one pretense added to the thousand already at work; minus a few. After all, what kind of world was it if the deck cleared of a thousand conversations that you'd enjoyed across the kitchen table, just because one of you couldn't pretend any longer? But it was sexy when a woman read your play and liked it, and pretty sexy, too, even if she didn't.

Sleeping with a friend was different from sleeping with somebody who'd later become a friend, or a woman who was also a friend—"With *privileges*," in Fitz's phrase, who'd slept with Roxie and Hankie and almost any woman friend he'd ever known, the privileges understood. Everybody knew what Fitz was about. But for all the times Presner envied him, the sex and the clout and the elocutionary talents, did Fitz get to hear the nice stuff Presner heard? Hear it the way *Presner* heard it, even if it was only the stuff everyone hears in these situations, things that for all he knew Lisa told him because she wanted him to whisper in her ear nice stuff back. The two took turns extolling each other's virtues, pointing out their flaws, though in the landscape of the virtues, the flaws became virtues themselves, stuff you *wanted*, like the warp in the Navajo blanket that allows the soul to breathe. The choices he didn't make out of cowardice, opacity, or phoniness, in the telling became stubbornness, a steadfast stoicism against the fates. Caner's own insecurities became the lifeblood of her extraordinary talent. No more or no less true than the stuff Fitzhugh was known to say, Presner imagined, mouth-to-ear with Hankie or Roxie or a hundred others. More than a few of his pal's ex-lovers had gone out of their way to talk to the bruiser over the years about Fitz, feeling him out. Fitz never broke it off with women, he just broke off the round, and that's what Presner would tell them when they'd call and want to meet him for coffee to discuss the guy.

No more or less true, but the boost was extra coming from Lisa Caner.

"I've wanted this forever," Presner admitted. "I dreamed about you."

"You knew that this would happen?"

"Well, dreams aren't prophecies, they're wishes."

"I like your body," Caner said, kissing his shoulder.

"I like your body."

Later, Caner said, "I didn't get the part I was practicing the other day when you came over. For Nora? They may offer me Christine."

With Caner in his arms, he had *responsibilities*. The bruiser webbed his hands behind his neck and stared at the ceiling. He thought about offering to beat somebody up or make a few calls. "You're the best."

"You like saying that, but I'm not. Know what? I don't make a creed of it. I really try. I'd love playing Christine, but don't you think I'd rather be Nora, whom everybody falls in love with? I'm never quite what they're looking for, or I am but they already have somebody else in mind."

"They're idiots," Presner told her flat out.

"They'll give me a call when they need somebody for a staged reading. I'm *great* at staged readings. Or else Christine's what they give me when I audition for Nora. It's not artistic expression or integrity or anything like that, it's what I *get*." Still, Lisa laughed in his arms. "You think I'm a lot better than anybody else thinks I am."

"I know what I see and hear."

Lisa kissed his forehead and leaned above him, stared briefly into his eyes then gazed past Presner to the row of posters in the hall by the kitchen. "Thank you so much for always saying that. Know what? When you were out yesterday, before I read the play, I looked again at the Bellows over there on your wall. The one you rhapsodize over. It's the first time I've really looked at it. I remember what you told me about it the other time I was here. Do you mind if I say this? It's second rate. That dark green coloring is awful, it's *artificial*. Have you ever seen a color like that in nature?"

Presner blew into her ear. "A lot I haven't seen in nature. It could be that armadillos look that way in the shade. Or magnolia leaves."

"Don't blow into my ear." Lisa webbed her hands behind her neck and stared at the ceiling, elbow-to-elbow with Presner. "What's the boxer's name again? Firpo?"

Presner nodded. "But you miss the point. He refuses to let himself dream. Can you imagine what that must be like? There's dignity there."

"You're a good guy, Presner," Caner said softly.

"I know it's not great art."

Lisa thought it over. Unlike the bruiser when he got going, she didn't just spout. She looked through the moonlight, across the bedroom to the row of posters. "I think you're right, he's a great character, but anybody can deny themselves illusions. All you have to do is live in the moment or pretend that everything's shit. As Beckett would say, 'Their illusion is that they don't have any illusions.' I remember you told me that Firpo ended up in a traveling circus? Know what dignity is? If the boxer really knows that's his fate, I like him because he's in the ring anyway."

"Glad you like it," Presner said.

It turned out that she thought he was like Firpo—and herself—firing away though you knew how the deck was stacked. "You're not Tennessee Williams, but does that stop you from writing your play and sending it out? You've got guts."

"Thanks. That's the way I spin it," Presner admitted. "But that doesn't mean *you* have to."

Lisa looked in his eyes. He couldn't see the pale cerulean, but in the faint light her eyes flashed like a cat's. He wondered, if he let himself go, if he would get lost there. "It's not spin, I mean it," Lisa insisted. "You're a really bright guy. You could do a lot of things. You're an attorney, but you didn't practice the law so you could work on your art. You think guys like that are everywhere?"

"I didn't have the guts to get into drama when I was a kid, and I didn't have the spirit for the law, especially after Sara died. That really took the starch out of me, but I was backing off before that. Then the shit hit the fan. I couldn't find anything I was able to stay with. I had interests, I'd get fired up about this or that for a few days, but it turned out I was just changing costumes. For years I was the guy Beckett's talking about. Worse, I let everybody know it. Two years ago, I walked into the Continuing Ed class on a lark and saw you."

Caner said, "You've moved on. Anybody can have the guts for stuff like that when they're a kid."

Later Presner asked, "What do you figure Chekhov's illusions were? I mean beyond the usual?"

Lisa sat up and raised her knees to make a small tent. Sometime during the night, she'd found her way into one of the bruiser's t-shirts. They were easy to find, piled on the floor, but the intimacy rattled him. "Beyond that death's unimportant and misery's ennobling?"

"Also, beyond that everything happens for a reason."

"Did I mention that good things happen to good people?"

"I was really thinking more of the illusion that audiences would laugh at his comedies."

"I've been thinking this over, since you're always going on with your 'Chekhov this's and Chekhov that's.' Chekhov ridicules people for being ineffectual dreamers. He doesn't mean to be cruel. He thinks it's funny. Of course audiences never *get* it."

"But you see his point," Presner said.

Lisa kissed her finger and softly traced his lips with it. "It hurt when I didn't get the part."

Presner licked her finger. "I'm always going to write plays. Without that I'm jack shit."

"Thanks for showing up at Continuing Ed on your lark."

"Thanks for being there."

The phone rang once or twice. If he thought it might be Fitz in the event Fitzhugh wasn't out tripping the light fantastic, he wasn't inclined to disengage his limbs from Lisa Caner in order to discuss payment schedules.

Presner dreamed but forgot the dreams upon realizing he'd been dreaming.

Presner was usually such a light sleeper that when somebody sneezed across the street he popped into the air and flailed his arms as if swatting flies, but she was dressed by the time Presner awoke the next morning. There was no production about using Presner's towels, no wistful gazing at the bruiser's sleeping hulk. Lisa smiled at Presner and left the room. *Gravitas?* A week ago, he had neither a career nor a woman. Now he was a playwright—pending the other shoe falling from across the ocean—with a beautiful actress in his bed. Actually, Lisa was leaning back in the easy chair again, thumbing through his play. She wasn't lingering over the words this time, and he resolved if he ever wrote another play, he'd do it right, not just with dramatic structure but phrasing the dialogue just so, so someone like Caner would read it the next day, even after sleeping with him, the many mysteries diminished, a few more set into motion, and still pause the second time through.

Presner walked into the kitchen—Lisa already had a pot of coffee going—and dialed Fitzhugh at home, nobody there, left a message, filled his favorite cup, and returned to his living room. He sat across the table from her. Caner looked up from the script and furrowed her brow.

Presner explained, "Comedy's one of those words, like epistemology or existential, that you can use to modify anything. It doesn't mean you'll *laugh*."

"Phenomenology."

"What?"

"Phenomenology's one of those words too," Lisa said.

"Chekhov too, I guess. Damn near anything's Chekhovian. Not with the Chekhovian pressure of life bearing down, of course. You can't find *that* everywhere. But the term itself. Comedy? Tragedy? All you have to do is to say it."

"The words are meaningless?"

Presner didn't like the way she waved the play in the air to emphasize the point. 'It's the music that counts; the interplay between the music and the words that loads the words in ways their syllables alone can't, and loads the music beyond what the notes are capable of.' All this Presner meant to say. Observations Lisa Caner could listen to and not scream or think him pretentious or pompous or grandiose, a deluded dreamer always off-kilter, far out of his depth, pretending to be somebody better.

Still, as for this particular observation, he didn't say it and later thought of calling her up to tell her—'One more addendum, please, Lisa'—then thought better of making the call (enough Presner being enough) and made a mental note of telling her the next time, even as he knew that the next time probably wouldn't be the right time anymore, or would be the right time but the mental note would have slipped into the void by then. "Couldn't have been too important," Presner's fourth grade teacher liked to say when somebody let something slip away that was on the tip of their tongue, but even then Presner thought the teacher was wrong. "Maybe it's *too* important," he blurted aloud once when a kid in class—Jerry Little, he still remembered—forgot what he was going to say. Everybody laughed—that's the way Presner's proclamations were met back then—or else with ponderous silence—but he'd felt like he'd stumbled into one of life's homey truths, hitting him from nowhere in what would later prove to be the usual way, like a meteor. "I'm just saying the thing's a comedy," Presner said.

"Don't be so prickly. I know it's a comedy. Roxanne called earlier. I didn't want the phone to wake you, so I answered. I hope you don't mind."

"We're walking on eggshells around each other, aren't we?"

"I hope you don't mind that I made the coffee, either."

"Don't you know about *boundaries*? Personal *space*? Didn't you ever learn about asking first?"

"I like to barge in and take over. That's my style."

"A ball buster's what you are," Presner said.

"It's why I'm not married," Lisa said, not looking up from the play.

"In addition to that you've been waiting for me."

"Don't say that."

Presner shrugged.

Later: "What did Roxie say when you answered?"

"She said, 'Honey, what escort service do you work for?'"

The bruiser liked the idea of Roxie musing: 'First he brings back Fitzhugh. Then he beds a gal.'

"I told her I came over to work on your play."

"And she said?"

"Hmm. Fitzhugh called her, by the way. There's a meeting this afternoon at 4:00 at the Nick. A conference. Everyone will be there, Roxie said. She said you'd understand. Did you ever go out with Roxie, by the way?"

"Only in my dreams," Presner allowed.

That afternoon he thought about calling up Fitzhugh before the big do at the Nick to strategize. 'Fitz, you haven't seen these guys lately. They're out for blood. Better have a payment schedule lined up, copies for each in triplicate, secondary payouts. You can't wing it with this gang.' He went so far as to call, but left no message; who knew? Fitz might fly to Bolivia. Also, he wanted to tell him about Caner face to face.

Come 4:00 the bruiser was at the Nick, as usual the first to show. Why should somebody wait on his account? Who'd reserve the table for six? He remembered that his dad would show up two hours early for airplane flights on the theory that the recommended one hour in those days meant one hour *before* the recommended time. "Otherwise, it wouldn't be one hour early," Presner used to josh with Sara. "It would be on time."

'If somebody has to wait around, better it be me. Or is it better it be I?' Presner wondered, the grammatical rule elusive. His dad used to correct his grammar so often—approximately every time they spoke—that even today the playwright skirted certain formulations. "Better be safe than sorry, as far as those formulations were concerned," he'd told Lisa Caner last night as they lay in bed, facing the ceiling, entangled, free associating, untangling only to reach for the night table and sip lemon waters before resuming entanglements and random associations. "You never mention your parents. What was your dad like? You don't have to tell me."

"I'll tell you." With his dad, you had to show up early and you had to speak right, and Presner had been doing both ever since.

The other thing worth knowing about Presner's dad is that he was the greatest man in history. While objectively the bruiser knew this to be unlikely—his dad was a CPA for a small firm, and outside work had few interests beyond reading the newspaper—he looked back on the stuff his dad would say to him, even throwaway instructions like, "Use some elbow grease," when young Presner could be spotted raking the leaves half-heartedly, as not only practical and metaphorical but ethically binding, worthy of a sacred text. The 614th Commandment. A lot of guys also felt the same way about their dads—Marx did, as Presner remembered from a conversation back in law school; Fitz did; Pepe *didn't*—"He's a prick," Pepe said, which Presner took to be the price you pay for owning Detroit. Perhaps there was a gender dimension? Few women he'd known thought of their mothers as the greatest woman in history, though in almost each case, from what he could tell, they were a lot closer to their moms than Marx or Fitz—or even Presner, who worshipped his dad as a child but was embarrassed by him as a teen; a stance he never quite grew out of—were to their dads.

The Nick used to be known as a Yuppie hotspot and disdained or celebrated accordingly, a venue of *faux* unpretentiousness, with animal horns protruding on the walls next to hastily installed Edward Munch reproductions, and locked chess sets at half the tables. Since almost everybody he knew outside Tyson's had a career—the alternative being eternal boyhood, or homelessness—in recent years the Nick was reduced—elevated, in Presner's view—to the status of mere hangout. 'The Nick? Why *there*?' Still a bustling place during Happy Hour. On the infrequent occasions that Presner was waiting for somebody, he enjoyed showing up early, hanging out at the Nick in the late afternoon. He'd watch the well-dressed office workers gather around the circular tables ordering their margaritas and gossiping. The listening was almost always as interesting as the watching, and sometimes the bruiser had the impression that they played to his rapt attention. One would meet his eye, and though the contact was in passing, Presner would envision her walking over to his table and saying, 'Hi, my name's Lori.'

The old gang was well heeled. Presner liked that. The few times he'd met with them in public in recent years—usually at the Nick—half the people in the place recognized Gary Marx—"I'll get you a check. No promises"— from the bus bench ads and TV spots, and the other half took in his chiseled anchorman's coiffure and were pretty convinced they placed Marx from somewhere. You could see tables full of women eyeing the guy. Half recognized Fitz, too, from his stint as the reigning media authority on all matters legal—"That's Norm Fitzhugh!" And while few in a given crowd had stood in court before Roxanne on the bench, Roxie cut a formidable figure—she expected deference these days—Presner figured you could see from ten paces that you better not get within ten paces of Roxie. Pepe usually didn't show up at all—family obligations—and Hankie, worn out from her skirmishes at the Public Defender's, looked like the placid, buxom, tired, spirited wife of somebody prominent. Everybody watched the group at Nick's, they were the center of everybody's calculations, and Presner had this way of leaning back during the give and take—Fitz holding court, Marx rolling his eyes, or Marx rattling on like an anchorman filling time—and took in everybody in the crowded bar and grill taking them in; one spectacle mirroring the other. Perhaps there was a third spectacle elsewhere, mirroring both? That too seemed likely at the Nick. "When you sit with these guys," he told Lisa Caner once, "you feel credentialed."

"Good talk?"

"Good but not honest." Presner thought it over. "It's mostly spectacle."

Presner ordered a pitcher of the famous margaritas, then poured one for himself and stared at it.

Roxanne and Henrietta showed up first. Both were dressed from their day in the chambers, which distinguished them not at all from the women who were dressed to kill the likes of working stiffs like Presner. "You guys look gorgeous, dressed to the nines."

"We're professionals," Roxie said as both slid into chairs across the circular table.

"Fitz told me he keeps a fancy suit in his office closet for court and media appearances. Otherwise, he's dressed around the office like a slob."

"You can do that when you run your own office," Hankie said.

Presner nodded.

Roxie got to the point. "Was that Lisa Caner who answered this morning when I called? I could swear that you'd split up with her. Didn't you?"

"How many guys did you send to jail today? Yet you're mainly wondering if Lisa Caner spent the night. Tsk tsk."

"I have my priorities, yes."

"It was Lisa Caner, and two, it's hard to say if we split up since we were never together. Are we now? Time'll tell. She's complicated." That's what Presner had prepared to say over the twenty minutes waiting with his margarita, in the face of Roxie's inevitable interrogation.

"You're complicated," Henrietta said.

"I'm an open book."

"If that book's *Finnegan's Wake*."

"Do you want her?"

The bruiser shrugged ostentatiously at Roxanne. "That's a complicated question. Jeez Louise."

"That means no. If it's a complicated question that means you don't want her." This was Henrietta now. "If you really want her, it's the easiest question in the world."

Presner loved this. "Did you get that from the best loved adages of Dr. Ruth?"

"I'll loan you my copy," Hankie offered.

"Sure, I *want* her. That and a nickel gets me five pennies."

"A nickel gets you five pennies," Roxie said. "'I want her' gets you out of bed in the morning, then makes you comb your hair and run your miles and plan your little speeches." She patted Presner's hand.

"Except for combing his hair," Hankie added.

Presner discerned from the eyes of the women the next table over that the luminous Gary Marx was making his entrance. Or John Elway? Or the Pope, Presner thought. Though it could have been Fitz, too. Fitz had that presence, that command. Slovenly but also stately. The difference was that Marx, always a working proposition, knew it and cultivated it, while Fitz assumed the attention. The room wasn't the same when he left, or before he got there.

With Marx the swagger disappeared when he began talking. He embraced Hankie and Roxie and shook Presner's hand warmly, as he always had, even back in the days when he must have suspected that the bruiser could very well deck him with the free hand then kick him when he curled on the ground.

Marx released Presner's hand and took the seat across the table, leaving the empty seat beside Presner for Fitz.

"Presner and Lisa are an item," Hankie informed Marx. "How long now?"

"One day and counting. Gary, how're the wedding plans?"

"There are a thousand details, then another thousand. I understand now why you never got married, Presner. It reminds me of contract law. You always hated con law, didn't you?"

"It's not too late to flee to Tahiti. Don't worry, I'll take Jill out for a drink to break it to her gently."

"That's the kind of talk I like to hear," Marx smiled at Presner.

"That's why I'm here. To advise you of your options."

"I have one for you," Marx said.

That was another annoying thing about Marx. He'd let you bust his balls for a while, but then he'd bust back.

"Enough," Henrietta said,

"Enough of the pissing contest," Roxanne said.

Marx smiled his presidential smile. "Where's our guest of honor?"

Roxanne cleared her throat. Preliminaries were over that quickly. She had a formal and severe face when she talked like this, as if she were peering from a group portrait of legal luminaries, that made Presner wonder if everything he'd ever thought about her was wrong. Then she'd change back to the other face, the one she wore during the preliminaries that bore the worry lines over whether Lisa Caner spent the night with Presner. The Honorable Roxie face was sheer survival, he understood. When somebody was thrown into the ocean, they didn't act the same way as when they sipped martinis or played shuffleboard on deck. They swam like hell. "First, when Fitzhugh called last night, he said he was sorry for losing the money. I'm inclined to allow him that. 'Losing the money,' Fitzhugh phrased the act, as if a few coins and a cancelled check fell out of his wallet onto the street and he's done nothing but retrace his steps ever since. Second, he said that everything he ever told us was true."

Marx laughed.

"It's gone," Henrietta gasped.

"You knew that," Roxanne said to Henrietta.

"Not until now. I really thought—"

"*I* knew it," Marx said.

For ten seconds Henrietta sobbed, then collected herself and stared at Marx across the table, and then at Roxie, and then fell apart again. Marx reached across the table and squeezed her hand. She frowned back at Roxie then looked at Marx then back to Roxie, then tremored and sobbed. By now both of them were talking to Henrietta so quietly that Presner couldn't hear without leaning forward, but this wasn't for him to hear so he tried to look at the group of women at the next table. There were only three of them left now. Lori had left without stopping over to say hi. Presner could never look at women across a barroom without thinking it was a miracle that he'd ever talked one into sleeping with him, and it surprised him to remember that he'd slept with one last night, that's what he thought with Henrietta sobbing and the scuzzbucket—Marx—comforting her and Roxanne looking on, not knowing whether she was about to pronounce sentence, or had just done so.

Marx leaned across the table and held Henrietta's hand, whispering as if his words and flesh were a lifeline to a secret universe they'd never entirely left, though it had been a long time since the year after law school when she'd taken up with Shrady and left Marx biting the dust. Live and learn.

"We're out of our league," Presner said softly to Roxie.

Roxanne nodded.

"How come they never got married?" Presner said this softly too, though he could have shouted, for all Marx and Hankie would hear from the secret universe.

Roxie shrugged. "How come anything?"

The bruiser nodded, then looked at the door waiting for Fitz to swing through.

Roxanne coughed ostentatiously and clapped her hands, then tried to change her voice back to legal mode. "If anybody's interested, as you know, Presner did drag him back. Fitzhugh said that he wanted to talk to all of us tonight."

"I didn't *drag* him back. It was his idea. It's not my money so I won't say that anybody's overreacting, but he'll be here momentarily."

Marx laughed.

Back from her journey to Marxland, Henrietta looked blankly at Presner. "You said he'd pay back every red cent."

"He will."

"I'm such a fool," Hankie swallowed.

"He'll pay you back," Roxie promised. "We'll all see to it."

"The fuckface better," Marx said.

"Call him 'fuckface' and see where that gets you with the payment plan."

"He's always been a fuckface."

"That makes you a scuzzbucket."

"That makes you a fuckface yourself."

Presner half stood and pointed at Marx. "He kept you awake in law school, to which we owe your face on bus benches. Don't forget that, Ambulance Chaser."

Marx half stood and pointed back. "Fitzhugh *pities* you, Tarzan. Asshole."

"Shmendrick."

"Enough," Roxanne ordered.

"He helped me with my sister," Presner got in.

After an hour he knew this wasn't a scheduling misunderstanding or crossed signals or getting lost in traffic or the thousand things that always got in the way when you need to be somewhere. Fitzhugh wasn't going to show up. Still, every time somebody pushed through the door, he looked up expectantly.

Long after Marx left with Roxie and Henrietta, Presner waited.

<hr />

When the worst hits, it hits from a thousand directions. If not simultaneously, then on timed delay.

Presner worked the late shift at Tyson's but woke up early, lifted, ran, lifted again. Because symmetry to the equation was inevitable, he ran again after lifting, strained a calf muscle the second time around, forced to walk the last few blocks. Fuckface.

In the afternoon he took the bus to the bungalow where Fitzhugh practiced law and lived when he wasn't traveling. Presner knocked on the door beneath the granite-plated *Norman Fitzhugh, Attorney-at-law* shingle, rang the doorbell, eased his way to the window and peered through. As substantial as the bungalow appeared from the outside, he knew the inside had lapsed into a state of disarray as quickly as any bachelor's place since Fitz had cut back on his local practice. No sense straightening up when tomorrow he'd be off to Pompeii. Still, he couldn't see anything through the window. He knocked on the pane. "Fitz, open up," Presner said softly, then louder. For twenty minutes he waited on the steps, until he saw an elderly lady walking into the next bungalow and hobbled next door on his strained calf. The lady looked up from her shopping cart and watched warily as the bruiser approached. "Are you okay, Mister?"

"I strained my calf. Nothing serious. Have you seen Norm Fitzhugh around? The guy who lives there?" Presner motioned with his head toward the bungalow.

"Was it yesterday or two days ago?" the woman wondered. "He's been away a while. He usually is. But he's back." She looked suspiciously at Presner. "Are you a lawyer, too?"

"Friend."

"Your friend stops by to say hello whenever he's in. Tell Norm to stop by Marie's if you see him."

"Sure. Tell Norm to call Presner if you see him first."

Presner took a deep breath and called Caner, whom he hadn't talked to since she'd left his place yesterday.

"Hi, Presner."

Presner considered it promising that she didn't immediately tell him she was busy for the next month, or that they needed to talk because she'd been thinking things over. What it promised, he couldn't say.

"Fitzhugh's gone. He told me he was going to take care of this business. 'Every red cent plus interest.' We talked payment schedules. I flew back with the guy, dropped him off at his place. You knew that we were going to meet—all of us—last night to hash it out? He didn't show. What was he afraid of? The worst it got they called him 'fuckface.' Sheesh, he hears worse than that from his mom."

"He was afraid of humiliation."

"It must be a complicated form of humiliation that throws the guy. He entertained us with his entanglements for years."

"He lied to everybody else. Why wouldn't he lie to you?" Lisa said.

"Why wouldn't I lie to him?"

What's Fitz *afraid* of? That was the same question, more or less, that Roxanne posed when she called after he hung up with Caner to tell Presner that she was going to schedule an appointment with the U.S. Attorney that afternoon. "Don't act disappointed in me or shocked and furious."

The bruiser closed his eyes for a moment. "Give him another few days. I got him back here. That's a start. I'll find him again."

"He didn't take your $50,000."

Presner needed to remind himself that he was a peripheral figure, and everybody else needed to remind him as well. "I know he didn't take my $50,000, but once you see the U.S. Attorney you can't put the genie back in the bottle. Wait till Fitz gets back to you, anyway. He'll tell you a story about a normal deal which went south but don't worry, you'll see through it. What if there's an innocent explanation?"

"You always think there's an innocent explanation. I've always envied that about you. I think that's why you didn't practice the law, Presner. You're a dreamer. You wanted to keep dreaming. It's not only Fitz. You've always seen the rest of us as being better than we are, even Gary, whom you profess to hate."

"Marx is a fuckface."

"It was very nice to hear you two sound like mature adults last night," Roxie said.

"Marx said it *first*."

Roxie sighed.

"That means there's precedent," Presner added, without conviction.

"In case you want to know, it was Gary's idea to have you talk to Norm first. 'He'll listen to Presner,' he said. He has a high opinion of you, despite your attitude, so let it go."

"Marx doesn't think I can chew gum and fart."

"Don't kid yourself, he admires you. He wishes he didn't have re-sponsibilities and could walk around free as the wind, cultivating his grievances with the world, railing against hypocrisy, calling everybody to account, one day an artist, the next a saint. What guy sitting in his office making cold calls wouldn't envy that? It just raises his ire when you call him a scuzzbucket."

"The truth hurts."

"Also, you can be amusing."

"Don't call the fuzz," Presner hissed.

Later, reading over his play for the thousandth time, for the hun-dredth time the playwright wondered if he should burn the thing. Maybe out by the flagpole. He'd have to find a flagpole, but figured schools still had flagpoles. It wouldn't be that hard to find a playground. Even if it were a melodramatic gesture, Chekhovian in its implications, who's to say it couldn't also be cleansing?

Whatever came of Fitz and Cecil and Richard overseas, Presner promised himself that he'd always feel sentimental about the thing. Whereas he'd awakened most days as an imposter, the thing made him feel legitimate for hours on end. Also, if the play turned out to be a dis-aster, it was worth remembering that it got him a night with Lisa Caner.

He wouldn't burn the thing any more than he'd burn that. (He could hear Fitz saying, 'What is it that—who was it?—*Freud* said about why *artistes* like you operate? 'Fame, money, the love of beautiful women?' 'I read that,' Presner would say. 'And not so beautiful women, too,' he could hear Fitz add. 'Are you saying she's not beautiful?' Presner would bristle.)

The playwright thought of his next play. This one wouldn't be about what Fitz would do, but what he did. A colorful guy who bilks his friends out of a quarter million dollars. Everybody's mad at the guy, but he's such a great guy the worst they do is call the guy a fuckface. They don't press charges, despite the fact that they're a bunch of judges and lawyers, litigious by inclination. One night they get together in a bar to discuss why the colorful guy would have so betrayed their trust and what makes him tick. Each provides a theory.

The climax? The colorful guy enters the restaurant—in fact, he's been sitting at the bar all night long listening to himself being raked over the coals.

Now he knows what they think of him when the chips are down. Knowledge but—a Chekhovian twist—at such cost. This is communicated to the audience not through dialogue but the look on the colorful guy's face.

But it doesn't end there. The colorful guy turns the tables. He slowly slides off his stool and walks over to the group. He tells them *why*, exactly why—pointing out, unknown to them, that they weren't pure as the driven snow themselves—and then returns the money—it turns out that another deal has paid off in spades—every red cent plus interest.

It would be like one of those old movies where everybody gets together in the last scene, and the explanations are offered.

Presner went over to Fitz's the next night, unannounced, and knocked on his window. Nobody. One more day and he'd break the window and crawl through. There was a light on at the bungalow next door. He thought about limping over and asking Marie if she'd seen Norm around, then went home and waited by the phone.

He slept on the couch by the phone. When the instrument rang it was Roxanne. Before she could gleefully update him on her progress with the U.S. Attorney, he told her that Fitz wasn't answering his door.

"What do you expect, a forwarding address?"

"Roxie, I don't think he's left town. He's there."

"Well, you do have an active imagination. I have an extra key. If it'll make you feel better, I'll look around later."

"I was going to break a window and crawl through. You may as well give me the key. I can call in sick. You have a full docket."

Presner called Tyson's and said he'd be an hour late for the shift—standard practice, swapping shifts, requesting adjustments, though he'd never called in late in thirteen years—then walked over to the County Courthouse where Roxie said she'd leave the key with one of the deputies who ran the metal detector.

He broke into a slow jog, half running, half hobbling on his strained calf through the Golden Triangle, past the small galleries and chic restaurants until he reached the bungalow, then stopped and caught his breath—he could run ten miles in his jogging shorts and running shoes, two miles at best without the uniform—then took a second breath and slowly ascended the porch steps.

The bruiser paused momentarily and wished that he could stand on the porch poised before the door waving the key in the air for another twenty minutes, lingering in a limbo world where Fitzhugh was still alive. But this wouldn't be any easier in twenty minutes or an hour or five seconds, so Presner fit the key in the lock and turned. He walked down the foyer past the receptionist's desk still fearing the worst; he steeled himself against the wave of nausea he knew would overcome him like a cloud of sulfuryl chloride in a high school chemistry experiment; he turned to the right, into the large, messy bachelor's room with the dark paneling, then walked over the thick green throw rugs on the hard pine floor to where Fitz sat at his desk leaning forward as if poring over documents, until he saw that Fitz's head touched the oak.

According to Viktor Frankl, pain is like a gas that fills the human vessel.

He glanced at the dried swamp of vomit crusted on the oak finish. He saw a blue bruise on Fitz's cheek where the blood had already settled. He touched his friend's cold face, then felt down his neck for the pulse. The bruiser would have thrown Fitzhugh to his back and applied CPR if it weren't so pointless. He thought of doing it nonetheless so that in twenty years when he thought of this moment, he could assure himself that he'd left no stone unturned, that he'd done every last thing and beyond for his friend, he'd run through walls, he'd beaten his fists against the floor until his hands smashed to chips and finally powder. Where would it stop? He'd sue the EMTs if they couldn't spark Fitz back to life? There was a point at which you'd done everything you could, and beyond that a point—no less overwhelming for its being metaphorical—that you could never reach, where you could never do enough. But you still kissed your friend on the crown of the head and told him that you were so sorry for this, and so sorry for everything.

Presner placed his hand on Fitzhugh's head and rubbed his thick hair and again rubbed it—"with elbow grease," as he could remember his father saying—then called 911. To the first question, he couldn't remember Fitz's address, so he walked outside, couldn't find a number, then walked to the two adjacent bungalows. "It's between 957 and 969," he told the dispatcher, then reeled in the other incidentals while trying to hold his breath, spelling Fitzhugh's name three times and his own twice, then before the dispatcher was through asking questions said that he'd wait outside for the ambulance.

"Don't get testy. I have a job to do here," the dispatcher said.

Roxie was about to walk into session when he called. "Oh fuck, I wasn't expecting this. Presner, I have to make some calls. Shit. I'll call Henrietta. You call the others. I'm sorry. Call me later."

He placed his hand on Fitzhugh's shoulder and squeezed, then walked out to the porch where he sat on the steps to wait for the EMTs. Immediately he stood up and hobbled back inside. What had he been thinking? Fitz was inside.

He'd wait beside Fitz.

"He was a big guy under tremendous stress. His fibers burst," Presner wailed when he called Roxie later. This was after he'd returned home from the hospital where they'd pronounced Fitzhugh gone. Heart attack, although questions would remain. Forty years old, like Presner, according to his driver's license, though Presner knew his old pal to be two years older. "The kind of stuff I said to him people can't take. You should have heard me on the plane. He didn't need that from me, his old pal. He had enough troubles without that. I'm sure his heart burst and gave out."

He'd been home for an hour before he called her. "How are *you* doing, Rox?"

"I don't know." She sounded okay. She always sounded okay. Hankie when she heard would be down on all fours crawling across the kitchen floor, but it was the same as Roxanne sounding okay.

If Presner himself was the kind who sounded as calm and distant as the faint siren of a fire truck on the other side of town, it was also the same as Hankie and Rox sounding okay. "Do you want me to come over?"

"Why? I didn't think this was going to happen, Presner."

Presner thanked her for the key and called Hankie, whom Roxie had already called. It sounded like she was still crawling across the floor. They talked for a while, and then he called Marx and Pepe, as Roxie instructed, leaving messages. "Call me if you feel like it."

They wouldn't.

Presner, still hobbled by the calf strain, limped through his route. For a brief second considered throwing himself into the river. Not the Platte River, exactly, but some other river where he couldn't swim to shore so easily no matter how he tried. He knew he'd try to swim to shore, or hoped he would, so it would have to be the Mississippi, or the Amazon. He thought a thousand things about Fitz, and all along he expected Fitz to rise like an apparition from the surface of the Platte.

He called Lisa Caner and left a message.

Roxanne called again after he hung up. She wanted Presner to come over, after all.

The judge lived in one of the few high rises in downtown Denver, a new place designed to look like a chunk of downtown Barcelona. Presner signed in, the door guy called up, and the playwright took the elevator to the seventeenth floor. On the elevator wall was a Gauguin reproduction. Something about it was elusive. The irony was too easy. In a city, taking the elevator to the seventeenth floor, a reproduction of the South Seas? Perhaps it was a statement about the imagination. Perhaps you could get as far away as you want, wherever you are, or remain as close by, though—one more level of irony to slam your heart shut—you really weren't anywhere but where you were, whatever you thought.

Roxie hugged him at the door. Presner followed her to her huge dining room table. The table was piled with papers and correspondence and pamphlets and books. The two times he'd had dinner here the table was cleared off. He wondered now where she put the piles, which appeared to be meticulously maintained—or knowing Roxie they'd be, so perhaps he only saw it that way—the bruiser was beginning to wonder if he knew any more about Roxie than he did Fitz, or the South Seas. She probably piled them into the pantry when she cleared them off the table.

Roxie was crying, but mostly she looked pale and sick. Presner imagined if he looked closely enough, he could locate a malarial tint. "You look awful," Roxie said as Presner sat down across the table. "I'm sorry that you had to find Fitz like that."

"He would have made good. The payment schedules, the contrition, that stuff was all true. He saw a chance and thought of you guys and never thought it would go south. He never meant to hurt anybody in a thousand years."

"You know better than that."

"He was going to meet us last night, as promised. Fitz to the rescue."

"Presner to the rescue."

Touché. He nodded.

Roxanne cleared her voice. "Well, as you see here, I have a mess on my hands. You know the worst thing about messes? I never have time to clear them up. You may not know this, but I was—am—Fitz's attorney of record. All stuff we settled a long time ago, before my appointment. Mostly he represented himself. A pro forma arrangement, really. Anyway, I'm busy. I just don't have the time. Everything's a mess. I'll be candid, I've asked Gary. I've asked Pepe. They're too busy. Anyway, Presner, there's really no choice." Roxanne looked at him nervously, but she was the judge. It was her court. "You're a member of the bar, I understand. You were his best friend."

"Roxanne, I don't know jack shit."

Roxanne shrugged. A day didn't go by when she didn't make similar observations about the guys appearing before her. "You'll learn. You don't have to, of course, but there's nobody else. Even if there were, I'm signing this stuff over to you. Be a lawyer."

That evening the bruiser/attorney left the Belvidere with a box full of papers and the key to the bungalow, where the next morning he'd pick up the chair where he'd found Fitz slumped over. The EMTs had knocked it upside down. The police had also searched the place thoroughly. Presner appreciated that they would have searched him thoroughly, too, and also closed off the building for several days, if Roxie hadn't made some calls as soon as they'd hung up. But he knew it would be up to him to scrub the mess Fitzhugh had made from dying, and to scrub the mess the police made from investigating why.

He'd spend most of the next several days—when he wasn't at the wedding or attending to Fitz's funeral—at the bungalow. First, though, he walked into Tyson's for his shift, served it out, then called Mr. Tyson. "An emergency came up. I need vacation time. I have some coming."

"Take all the time you want," Mr. Tyson said. Presner knew it wasn't that the patriarch, whom he liked, was so understanding. Guys came and went all the time without filling in the niceties, but he wouldn't find many like Presner who needed it so much; who'd manage the place for a decade, afternoons or graveyard, and hang out—host?—the place in his free time, if not like a fantasy park then as something other than the foreman of a ball and chain crew. "Take all the time you want. I owe it to you," Mr. Tyson repeated. "Then do yourself a favor: Don't come back when you're done."

After thirteen years, you'd think there'd be more to it than that. Announcements, bells and whistles, a confetti parade, gold watches, plaques, sentimental speeches. But the patriarch was right.

Being a lawyer wasn't much different than cleaning your house then doing your taxes once everything was spic and span and you did a thousand other things before you got around to it. Fitzhugh's files were extensive—Presner had to wade through each—but Fitz had been telling the truth at least about shutting down the practice. Most of the accounts were settled long ago. Presner sorted through the catacombs. There were contracts with the local news station that had expired, and contracts—also expired—with local businesses. No rhyme or reason. Fitz took what came through the door. He specialized in whoever he looked at. There was no record at all of the sexual harassment lawsuit that made Fitz famous, no financial records of personal funds, which meant that the new practicing attorney had to turn over every straw in every haystack. No Fitzhugh Limited Fund, needless to say. Nothing, of course, from Richard and Cecil about a certain play under consideration. So much for that delusion. Still, he enjoyed the concentrated tedium of looking through Fitz's effects. Not that it kept Fitz alive, but it kept him from thinking about Fitz; Fitz an object he was investigating, not the guy he knew, and for the time being he needed the guy to be an object. There was a listing of the contents in a safe deposit box and a key. Presner drove over to the First National Bank and showed the manager the papers, then waited in the anteroom sucking on a complimentary mint until the deposit box was delivered. The thing was empty except for a diamond ring.

Ah Fitz, Presner thought. Certainly he would have *known* if the guy had ever been married, but, leaning back in the anteroom, closing his eyes, he knew it wasn't unlike his old friend to hold a ring in stock in case the right woman came along, Fitzy needing to act fast. Of course, like most gestures, this one would be symbolic. Presner figured the guy was spontaneous only when he sat still. The other stuff—that seemed so spontaneous—was as studied as a state of the union speech, was strategy and rhetoric and sizing you up for the pressure points. Fitz wouldn't marry on a whim any more than Presner would run for Mayor of Denver on a whim, but wasn't it nice to have a diamond ring in stock? If she walked into view, you were ready.

At the bungalow, Presner called Roxie. "Oh yes, the ring. It was his mom's, a family heirloom."

"I've been looking for a number, by the way. In fifteen years, I don't think I ever got a straight answer from him about his folks, other than that his dad's the greatest guy in the world."

"You know his mom died when he was a kid. His dad's in a nursing home in Cleveland. He has Alzheimer's and hasn't remembered Norm for years."

Presner lifted the phone away from his ear, rattled it in the air before bringing it back. "I guess the ring goes to his dad. It's sad that there's no more family than that."

"He liked the way you got along with Sara. Maybe he idealized you a little, too. That may be why he adopted you."

"He didn't adopt me."

"Look for an insurance policy, if you would."

If there was an insurance policy in the office it would have turned up by now, but Presner looked again. A couple of times he thought he'd found it, but instead turned over another expired contract. It would be nice, he thought. An insurance policy for a quarter million, for example, naming Roxie, Hankie, Pepe, and Marx as beneficiaries.

The new practicing attorney imagined he lacked a lawyer's imagination. There were no records of Fitzhugh's offshore activities or intermediary contracts or the export/import schemes. Perhaps Fitz maintained offices overseas other than his coat pocket, but he suspected the records for these contracts could be found in the same place as the records for the Fitzhugh Ltd. Fund. For the record, Fitz was destitute except for the ring.

Norman Fitzhugh's obituary ran the next morning on the front of the *Post*'s feature section. Fitz looked vigorous in the picture, where he held a microphone facing the camera as if in the next second he would begin to explain everything, or take off on such a riff that you didn't care. All you wanted—if you were the bruiser—was to hear. Fittingly, the article emphasized his media expertise. "Concise, comprehensive, and offbeat," the 9 News director was quoted as saying. "Norm was an operator, but in a charming way." Nobody else was quoted. No survivors listed—the bruiser half expected himself to be listed, along with the old gang. 'No family,' that article would say, 'but the guy had a frame of reference.' As he read the paper, he had this vision of the reporter calling dozens, none of them willing to comment for the record. 'He broke a thousand hearts,' Roxanne would reveal, possibly clutching her own left ventricle.

'An operator but charming, except for the charming,' Marx would insist.

'He bilked us of a quarter mil, but would have paid us back plus interest. Except his heart gave out,' Hankie would say.

At the wedding that evening nobody said anything beyond, "Did you see the obit?" Presner, Lisa Caner beside him, had the impression that the group was looking at him hopefully, as if he might yet locate an insurance policy or discretionary account. Henrietta mentioned it. It was striking—Presner's projection here perhaps was monumental—that Henrietta was nervous with Lisa Caner beside him. In her sleeveless pink dress, even Fitz would approve. The man of the hour worked his way over to say hello and meet Lisa Caner. "Presner with a woman," Marx shook his head. "I hear you're a lawyer now, too."

"Temporarily."

"I may have some work for you if you're interested. Give me a call when I get back from Tahiti. By the way, Roxanne said there may be a policy."

"Thanks for the thought. And I haven't seen a policy. If it's there I'll find it. You know me, Gary. No stone left unturned."

"I saw the obituary this morning," Marx said. "It made me think he wasn't such a fuckface."

"Preparing for his wedding and still takes the time to check the local obituaries," Presner observed to Lisa.

"What can I say? I'm a *prince*." Marx clapped Presner's shoulder and winked at Lisa Caner.

"Nice to meet you," Pepe said to Lisa Caner, after he'd made his way over, then soon walked back across the ballroom to his wife. Pepe whispered in her ear—Sandra waved across the ballroom floor to Presner—and then Pepe—Peter Murray—moved on to a dozen other conversations within ten minutes. ("Nice to meet you." "Good to see you again." "I'm Peter Murray.") Contacts, not friends, though the temporary attorney wondered. Networking even on a day off. An integer in the same equation as a million other integers, cancelling each other out. He thought he could have predicted that Roxie became Roxie, Henrietta Henrietta, Marx Marx. But even compared to Fitzhugh, this Peter Murray came from outer space. Presner watched him work the room, not without an envy that surprised him.

"I meant it when I said temporary, by the way."

"Sure. Your friends are nice."

"They're not my friends."

"Okay," Lisa Caner squeezed his hand then released it. "The All-Stars are nice."

Still, the bruiser found the wedding stirring. Even the Rock Cornish game hen, even the floral arrangements, even the chamber music and the exchanged vows, which Gary Marx delivered as passionately as if he were taping another ad: 'I'll get you a check. No promises, just results.' Lisa cried although she'd never met Marx and Jill before, other than as names in the stories Presner told.

Pepe was best man and gave a toast that made Presner think, for a moment, that he wasn't coming from outer space but inner-city Detroit again, the same Pepe he knew back in law school who'd shred the pretensions of the privileged class, with the same pronounced scar on his forehead, long since a target of plastic surgery. The guy who was a friend, not a contact or opportunity. But then Pepe became Peter Murray again, rolling his eyes as if he and Marx were young idiots together who miraculously survived their youthful decadence.

Boys will be boys.

Peter Murray paused at the end of the toast—in that instant Presner thought he was about to mention Norman Fitzhugh—a moment of silence to recall the guy who couldn't be here due to a fatal heart attack—and the bruiser imagined in that instant that there was nothing else for the Pepe he knew to do but to become Peter Murray, if for nothing better than symmetry. It wasn't from outer space but the other side of the same coin he'd flip a thousand times in the air before letting it land: Heads or tails? If it was tails before, it was heads now. Who doesn't strive to make an art of their various lives?

"It's not an ending, it's a beginning!" Pepe held up his glass after the pause.

Most of the 250 friends and relatives and contacts and guys they used to know holding hands with their dates groaned lavishly.

"For the luckiest guy in the world!" Pepe shouted.

So many people to say hello to, so little time.

The new practicing attorney broke fast from the field. Was there a moment when it turned for the bruiser? If there was one instant, there were ten. Correspondingly, if there were ten there were none. Still, when he stared down the wind, he felt less like he was bluffing.

The toxicology report came back the day after the wedding. The coroner issued a report—by phone and fax—to Roxie, as attorney of record, who called her stand-in, who hustled over. "Sit down. Fitzhugh died of a heart attack, as we suspected, but it wasn't due to stress. Not directly. A salicylate overdose. I'm reading from the report. They measured for blood and urine pH, blood PC02, serum electrolytes, blood PO2, HC03 concentrations. There was elevated arterial blood gas. There were clumps of aspirin tabs in his bowel. As many as 800 or 1,000 aspirin all told, dissolved, apparently, in a glass of water they found in the bathroom. Torched with gin, of course."

"I'm missing something."

"He killed himself, Presner."

Presner didn't know what to do, so he took a deep breath.

"Draw your own conclusions," Roxanne said. "But I've had it with Fitzhugh. Even if there's a policy they won't pay off for a suicide. You know that. And don't 'the poor old fuckface' me, Presner. 'Would have paid us back plus interest but his heart gave out.' The coroner looked at foul play. I can only assume we weren't the only ones he fucked over. The only ones he defrauded, bilked, screwed royally. There's probably a line extending across the Front Range. That's why he had to go to Europe. He wasn't there for the exchange rate. Anyway, he came back. You made him come back." For a second Roxie's face turned a thousand directions, then focused on Presner across the table. "There wasn't any note, but nobody executes somebody with 800 aspirin and a glass of gin. There's no evidence anybody else was in his bungalow to see he took the cocktail."

Presner breathed outward.

"Fitz was a cheat and a coward."

"Is that in the report?"

Roxie walked Presner to her door.

The bruiser felt as he once had years before when he broke up with a girl at her place. She'd walked him to the front door. There wasn't a lot to say that you hadn't spent hours saying, but still you stood face-to-face with somebody you'd been close to, and when you stepped through the threshold, you'd never see each other again, at least not in the same way. It was true; he never saw Jane Bartel again. "Aren't you going to hug me," Jane had said as they looked at each other. Presner hugged her for a long time—over a minute—and then they let each other go. That's how it was, staring at Roxie by her door, but she didn't move in to hug Presner and Presner didn't move in to hug Roxie, but nodded and smiled. Roxie's face again turned a thousand directions at once, then the honorable judge nodded and smiled back.

"Counselor."

"Your honor."

The attorney suspected that Fitz wanted to be cremated. It didn't seem right to cremate somebody because you suspected they might want that—or you suspected *you'd* want that—too large a step to base on suspicion—so there'd be no cremation. The funeral director explained the casket and floral options. "Is this a relative?"

"I'm the executor."

As the executor he would receive a fee from the estate, which would be nothing—a pauper's funeral for Fitz, plus whatever extras Presner could afford—no monthly maintenance fee as he paid for his parents' and sister's plots—but that morning the attorney found a deed at the bottom of one of the haystacks. He'd spent the night looking. It turned out that Fitz owned the bungalow. As executor, Presner would sell the bungalow, subtract final expenses, give the rest to the creditors—Hankie, Roxie, Marx, and Pepe, though you didn't know who else would emerge—and whatever was left over would be sent to the nursing home in Cleveland. Fitz's equity in the house didn't turn out to be what was wished—not surprisingly, he paid as little up front as possible—but the attorney would see to it that most of whatever was left after expenses they'd all agree to give to Henrietta.

Even with that in mind, he didn't order the cheapest casket. Everybody has to make a living. He looked through the yellow pages and called a rabbi—the same guy, he remembered, who buried Sara—to officiate. "He's not a Jew," Presner admitted immediately. "Except under the skin," he added.

"Then why call me?"

He hadn't seen the guy for a dozen years and hadn't known the rabbi before then. He thought of saying, 'I was the guy he was closest to. It's for me,' but that wouldn't get him anywhere. "I'm his attorney. You're the only one I know," Presner said. "Plus he's a Catholic, a suicide. *Possibly* a suicide. Would a priest do it, *nu*?"

"We've met?"

"You buried my sister twelve years ago. Sara Burton?"

Rabbi Bergdorf said he remembered, though he'd say that anyway.

"You met the guy. He took care of a lot of stuff. You talked to him for half an hour after the service. Big guy. Red face."

"It's a *Jewish* funeral you want?"

If Rabbi Bergdorf was taunting him, Presner didn't blame him.

"Whatever you can come up with," Presner said. "It's *meshuggener*," the attorney agreed. "*Uggavalt. Farblondget.* Just some words in Hebrew to gussie it up. It doesn't have to be *official*. Cut rate's fine."

The rabbi considered the hustler's pitch. "It won't be official," he said after a while. "Or cheap."

He called everybody that he could think of to tell them about the service, including the News Anchor at Channel 9. He called Roxie, Pepe, and Henrietta immediately to explain arrangements, then attended to a thousand other details, the stuff Sara mostly took care of when their parents died, the thousand details he'd mostly forgotten that Fitz handled a dozen years ago for Sara. He thought of calling Marx in Tahiti, but judging from the silence on the other end when he talked to Pepe, Hankie, and Roxie, Presner saved his quarter.

At dusk, the night before the service, Presner met Lisa Caner in Washington Park. He wasn't certain why he'd asked her to meet him here and, if for no other reason than force of habit, was a little surprised that she'd accepted. He could free associate as easily on the phone, and he'd have more time to polish his thoughts after he got Fitz buried tomorrow. But it had to be *now*, and the bruiser wondered if he'd really turned a corner—or else was selling himself a bill of goods in order to bolster sagging spirits—into a future where he could never let up, where everything would have to be now or not at all, or else he'd lose this spirit that had seized him lately, that he'd seized by the dangling threads.

Caner sat beside him on a rolling grass hill above the lake where joggers ran by them on the path ten feet away, alongside young women pushing baby carriages and couples holding hands. The attorney thought that the lovers made Lisa anxious, as if she thought he might choose this setting to propose marriage; that explained the trepidation in her eyes. "I'm an attorney now," he began.

"I thought that was just temporary."

Presner shrugged. "Fitzhugh used to tell me that a big part of being a successful lawyer involves taking something which doesn't seem to fit the criteria at all and making the case that it does perfectly, and then taking something that seems to fit the criteria perfectly—that's the other guy's motion—and trying to persuade the judge that it doesn't at all. Apples and oranges. Basketball and bingo. Fitz thought that was a good thing, the heart of the adversarial system; the laws won't bend, so you turn what happens—objective reality, I mean—into an abstraction, then bend the abstraction to fit the law."

"That's what everyone pretty much does with everything," Lisa Caner said. "It's called living with yourself."

The bruiser nodded. He wondered if a dozen or twenty years from now he'd find himself having a conversation with Caner and she'd still take most of what he'd say and reduce it to a cliché. "That's my point,

Lisa. But I can't do the abstractions anymore." Presner stood up and stretched gingerly. His calf was still sore. Still, he entertained the idea of breaking into a sprint down the jogging path, of never stopping and never looking back until he reached a town far away where he'd become somebody else, somebody rumored to be great, not just Presner in different clothes but with a different past he wouldn't cling to—or that wouldn't cling to him—like a lifebuoy. He had the idea that if he held onto the buoy he may not drown, but he wouldn't reach shore either unless somebody happened to save him; who would go to the trouble?

He looked back at Caner. How much of what he was going to say was part of the new hustle, and how much depended upon knowing the difference but saying it anyway, dunking it in sentiment until it glistened? Tonight he knew the other choices weren't choices at all. "I don't know where I'm going to get the money. I can get better as a lawyer. Fitz got better, I'll tell you that. He looked awful in overalls. If I ask Roxie she'll throw me some crumbs. Marx will, Pepe will. They may hold their noses, but they will. And Mr. Tyson's offered me a severance 'loan.' 'For Chapter Two,' he says. You get enough crumbs pretty soon you'll have kugel." The bruiser coughed. Lisa Caner was looking at him as she had dozens of hours across her kitchen table as they'd discussed Chekhov and the arc of tragedy, the bitterness of comedy and the way that the most subtle of inflections can destroy or create meaning; looking at him as she had their one night together. "The Sara Burton Theater. That's my idea, capeesh?" The bruiser frantically tried to reel in what Fitz had pitched to Richard and Cecil. "It's the myth that sells the play, that jars and salves the imagination. Anyway, we'll start in a tent if we have to. We'll start in the basement and take the dozen paying customers out for pasta afterward. We'll begin in my living room or your kitchen if necessary but that's the point: We'll begin. It's a start. We'll develop a core group. Maybe not. We'll *push* ourselves. We'll struggle and learn. I'll get the money and put up the posters and make the publicity calls and you'll get the actors and pick the material. Or if that's too much—I'll understand if so—I'll get the money and put up the posters and make the publicity calls and recruit the actors and pick the material, and I'll begin. I'm beginning, anyway." Presner looked at her and shrugged. "I'd be honored if you'd act."

He'd hoped to fly in Fitzhugh's dad from Cleveland, but the representative of the nursing home said that Mr. Fitzhugh was too deep into dementia to register events and was liable to be upset by the travel. "It's his *son*. Don't you think it's necessary for him to come? Don't you think his son would want his dad there?" Presner railed into the receiver.

"We deal with these situations all the time," the representative said, and went on to explain that while they had no problem with the symbolism Mr. Presner mentioned, they were the ones who had to live with the reality of a frightened old man. Presner suspected that mostly they didn't want to be inconvenienced unless there was something to make it worth their while. The representative droned on. Presner let himself be talked out of it.

Why not idealize your friends? What a grim place the world would be if you didn't. And if you were living a lie, who wasn't? Wasn't religion a lie? Everlasting romantic love? Every good memory you had of your travels, overlooking the tedium, the short tempers, the toilets that wouldn't flush?

Lisa Caner showed up. Surprisingly, Hankie showed up and stood beside Lisa Caner, who stood beside the bruiser. The service was delayed fifteen minutes to allow for the arrival of latecomers. Rabbi Bergdorf gave the impression that he had all day. Presner liked that. Whether it was true or just a useful impression to communicate, he didn't need to know.

Still, they may have needed ten for the service. Presner tried to remember. Was a minyan necessary for a funeral? Did they relax the standard when the guy wasn't Jewish?

If the rabbi was nonplussed at conducting a ceremony in front of three mourners and two employees standing in the distance with their shovels, or at conducting a Jewish funeral for a Catholic suicide, he didn't betray it. A good hundred yards away were the plots of his parents and sister that Presner attended weekly. Usually, he'd bring along a bag of pebbles he'd place on the stones. Fitz's hole was by the access road, and the bruiser noticed every car that purred slowly by as the small group gathered.

Already Hankie was sobbing, and the sight of the second-rate casket beside the immaculate hole in the ground against the flowered backdrop was enough to make Lisa sniffle as she had at Marx's wedding three days before.

"We're gathered together today to celebrate the life of a man you all knew, and to ease his transition into the next state of being." Rabbi Bergdorf addressed his remarks beyond them, perhaps to the grave diggers or the cars driving by, or to where the other mourners, if there were any, would congregate. Presner, Hankie, and Caner locked arms and swayed back and forth as the rabbi prayed. Briefly a gust of wind lifted his yarmulke, though it landed back on his head. Instinctively the attorney pulled his yarmulke on tighter.

It was fitting that nobody showed up, and that the ceremony was conducted by a rabbi, and that they were standing a stone's throw—better yet, a *Herculean* stone's throw—from his parents and sister, from where he would someday lie, and that now he was standing with Lisa and Hankie, arms linked, swaying as the rabbi sang out: *Yisgadahl vayisgadosh shemay rabaw.*

And the bruiser sang out. "It's your funeral," some wiseass would always tell him when he was a kid, on the rare occasions he'd attempt something noble but patently foolish, beyond his reach. 'It's my funeral,' he wanted to say back now. 'Every funeral's my funeral and will be until it's my funeral.' Could he live like that? He promised himself he would, went on the record with Lisa Caner about his plans, though he already reminded himself of a toddler puffing out his chest. Already he'd let the nursing home in Cleveland talk him out of flying in Fitz's dad, which Fitz would have done were it the other way around, blindfolding the attendants then kidnapping the guy, hijacking a chopper so they'd get back in time, arranging for a limo waiting at the airport. Fitz—not that he was comparing, a game he couldn't win now that Fitz was already receding into mythology, and wouldn't have won before—also would have stood on this ground and counted up the mourners, six, but then run like hell to find four others, emptying his wallet, so the proceedings could be official, a minyan. *Six?* No doubt the rabbi wasn't above taking shortcuts, under the circumstances. Presner wouldn't accuse anybody. According to the mishnah: "Whoever thinks about four things, it would have been better if they were never created: What is above? What is below? What is before time? What is after?" Interestingly, that didn't go for the guys who studied the mishnah. Not for them. *They* could contemplate Paradise, they lived for those questions (along with cali-brating ethical mandates), but the others might be misled, deceived, get the wrong idea, worship false idols, not fully appreciate the paradox at the core of every grain of sand—which is as useful a symbol for existence as Presner could think of. You could lie down and let the granules run through your toes, or, though it may take an hour or a life and wouldn't last, you could build a castle. Chekhov knew which was the bigger waste, which is why his plays could tear out the bruiser's heart. Mislead? These guys saw *messiahs* around every corner. Akiba, the genius of the oral law, thought Bar Kochba, a general, a revolutionary, was the messiah; Presner knew that, considering everything, he would have, too. *Fitz* would have. How do you get by? Every dove was the hope of peace, every son was everlasting life, every life the world eternal, every sinister face you pass a potential hidden saint, the bitter herbs were slavery, the challah the sweetness of life, the prayer for the dead a valentine to the living world.

Ah Fitzhugh, fuckface. You helped me with my sister. Nobody else did. I didn't ask, you insisted. You flew me to England because you figured I needed a lift. You insisted. I didn't ask. When I was in the dumps, I thought of how you'd be and could suddenly imagine myself down as *spectacle*, not statement. You were two sides of the same strange coin. You were a scammer and I'll remember your generosity. You had the energy and the nerve. You were a tough nut but a softy at the core, that's why I'm here. You looked lousy in overalls.

The rabbi looked up, not at the empty expanse where the audience never materialized, but the three mourners holding hands. "Excuse me, does anybody have something that they'd like to say about the deceased before we lower him back to the earth whence he came?"

Presner stepped forward, and then he spoke.

About the Author

Don Eron lives in Boulder, Colorado. He is the author of *And Go to Innisfree*.